JUNO & JULIET

JUNO
&JULIET

Julian Gough

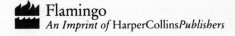
Flamingo
An Imprint of HarperCollins*Publishers*

Flamingo
An imprint of HarperCollins*Publishers*
77–85 Fulham Palace Road,
Hammersmith, London W6 8JB

Published by Flamingo 2001
1 3 5 7 9 8 6 4 2

Copyright © Julian Gough 2001

Julian Gough asserts the moral right to
be identified as the author of this work

This novel is entirely a work of fiction. The names, characters
and incidents portrayed in it are the work of the author's
imagination. Any resemblance to actual persons, living or
dead, events or localities is entirely conincidental.

A catalogue record for this book is
available from the British Library

Photograph of Julian Gough © Phil Rose 2000

ISBN 0 00 710809 5

Set in PostScript Linotype Galliard with
Optima and Photina display by
Rowland Phototypesetting Ltd,
Bury St Edmunds, Suffolk

Printed and bound in Great Britain by
Clays Ltd, St Ives plc

'. . . man has the advantage of choice, woman only the power of refusal . . .'

Mr Tilney on matrimony and dancing, from *Northanger Abbey* by Jane Austen

'I like to teach,' Angela said. 'It's easier than learning.' From *Couples* by John Updike

Part One

GALWAY

1

When Juno and I stepped off the bus in Eyre Square we were
armed only with an enormous rucksack each and the scribbled
address of a distant cousin. A blizzard of youth-hostel flyers
immediately engulfed us, clearing only to reveal a blizzard of
youths, smiling at us in French, Spanish, English and Italian. Juno
told them we didn't need a hostel, but thank you anyway. I told
them we didn't need a hostel, so fuck off.

And there I think you have, neatly illustrated, the essential difference between her and me.

I had, to be fair to me, not enjoyed my journey much. The
peace had held all through the morning's packing, but on the way
out the door I managed to have an almighty row with our father.
What was it about? Ah, what are they ever about. It was about
nothing. All the way up on the bus I had stomach cramps and a
headache. A drunk behind us spewed against the back of my seat.
Then he tried to make light conversation. The driver spent the
entire journey with the radio on at full blast as he attempted, with
an ever-increasing lack of success which would have disheartened
a lesser man, to tune into a country and western station that
seemed to be making its last, faint, desperate broadcast from somewhere beyond the edge of the solar system.

Things rapidly improved once we'd got off the bus and through
the blizzard. Pausing only to shovel fistfuls of flyers into the big
yellow litterbins that disfigured the edge of Eyre Square, we
headed for the nearest coffeeshop. Apart from a couple of buskers
and another drunk and a spotty boy with a clipboard who promised
not to take up much of our valuable time and didn't, nobody
bothered us for money, our names, or a kiss in the hundred yards
to the GBC coffeeshop and restaurant.

Some kind of record.

I should probably explain that Juno began to be beautiful

around the age of fourteen and the process shows no sign of stopping. Her beauty refines and upgrades itself constantly. At the time this story begins, she has just turned eighteen and it's almost ridiculous how beautiful she is. No, it is ridiculous how beautiful she is. She's beautiful to the point where it might as well be a disfigurement. She's invisible behind it. It's all people see. Not just men. Everyone. That doesn't mean everyone's attracted to her. It just means everyone has an attitude, an opinion, before they know a damn thing about her. It's nobody's fault. It's the way we are. It annoys the hell out of me.

I should probably also explain that Juno is my identical twin.

We got a seat in the nook at the back. The coffee was lovely. My cramps and headache faded. We'd left home. I felt great. Eventually we paid up and went to look for the house of our distant cousin.

We found it.

2

The front door of 14 Bishop Casey Terrace swung open and we stepped trustingly into what might as well have been deep space. It was so dark I had the sensation of falling and grabbed Juno. Seconds later, as our eyes adjusted, we found ourselves blinking in the centre of a kind of smoke-blackened igloo constructed entirely from plaster statues of Our Lady of Perpetual Sorrow, in assorted sizes, and large, framed pictures of Pope John XXIII. Turf dust covered every flat surface an inch deep. No light came through the shroud-like curtains. A tiny turf fire in the grate sent a little light halfway across the rug, while the small, sinister, glowing Sacred Heart lamp on the far wall did its job of flooding the rear of the room with darkness. Our distant cousin was now close enough for us to count her teeth, even by that light.

Five. Three up on top.

She spoke in tongues, and vanished. I was terrified.

'What the hell was that about?' I asked Juno.

'She's gone to put her teeth in and put on the kettle' said Juno, who'd always been better at languages. 'She hopes we had a pleasant journey.'

The tea was actually grand and over the course of it our cousin slowly turned into a human being, although a very old, very religious human being with no sense of humour. That didn't stop her being very funny, it just stopped her from noticing the fact. We had to turn a lot of laughs into coughs, to the extent that she gave us both cough-sweets which she took with a creaking of bones from the top of the dresser, half a packet of them softened with age into a thick paste in their paper wrappers. They came in some obsolete, unrecognisable flavour, probably that of a long-extinct plant. Gobi Water-Lily. Sabre-Toothed Parsley. We liked her. We even ate some of the sweets for her.

She had left Galway twice in her life, once to go to Lourdes (the Mecca of the Irish) and once to go to Sligo (the Sligo of the Irish). She thought both places overrated, which, given that Sligo has a global reputation as one of the three wettest, dullest towns north of Antarctica, was a pretty harsh judgement. I coughed enthusiastically and declined another sweet. A cat, half-blind with age, jumped up on the table and began to lick the butter. Juno coughed, and declined a scone.

We hadn't come to Galway to live with our distant cousin. We'd come to Galway to go to university and study English. We were just staying with our cousin until we found somewhere to live. She was lovely, and after five minutes even I liked her. Juno liked her instantly. Juno tends to do that. Living with our cousin was out of the question, though. Her house was a classic Galway terrace house, the kind in which Nora Barnacle and her countless siblings grew halfway up (bad diet, short people). The bottom floor comprised a small living room. The top floor comprised a small bedroom. That was it. Her periodic vanishings to the 'kitchen' were only made possible by the almost total absence of light in vast areas of the tiny room. The 'kitchen' was a gas cooker, installed strategically under the stairs long before we were born to ensure fatalities in the case of a chip-pan fire. Sadly, everyone had grown up and left or died of natural causes before the cooker could fulfil its destiny. Now it probably wouldn't bother, with only our cousin to operate it and nobody else to be trapped upstairs.

I shall draw a discreet veil over the defects of the sinister, pre-war plumbing. Suffice to say, everything lurked in a shed the size of a wardrobe in the tiny yard out the back. Before retiring for the night, we were introduced to the facilities, a stiff breeze caressing our ankles, in the dark. We returned shaken, traumatised, but alive. Let us pass on.

We spent our first night in Galway in sleeping bags on the living room floor, lulled to sleep by the reassuring hiss of gas leaking from the perished rubber tubes joining the antique cooker to the rusty cylinder, and by the comforting weight of cats lying drowsily across our feet.

'Night-night, Juno.'

'Night-night, Juliet.'

3

We awoke at what felt like dawn, though of course it was still dark in the living room. Our cousin was making us breakfast. By the time we'd thanked God that we couldn't see the state of the plates we were eating off and had eaten an enormous fry, our eyes had adjusted enough to see the state of the plates we had eaten off. They were practically trimmed in fur. We thanked her very much, enthusiastically declined to visit the chamber of horrors out the back, and headed rather urgently out into an explosion of light to look for somewhere civilised to piss. And, once we'd carried out our priority mission, somewhere civilised to live.

We had turned up in Galway a week and a half before the start of college to make sure we would have plenty of time to find a place. So had several thousand other people. These were the late arrivals. Many thousands more had already been in Galway for quite some time looking for places, with far from universal success. A lucky few had parents with the foresight to give birth to them in Galway, but even some of these were struggling. Galway is a small town with a large university. All that Thursday we saw people fighting for bedsits a wino's dog wouldn't tolerate. We saw flats that seemed hewn from the living mildew. We didn't see them immediately. First we had to queue. We saw cookers that would have left our distant cousin exclaiming 'How quaint! An antique!' We saw electric heaters that were obviously prototypes from the dawn of the age of electricity, and slightly before the dawn of the age of tenants' rights. We saw Mesozoic lino. We saw pre-Cambrian carpets.

We saw armchairs with no arms. We saw tables with no legs. We saw young men fighting and dying in a senseless war over a few square yards of worthless ground, and the winners spending half their grant on the deposit.

We saw our lives flash before us.

We had to sit down.

'Jesus, this is awful' I said. I had begun to feel very far from home. Every place we'd looked at had been disgusting, expensive, and taken. Our parents didn't have any more money, I wasn't even sure how they'd gotten what they'd given us, and it wasn't enough. Our grants weren't going to come through for weeks and all we had to last us until then would barely cover a deposit. If we could find a place. And then how would we eat? How could we buy books? Were we beaten? Was it over before it had started? Would I ever, ever, ever get away from Tipperary and my parents and my school and my life? I started to cry.

Juno held me as we sat on the wall of a tiny house in New Road that had been subdivided, with sturdy cardboard partitions, into five 'bedsits', in all of which you had just about enough room to prove the description truthful by sitting on the bed, as long as you didn't try anything recklessly space-consuming while you were at it, like crossing your legs, or removing a hat. The last one had gone, for a suitcase of used notes, a kidney, and some share options, ten minutes before we'd arrived. We'd looked, wistfully, anyway. 'Oh Juno, I'm homesick and I don't want to go home' I sobbed. Juno held me tighter. 'Hey, 's OK baby Juliet. I'm here.' That's one of the nice things about Juno. She understands me no matter how little sense I'm making, and she never goes for an obvious joke at my expense. And when I feel like a baby she never stays tough. Me, I stay tough. I'm awkward when she's sad, I feel useless and I can't say the things I know I should. But she's good with me. She's really very good.

When I'd stopped crying we went back to our cousin's house. It was after seven p.m., we'd been looking for a place since we'd picked up the new *Galway Advertiser* that morning. Our copy was in bits, the big Accommodation Available section was covered in scribbled phone numbers and directions and prices, we'd used up two phonecards and walked ourselves stumpy. Time to go home.

Our cousin gave us tea and sympathy and a red-hot tip. 'I'm sure old Mrs Flannery has rooms to let, I'm sure of it. You should try her tomorrow, first thing. She has a house down by the docks, half-empty for months. I'm sure I have her address

here somewhere, yes you must call on her tomorrow and enquire.'
Our cousin hesitated. 'Ye might find her a little . . . old-fashioned.'
She frowned. 'And she'd be a bit too religious for my taste, now.'
We gulped. But we went.

4

We bearded Mrs Flannery in her lair, armoured by our innocence. She lived a good mile from the docks in a house in Renmore that bristled with old ladies of uncertain function. They could have been friends, relatives or servants. It was impossible to tell from Mrs Flannery's erratic manner, and she didn't deign to explain. All through our interview they flitted in and out of the half-dark of the drawing room, bringing us fresh tea and bearing away the old cups. The tea was lovely. Biscuits were provided by swift, silent figures. Soon we were ignoring them with the same serene composure as old Mrs Flannery herself.

Old Mrs Flannery (so-called because of the existence of a young Mrs Flannery, her daughter, a victim of coincidence or inbreeding) indeed had rooms to let. Not just that, the house down by the docks had been half-empty for months, not because it was uninhabitable (our first guess: why else would a house be half-empty in Galway?), but because old Mrs Flannery didn't believe in advertising and anyone who'd heard about it by word of mouth had also heard the stories about old Mrs Flannery and was afraid to go near her. We tut-tutted, people were terrible. I wondered if we'd get out alive.

She was crazy as a loon. She talked to us for twenty minutes about the worldwide Jewish/Communist conspiracy against Catholicism. She offered us more tea, which arrived instantly. She told us for a quarter of an hour about the profound evil of usury, and for ten minutes expounded on the Satanic nature of the Bank of England. She passed the biscuits. Then, after a quick history of the Masons, she told us what fine young ladies we appeared to be, warned us against the heresies of Martin Luther, and gave us the keys to the house near the docks. The top floor was ours if we wanted it, forty pounds a week (each? no, for the whole floor: two bedrooms, living room/kitchen and bathroom). She was sorry about the rent, it had been thirty-five pounds but, thanks to the Jewish/Communist economic conspiracy against Catholicism, money wasn't worth what it once was. We made noises that indicated an understanding of the words said, without necessarily indicating an agreement with the sentiments they expressed. We were pretty good at these noises by now, after an hour's practice. Juno handed me the keys to put in my pocket and we left.

The place was great. We took it.

Thus it was that we snatched the finest flat in Galway from beneath the noses of an astonished world.

5

By the time university started, we'd settled in nicely and I was in love. I was in love with Galway, I was in love with our fabulous fourth-storey flat, I was in love with our view of Galway from our flat, I was in love with buying brillo pads, I was in love with freedom.

I would wake Juno or Juno would wake me and we'd get up and wander in and out of the bathroom and each other's rooms, and shower and dress and eventually have breakfast together in the living room, looking out high over the harbour and the sea. The coast of Clare would shimmer in the haze across the bay (and much later, in the winter, would disappear behind walls of rain, reappear, and disappear again). I never tired of it, and I don't think I ever would have. We'd walk into town after breakfast, buy the makings of dinner, explore the shops, talk a lot.

I began to know Juno much better in those conversations. It sounds stupid, when she was my twin, when we'd lived in the same house and often the same room, for all of our lives. But how can you see something that's always so close? My picture of her grew much clearer against an unfamiliar background. I'd loved her absent-mindedly. I began to love her more.

Wait. Slow down. This makes me sound like I was full of love, that I was a casual user of the word, that I was comfortable with the idea. Not at all. I was full of confusion, anger, angst. The usual. I was just eighteen. I wouldn't even have used the word. But looking back, I would call all these things forms of love. For Juno, a respect gone wild, a kind of love. For my freedom, a passion, a kind of love. For the view, an awe and fascination that didn't wear out, a kind of love.

At the time, I didn't believe in love. Juno believed in love. Believing in it didn't protect her. Not believing in it didn't protect me. It was an interesting year. This is the story of it.

6

I was disappointed by the University, and vice versa. My fellow students, my comrades in the classics, turned out not to be the dedicated seekers-out of knowledge I'd envisioned. Not only did they not seek out knowledge, many of them hid when it visited. I went to a lot of introductory lectures in the first week of my first term, even in subjects I knew I wouldn't do, or couldn't do because they clashed with English or Philosophy. Those two I knew I wished to do.

In all the introductories, as the lecturers explained the subject and the work that they would cover that year, I looked around me at my fellows. It was a sight to tear at the hardest heart. Anguish and horror ploughed furrows across their low brows as it sank in that they were being asked to read, and not just read but read books, and not just read books but read books with no pictures. By the end of the tougher introductories, whole rows of jaws had slackened in dull horror till they hung like ripe fruit above their owners' laps, swinging in the mouth-wind, dribbling a little now and then. The attached heads sank slowly between shoulders now drooping, postures melted and slumped like lead figures in an oven. They took it pretty badly. It was like watching evolution in reverse.

After the lecturer had called for any questions, and received no response from the ringing, shell-shocked silence, and left, they would crawl erect and drag their knuckles out of the theatre, quizzing each other fiercely.

'Are we to do all that in one year?'

'My God, so many books, surely we don't need them all, does he think we're made of money?'

'If she expects us to read all those she's mad. I'm already going to be doing History and Archaeology, sure you'd want three heads.'

They'd go to the canteen and I'd follow and hover, fascinated. The complaints never stopped, never slackened. The price of the meals, the taste of the coffee, the workload, the booklist, semesterisation, repeat fees, bad holiday jobs, dole regulations. I'd drift from table to table, past clumps of frightened first-years and second-year couples and bearded survivors from another age, repeating their final year for the second-last time. The only constant was the white noise of complaint. I gradually got the peculiar impression that they'd all been promised a three year holiday in Disneyworld, but had been brought here by cattle-truck instead.

'This pizza's shite.'

'I'd piss better coffee.'

'Your man's a fuckin' eejit.'

'Bogroll here's hardly worth fecking.'

'I won't even get a job at the end of it.'

'She won't give me her notes, the bitch.'

'There's no paper in the toilets.'

'He won't tell us the questions.'

'It's too hard.'

'It's too easy.'

'It's too boring.'

The constant whine of self-pity from the student body began to drive me frantic, like a mosquito in my ear. Who were these people? Why had they come here? How was it they were so offended by their own choice of life?

I'd so looked forward to leaving the cultural wasteland in which I'd half-grown up, and in my last year at school I'd fever-visioned a dreamy, sunlit university-state peopled by the brightest and the best. I'd half-lived there for the final school months, it had seemed more real to me than the town outside. To get to the University and find it had fallen into barbarian hands, that its halls were full of the very peasants and savages I thought I'd left behind, still talking about how their new shoes had split on the second day, and of the TV shows they'd missed, and the terrible price of twenty cigarettes . . . it was a bitter blow.

I still hadn't made it out of town. The town limits expanded as I travelled, ahead of me.

Then Juno met Michael.

OK I know I should be modern and not really tell you anything directly, and imply everything, and be subtle and oblique, but I'm no good at that. If I feel I should tell you something I'm afraid I'm just going to tell you it. Another confession: my vice is the Victorian vice of sentimentality, not the modern vice of irony. If I slip, it will be in the direction of old-fashioned sentiment. For this, I apologise in advance.

7

Juno met Michael Fowler in a disco. I know I should say 'at a club' but you know I'm old-fashioned. Dance music was enjoying one of its periods of universal popularity when we arrived in Galway and many of the clubs were so full of a sense of their own cultural importance that they could barely find room for the paying public. I couldn't take them seriously, and quickly got into the habit of calling them discos because it annoyed the more dedicated club-bers. I had a talent to annoy. They didn't expect it from me, which was useful. I didn't look like the sort of person I was. I had the same serene beauty as Juno, though I cooperated with it less. My hair was cut quite severely, while Juno's was long. Also, my posture was lousy, whilst Juno could have descended a spiral staircase in an earthquake with the National Library on her head.

But in this disco, in the Castle one Thursday a couple of weeks into term, it was me that Michael Fowler first approached. I don't even remember what he said, it was nothing offensive, just a tenta-tive line that could have been read as a chat-up from the tone, or left as it seemed on the surface with no embarrassment. Nicely balanced. A request for a light? The time? It's gone. I forget.

I was rude or perhaps not rude, but very abrupt. His face regis-tered a little pain but he took it well, and I felt a little guilty stab, damn, he didn't deserve that, as he turned away. You can tell some people are nice almost instantly, God knows how, but you can. He was nice. Juno stood up and took a step and halted him and gave him a light or the time, and they stood there longer, talking. Not a light, Juno didn't smoke. It must have been the time. When he moved off she sat back down and we talked about him for a while, Juno liked him, he was funny and fast, and then a song came on that we actually liked and we danced.

Later as the lights came up, and the cave of deep bass and strobe-lit statues collapsed back into a hall full of blotchy-faced boys and girls with their hair stranded across their faces by sweat, trying to find their coats and each other, Michael came over to our seat. He was funny and direct and unembarrassable and the three of us left together. It was quite obvious he wanted to sleep with Juno even before he said

'Christ, you wouldn't believe how much I want to sleep with you, Juno.'

Juno reached for his hand and looked into his eyes.

'And I'm afraid you wouldn't believe how little I want to sleep with you, Michael.'

Michael sighed and turned to me.

'Christ, you wouldn't believe how much I want to sleep with you, Juliet.'

I laughed. What was funny, and very disarming, was that he was quite serious, but entirely aware of how he was coming across. It was a strategy Juno and I were both familiar with, a kind of bizarre elevated honesty that mocked itself, but he did it very well. Somehow it was flattering, it was charming. It wasn't likely to work, but it was very entertaining.

The three of us walked back into town along the seafront. There was a sliver of moon, it was lovely. Michael linked his arms with ours. I unlinked mine. Juno didn't.

'So you will sleep with me then' he said, delighted.

She unlinked her arm from his.

'No' she said.

'Ah well' he said, and they linked arms again. I coughed.

'Perhaps I should pretend I have to tie a shoelace, and fall behind a bit' I said.

'You're a genius!' said Michael.

'No' said Juno.

'I suppose both of you together is out of the question?'

'Yes.'

'Yes.'

Michael sighed and we walked and talked on.

There was a lot to talk about. Rumours of a ceasefire. The collapse of Catholicism. *Home and Away*.

At the door we said goodbye and then somehow we were all upstairs in our living room, I was making three mugs of coffee and Michael was lying on the floor in front of the bookcase saying 'wow' a lot and asking if he could borrow Juno's copy of *The Letters Of Groucho Marx*. He took milk, one sugar.

At four in the morning there was still no sign of his leaving and I had a lecture at ten so I went to bed and left them to it.

I got up at nine and stumbled into the living room, where I assembled a breakfast of cereals without at any point opening both eyes at once. Juno's door was closed, no sign of Michael, no clue as to whether he'd stayed or gone. I munched meditatively. Curious emotions swelled in me, small, nameless and contradictory. I had a quick shower and sprinted for University College Galway. (*Sprinted*: Old English Student word, meaning *walked faster than usual*.) The lecture was in Sociology and Politics, known in the Golden Tongue as Soc and Pol. Juno hadn't chosen it as one of her subjects because saying the word 'sock' made her laugh. I burned with curiosity till lunchtime when Juno wandered into the canteen through the usual swirl of glances, sat beside me and took a spoon of my apple crumble.

'It tastes like . . . Johnson's Baby Shampoo?' she said.

'Don't start' I said, 'You'll turn into one of them. It's lovely, and it's very cheap. Sometimes they don't rinse all the washing-up liquid off the dishes, that's all.'

Juno sighed. 'There's nothing wrong with complaining when there's something to complain about.'

'Oh Juno, there's *always* something to complain about, so don't start.'

She took some more crumble, this time from the middle.

'Not bad. And no, he didn't stay over, I can tell you're dying to ask. With great difficulty I managed to get him out of the house at five thirty. I like him a lot, but the persistence got wearing. And I did fancy him, yes, but if he'd got what he wanted last night I'd never have seen him again and he's too entertaining for that. It would have been a waste. I'm meeting him at nine in the Crane and I want you to come along.'

I cocked my head. 'Gooseberry?'

'No, if you're there it'll be a conversation. If it's just him and me it'll be judo. He's promised to show me some of his cartoons, you'll enjoy it, come.'

'But you want him, don't you, at some stage?'

Juno stared into an ashtray full of tiny ripped-up pieces of polystyrene. 'Maybe . . . no. He's not boyfriend material. But . . . I'd like to be his friend. I don't know if that's possible . . . Come along.'

'OK' I said. 'I'd like him as a friend too.'

8

The first obscene letter arrived that day by second post, while we were out. We didn't know it was an obscene letter at the time, but the later ones made it so. We just found it rather peculiar, maybe flattering. Yes, we did find it flattering, only the things that happened afterwards soured that. The first letter was a nice thing to get, a puzzle, very shy. We thought it was embarrassment and shyness that had led to the writer's leaving it unsigned. Perhaps it was, at first.

It was addressed to Juno, and one of the strange, mouse-like downstairs tenants must have picked it up and left it on the hall table inside the front door, among the postal silt of all such buildings, the dusty junkmail and bank envelopes of long-departed tenants. We almost didn't see it, unaccustomed as we were to receiving mail, a standard small, white envelope, nondescript. I'd been hoping for a postcard from a friend who'd gone to London. I glanced at the surface layer on the table and moved past, stepped back, picked it up and handed it to Juno,

'For you. Nearly missed it.'

A neatly printed address. Juno Taylor, 14 McDonagh Quay, Galway. She opened it in the hall, read it going up the stairs.

'Who's it from?'

'I don't know.' She kept reading.

'Who signed it?'

'Nobody.'

She handed it to me, and unlocked our living room door. I sat at the table and read

> *Dear Juno*
>   *I know that you do not know me, and I do not know you. Maybe you will think this letter is stupid. That's OK. All I want to say is that the other day when my life had got so dark and black I could not stand it any more, I saw you pass, you*

shone. I followed you. I know I should not have followed you. I would have thanked you but I was afraid then. I want to thank you now. Looking at you, I cured myself somehow. Your beauty pulled me through. That is all. And I thank you.'

The paper was ordinary, white, a single sheet, folded and folded then folded again to fit the small envelope. The black ordinary print of any letter written on computer. The look of the letters so ordinary. Times I thought calmly. Times Roman. The one you get unless you ask for something else. I carefully refolded the page along the original creases until it was a little white pillow of energy small enough to pack into its envelope. I turned the envelope face up. Stamp. Galway postmark.

'Juno, you do attract them.'

'It's creepy.'

'It's almost nice, for a creepy letter. Polite. Weird prose style, though. And whatever happened to illiteracy and green ink? The guy writes like a computer in love.'

'If it's a guy.'

'Come on, it's a guy. He writes like a guy and you've never got weird shit from a girl. Guilty flirting or straight proposals, but not weird shit. Guy.'

'If it was a girl, that might be why she wrote instead of talking to me.'

'Nah. Guy. I'd bet money.'

'The printing thing, it's scary. The not signing it.'

'But there's nothing bad in it. It's not . . . threatening. Could just be someone shy, or with a stutter.'

'It reads wrong. Could be someone crazy.'

'Most crazy people are perfectly harmless. You've had weird admirers. So this is another one.'

'Mmm.'

'Maybe it's somebody foreign. Bad English. Doesn't know the social conventions. Thinks Walentine's Day is in Oktober.'

Juno laughed. Stopped. 'Our address. Whoever it was must have followed me home, oh God. Don't leave our door open any more, not even going for milk.'

'He, or she, whatever, doesn't sound dangerous. Except maybe to himself. Herself. Itself.'

We called it Juno's Pervert after that. A figure of fun at first. A shy hermaphrodite. We'd spot it shopping.

'That's your pervert there, buying the *Telegraph*. Look at the look it gave you. Definitely.'

And a startled old man would sprint from our interested stares, out of Eason's, bumping into tourists and blushing furiously.

'Look! It's buying the *Cosmo* with the "Sexual Obsession" article! What a giveaway!'

And we'd stalk some poor woman to the checkout. Bookshops and newsagents were good for this game, every purchase a clue to character. After a week or two we'd forgotten the letter, except as an excuse for the game.

9

'And now everyone's annoyed with Freud for being such a beastly patriarch and oppressor and for being totally wrong about everything anyway. Well, you know, what a crock of fucking shit. He was a Viennese Jew, for Christ's sake, a fan of cocaine with a theory of the mind. He couldn't have oppressed the world if he'd tried. People seem to be mixing him up with a chap called Hitler. Freud's theories spread because everybody loved them, they were sexy theories, it was a new idea, near as dammit. A new way to look at ourselves, and Christ we love to look at ourselves. That's all any form of therapy is really, a socially approved system of self-obsession. An excuse for talking about yourself to strangers. Fucked-up people are paying someone money to listen to them talk about how amazingly fucked-up they are. They don't want to waste valuable time being cured. If they were cured they'd have nothing to talk about. They'd be somebody else. They'd have to get a new hobby. Golf or something. As for "alternative" therapies . . . Jesus.'

Michael Fowler pulled deep on his pint. Juno and I looked at each other, and raised simultaneous eyebrows. One got the impression that Michael had not had a good day. Our meetings in the Crane were by now a regular fixture of the week, and Michael's conversational style did have a tendency to incorporate the rant as a major stylistic feature, but today it was scarcely a conversation at all. He had come in, got his pint, sat down, ranted about Galway City Council, ranted about modern architecture, dismissed modern popular music in a cogently argued six thousand words, gone to the toilet, returned with his flies undone and launched straight into a rant about the sort of people who attend therapy, finishing up with his analysis of the popular appeal of Freudianism. He put his pint down and began again.

'The bloody Silva method. You know it? Using coloured pens on pretty scraps of paper, you write out embarrassing, twee, positivist Christmas-cracker mottoes that would make a Care-Bear puke, and you stick these vile, offensive slogans on every available surface, at eye-level. I had a friend who attended a Silva course. Jesus. A sign on his fridge would be telling me that I was a happy and healthy person who ate only what I needed, while I'd be cursing and rooting around behind the vegetables to see where he'd hidden his beer. This was a guy who spent most of his day slumped across his work desk, stoned and giggling, under a big orange sign saying "I am a happy, productive worker, enjoying doing the work I like". I'd go for a piss and be told by the cistern that I was precious, valuable, unique and in the process of deservedly achieving my goals, as I pissed the shit-smears off the back of the bowl. Actually, I think he probably meant that one to be funny, he wasn't a complete moron. But you see what I mean? Therapy designed to make you feel OK about the way you are, while pretending to be therapy designed to make you a new, improved person. Most people aren't happy, healthy, productive people and a bunch of little stickers won't make them happy, healthy, productive people. Most people are dreadful, fucked-up, useless people who should just be honest and stick a My Little Pony notelet on their bedroom mirror saying "I am a dreadful, fucked-up, useless person and I will never change because I like it that way". Psychotherapy. Aromatherapy. Touch therapy. Colour therapy. Native American wanking therapy. A bunch of excuses for buying new clothes, getting your back rubbed and blaming your life on your parents and your starsign. Crap.'

'Michael' said Juno gently, 'what the hell is wrong with you?'

She took the hand that wasn't lifting the pint to his lips and he shivered violently.

'Nothing. Everything.'

'Well that narrows it down. Give us another clue' I said.

Juno frowned at me to take it seriously. Michael didn't seem to have minded, or noticed.

'A bunch of things' he said. 'Sorry, I have been talking complete shite. It's nothing. I'm sorry.'

The conversation slowly turned into an actual conversation but he still wouldn't tell us what the problem was. I had a shocking idea, but I was afraid to ask in case I was right. There was an awkwardness that wouldn't fade, and when we all left early he didn't come back to the flat with us as he usually would for coffee and talk. Juno went straight to bed, on the thin excuse that we had a ten o'clock lecture on Blake the next day. I almost asked her if we shared the same suspicion, but I couldn't bring myself to. After she'd gone to bed I sat up for another hour in the living room listening to *The Hounds Of Love* till the tape clicked off and I switched off the table lamp and sat a while longer by the window, looking out on a level with the high, bright, harbour lights at a fisheries vessel with tarpaulins over its guns, in close to our building, the width of the street away, its radar level with me, and behind it the long rusty bulk of a tanker, and across the harbour all the pretty little fishing boats named after wives and daughters.

10

UCG was built in the 1840s and the 1970s. The original, tiny and beautiful campus was built in the 1840s, to instruct a select few in the classics. The vast bulk of today's university was built in the 1970s, to instruct the masses in assorted categories of engineering, science, commerce and the liberal arts.

The original buildings were erected in stone, by hardy empire-builders who believed in fresh air and a standard twenty feet of headroom, from boardroom to toilets. The offices and passages of the Old Quad were therefore cool and airy in the summer and almost uninhabitably cold in the winter, as the stone sucked the heat from your bones and a combination of ground fog and low-lying light cloud obscured your view of the ceiling.

The modern buildings, in striking contrast, were designed and constructed entirely of glass immediately before the first great oil crisis.

Examined abstractly, objectively, with no clues given as to the intended function of the complex, you would have to guess that UCG was a vast heat-shedding experiment, a machine built on a tremendous scale to discover whether stone or glass could most efficiently transfer heat from the inside to the outside of buildings.

The modern buildings had the advantage there, in that they had far more heat available for transfer. The thermostats had been set high in 1971 and the secrets of their whereabouts, or how to alter them if ever accidentally found, were by now forgotten even by God. Slowly but surely UCG's oil consumption crippled our great Republic's balance of trade and brought the country to its knees, while downwind of the university tropical plants blossomed in a swathe across the rocky wastes of Connemara and carelessly discarded peach stones sprouted luxuriantly before they'd hit the ground.

Thus my thoughts as I snoozed through a lecture on Blake in

the balmy heat of the Kirwan lecture theatre on a cold wet day in November. Professor Flannery Ryan, a fierce rabbit of a man, was blessed with a high, thin voice, a lisp, and, on this particular day, a startlingly deep cough. As he leaped from bass to falsetto and back, neatly avoiding most of the frequencies available to the human ear, but causing consternation among the local whale and bat populations, I rested my chin in my hands and thought about heat and architecture, and the night before.

Juno dozed beside me, oblivious to Professor Ryan's whistles and booms. She hadn't slept well, had eventually given up trying, and had instead read for several hours before falling asleep at dawn. This she'd told me over a shaky breakfast. We hadn't discussed Michael.

I thought Michael was falling in love with Juno. And I thought Juno thought so too.

The heating vent beside me suddenly snored a warm Sahara wind into being, ruffling my sparse notes. Professor Ryan gripped the lectern firmly and loosed a cough like cannon-fire. The benches trembled gently beneath the sleeping students.

'Who, then, exactly, is this "prince of love"?'

(Cough, boom . . . echo . . .)

'This "prince of love" who

> "... loves to sit and hear me sing,
> Then, laughing, sports and plays with me;
> Then stretches out my golden wing,
> And mocks my loss of liberty."

. . . Eh? "And mocks my loss of liberty." Eh? Hey? Yes.'

He loves her.

11

Nothing happened for a while after that. I didn't talk to Juno about Michael and she didn't talk to me. I didn't know how she felt about Michael and, crucially, I didn't know how I felt about Michael. I couldn't bring the subject up because I didn't know what I'd say. I was, if I were to be honest with myself (something I was incapable of being at the time), terrified of my own emotions and quite in the dark as to what they actually were. I had a genius for hiding my feelings from myself, and I was working at the limits of my genius on this one. I knew that I believed Michael had begun to love Juno. I refused to think how that made me feel. If you'd asked me, I would have calmly denied I felt anything at all, and I would have believed that to be absolutely true. The day after the Blake lecture Michael went to Dublin for a week to work on cartoons and layout for a theatre festival, their posters and brochure and adverts and everything, and the crisis was postponed. Great word, postponed. Hoisted higher, on a thinner rope.

The morning before he was due to come back I was due to attend my first Modern English tutorial, in Room 315, Tower 2 of the Arts Block.

I woke early and wandered into the living room-kitchen wearing my favourite night gown, cotton and covered in pale yellow roses with black, shiny thorns on their long, delicate stems. Pouring the milk onto my cornflakes left-handed, because I was holding open Jane Austen's *Emma* with my right hand, I landed the milk in the bowl of the spoon, from which the milk curved back up again and lofted into my lap. Reflexively, my right hand moved, as though to stop pouring, while my left hand poured on. I thought to drop the book (a confused thought, that I could stop the pouring if I was unencumbered by the book), and dropped the carton instead, my hands and their actions utterly confused in my head by now.

Milk everywhere.

Mopping up with toilet paper, first the table because it was flat and easy, then the carpet, then me, I studied the night gown. It wouldn't survive much longer. It was faded and thin and the seams were beginning to go. The hem had lost its stitching almost all the way around. I was shocked at how aged it was. I hadn't really looked at it for a very long time, just assumed it still matched my image of it as it was when new. It had been one of the first items of clothing I had chosen for myself, years before, and it had been far too big for me. My mother had not been able to talk me out of it, literally, for I had tried it on over my primary school uniform. It had 'Night-Gown' on the tag and came in no smaller sizes. I told my mother I would grow.

I wore it for a while, tripping on the hem, then it vanished for a couple of years, reappearing on the foot of my bed one day with no fanfare when I was big enough to wear it. I had squealed with pleasure and ran down to the kitchen and hugged my mother. 'You grew' she shrugged.

I showered and dressed and threw the night gown in the wash pile and left the building. It was cool and foggy out, the tutorial was set for nine. Tutorials got all the awkward times, slotted in around the lectures after term had already begun, trying not to clash with people's other subjects. Juno's was at six on a Friday. She wouldn't be up till eleven today.

I loved the fog. Ships' masts disappeared up into it and I'd imagine them emerging into sunshine, and sailors in crow's-nests up there, waving across to each other, smoking a cigarette in the sun, and the vanished world beneath their feet going on without them.

No, that's not true, I'm romanticising dreadfully here. I thought all that once, and was immediately annoyed at myself for being so wet. 'Crow's-nests, huh' I thought to myself. Hardly anything of any size even had a mast any more. It's the mention and the memory of the night gown.

That night gown is now gone, as I knew that day it soon would be. All those years are gone with it, and while we can't weep for the years or we'd never stop weeping, we can feel a little sorrow for the things that don't matter, the toys and the clothes. That's safe enough. We can keep that under control.

I am trying to tell this story straight, but sometimes it gets coloured by what I'm feeling as I write. Sorry about that. It's only sometimes.

But I did love the fog, as I walked from the docks through Galway, on my way to UCG. No shops open yet, no cars on the streets, the occasional figures on the far pavement lost in fog and thought at twenty past eight in the morning. I was perversely early because I loved the fog. Any later and the clattering of metal shutters and hosing down of pavements and extension of awnings and putting out of signs and arrival of deliveries and staff and managers and customers would have begun to begin, ruining everything. I liked the muffle of early morning fog, the way the very occasional sound sank away completely and was drowned, leaving the pool of silence waiting for the next sound.

As I came over the Salmon Weir Bridge I stopped and my footsteps stopped and I stood looking over the bridge parapet into the white until I couldn't tell the roar of the blood in my ears from the roar of the weir.

A kind of ecstasy filled me then, or rather replaced me: I had disappeared. The world was fog and I couldn't tell the sound of myself from the sound of the world. In the roar of the weir and the roar of my blood with my eyes open and the world erased, I vanished.

Such moments, when they came, were very welcome. I had a turbulent self and was glad to be relieved of its burden for however brief a timeless moment.

Eventually a taxi came by, headlights dipped, very slow, and the delicate kiss of light and movement released me. I returned to the world and walked on.

12

Over the bridge and past the invisible bulk of the cathedral, feeling it like an increase in gravity to my left as I pass it, and along University Road, and across it.

Entering the university grounds now, keeping the low wall on my left, with all the trees in the world penned behind it. Not walking too close to the wall, though, because the sycamores overhang it a good deal, and as the fog condenses on the vast collective surface of their countless twigs and branches and the last autumnal leaves, it's raining pretty heavily under the trees.

Past dull buildings with interesting names. Past the Ladies' Club. Past the Terrapins. Past the Wind Tunnel.

On a whim, because I am early, I swing off course, walk parallel to the tennis courts, up the steps and, hopping over the high lintel of the small open gate set into the large closed gate of the Archway, I enter the Old Quad. I walk to the centre of it, and look around me. The grass fades into the fog on all sides, hints of the bulk of the surrounding buildings teeter on the edge of vision, I can't really see them but I can tell they are there. I pirouette. A small bird flies past me, low, at knee-height, and startles me. From somewhere close by and seemingly above me a big, slurring voice begins to sing a half-familiar piece of opera. Half-familiar to me, half-familiar to the singer, he lurches to a puzzled halt and a window slams before I can remember where I've heard it.

The gravel paths begin to crunch with arriving workers. I leave the Quad, nodding to the ghost-porter who is swinging open the big gate as I slip through the gap. It's hard to speak when the world's this quiet.

As I walk towards the Arts Block and its towers, ghost-students melt out of the fog and solidify into real students and the mood of the morning fades to white and vanishes. I enter the Arts Block as though I were modern too.

There's no fog in the building. Objects have edges. I take the lift to the third floor of Tower 2.

13

Room 315 was small, white and empty. Fluorescent lights, on. Ten black plastic chairs. One long table. I walked to the window and looked out. I was disappointed not to be above the fog, though it was thinner up here. I could see the pale disc of the sun glowing dimly from quite a different quarter to the one I'd expected.

I was looking into the dim sun when somebody came in and dumped a pile of books and papers across the table. I spun around, ghost-suns dancing in front of my eyes, the newcomer's face bleached and streaked and gone in the pile-up of after-images flaring and dying in the centre of my vision.

'Where's East?' I said, and a book tilted and fell off the table and hit the floor flat with a noise like a stomach being gently slapped. The static flared again as I blinked.

'There' he said and pointed past me at the sun. 'I think.'

'Yes' I said as he slowly grew more detailed and more real. 'It must be. Where the sun comes from.' And I felt rather silly. 'But I'd thought the east was over there, where the river comes from, when you can see it.'

'No' he said, 'I don't think so. I think the river flows south into Galway Bay, though the bay runs east to west and out into the ocean. One does tend to think of the Corrib as flowing west and out into the Atlantic but I don't think, on the maps, it does. Easy mistake.'

I could see him now, he looked embarrassed at talking so much. His hand shot out. 'David Hennessey, I'm taking this tutorial, I mean, giving it. I'm their new Modern English chap. I must say, I feel a terrible fraud. People have been calling me professor. Students, I mean. I've been doing Bellow and Updike and Nabokov with the third years and most of them look older than me and I can tell they don't believe a word I'm saying. One of the new boys is trying it on, they're thinking. I must knit myself a grey beard as a matter of the most extreme urgency. Can you knit?'

I didn't think he wanted a real answer, but he slumped into a plastic chair at the head of the table and waited till I said

'No, not really. My mother does.'

He gave a gloomy nod.

'I'm Juliet Taylor, by the way.'

He sprang out of the chair and shook my hand again, 'Sorry, sorry, didn't even ask. I always forget names, so I've never really gotten into the habit of asking. Juliet Taylor. Jolly good. David Hennessey, well, yes.' He sat down again. 'I'll forget, but I forget everybody's. Actually, where are the others?' He looked at his watch. 'Oh, early days.'

I hung my coat on the back of a chair and took *Emma* and a notebook and pen out of the right-hand pocket. It had pockets like shopping bags, which was one of the reasons I'd bought it. The other reasons were that it was rather nicely cut, that it cost only five pounds in the St Vincent de Paul shop, and that Galway had a rainy season that started with a bang in August and ran straight through till the following June. I carefully placed my novel, notebook and pen on the far end of the table from him, and sat down.

'Oh good, you brought *Emma*.' He'd noticed my bookmark, a Maltesers wrapper three-quarters-way through. 'How are you finding it?'

'Oh, it's brilliant, I think she's going to marry Mr Knightley, at least I hope she does.' I blushed furiously as soon as I'd said it. I was supposed to *know* these novels, I was supposed to be *studying* them, not treating them like Mills & Boons. 'I think she's going to marry Mr Knightley.' Oh God. But David Hennessey seemed delighted.

'You managed to skip that foul introduction, then? Thank Christ. It spoils the whole plot in two badly written pages. These bloody introductions to these bloody "classic" editions that tell you the ending and just ruin the book. A law ought to be passed. It's outrageous. Anyhow I won't spoil it for you. Knightley, hey? No, no hints, my face will give away nothing.'

I liked his smile, he did look rather young to be lecturing. A beard would have looked silly on him. A lot of the department did have beards. Professor O'Neill, the head of the department, had a pure white Santa Claus beard. Patrick Norris in Middle English had a black goatee. Donald Kruger (Modern English, though his accent meant you often had to take this on faith) from certain angles looked like a man drowning in hamsters. Even the department's Old English specialist Pamela Henderson cultivated a wispy moustache, which she would stroke fiercely as she read from *Beowulf* in a heavy Derry accent.

In fact, by the standards of the department, David Hennessey was extraordinarily presentable. He hadn't yet developed the bizarre, mannered, tic-ridden voice of the long-time lecturer, nor chosen from the array of twitches, stoops and puzzlingly meaningless hand-gestures that traditionally go with the job. He looked, in short, like a human being and though he did talk too much it seemed to be from nerves, and he seemed to be aware of it. I suspected that, among friends, he would be a good balance of talker and listener. As the rest of the tutorial group began to arrive he retreated into silence, arranging and rearranging his papers. I recognised some of the others from lectures but didn't know any of them well enough to start a conversation. A few of the new arrivals mumbled to each other, while a last straggler straggled in, looked around for somewhere to sit, left, and returned with a chair. Everyone fumbled intently with biros without catching the tutor's eye until it became evident that anyone who would be turning up had done so. David Hennessey coughed.

'OK, well, I'm your tutor in Modern English and my name is David Hennessey. I'm very bad with names, so if we all write our names on, ah, hideous scraps of paper and prop them up in front of us we will be saved a vast amount of embarrassment later on. Well, when I say "we", I mean I will.'

People tore paper and fumbled for pens. I wrote 'JULIET' in neat capitals on a page from my notebook, and wondered should I add my surname beneath, seeing as I'd already told him it. As I hesitated, the girl beside me glanced at my sheet of paper and wrote 'RACHEL' on hers. Seamus looked at hers, wrote 'SEAMUS'.

Jason wrote 'JASON'.

'KATHY'

'MAOLISSA'

'JANE'

'SIOBHÁN'

'TOM'

'TOM'

They looked at each other. The first Tom, annoyed and out of space, added 'FITZMAURICE'. The second Tom, triumphant, added 'FOX'.

'Everybody finished? Good. Well, as it said on the noticeboard, we're going to have a crack at Jane Austen today. Now I know not all of you have finished *Emma*, which incidentally is wonderful, so I hesitate to spoil the book by discussing it in detail before you've all finished it . . . How many of you have actually finished it, by the way? Oh. I see.'

Nobody had finished it.

'And how many have started it?'

Me, Rachel, and Tom Fox.

'Oh dear. Well, how many of you have, in a spirit of commendable perversity, started or finished any of Jane Austen's other books recently?'

I wasn't sure if I should put my hand up again so I didn't. Neither did anybody else.

'Hmm. Let's try to clarify this. How many of you have never read anything by Jane Austen?'

Six reluctant hands.

'Oh dear. Oh dear. I'm not here to insert a knowledge of Jane Austen's work into your heads via the ear. This is a tutorial, you understand, not a lecture. We are all supposed to *discuss* Jane Austen and her fine works, in particular *Emma*, which I recall asking you all to read on the notice, which I assume you read, telling you about this tutorial. We are meant to exchange views, to debate furiously the merits and demerits of her prose, to attack the plausibility of her plots, praise the clarity of her depiction of a male society from which she was so largely excluded, place her in her context and analyse her legacy. If you have failed even to bring sandwiches and a flask of tea to this Feast of Reason, then I cannot see how we can succeed in these modest aims.'

He stood, and frowned. 'If I was Robin Williams I'd stand on the desk and do this but we're not insured for it and the ceiling's too low. You may imagine I'm standing on the desk, though. And lit beautifully.' He cleared his throat. I felt an absurd urge to applaud, which I fought back.

'You have studied, filled in forms, undergone examinations, trials, ordeals, to win a place here. I have to assume you have within you a love for English Literature, or at least a capacity for such love. I have to assume that you actively wish to read these great books and poems and dramas, and will rush to do so at the slightest encouragement. Therefore I am now telling you that I expect you to have read *Emma* by next week's tutorial. If you haven't read it by then I would prefer you not to turn up. I have absolutely no qualms in expecting this of you, because I truly believe that the experience will enrich your lives. It will also enable us to have a meaningful discussion of the book at our tutorial, where everyone is equal and armed with the necessary knowledge to take issue with me and with each other as we tease our way through it and admire it from different angles in various lights. He leaned forward and put his palms flat on the table, looking us each individually in the eye, one by one, even the shy Maolissa, coaxed by the silence into reluctantly looking up from under his blond fringe. David continued.

I do not demand that you master the jargon of literary theory, I do not demand that you bury yourself in the major critics. I merely expect you to read the works, which will tend to be novels of the nineteenth and twentieth centuries. You are no doubt attending, or failing to attend, lectures and entire courses where you can get away with regurgitating half-understood literary theory and a fistful of quotes from the eminent critics without having actually read the text, but in my tutorials that will be a hanging offence. Yes, I will throw an assortment of critical theories at you in the course of these tutorials, a variety of specific and general approaches to the works, which I will expect you to ponder, evaluate, and either accept or discard in the light of your own reading of the works. But the critics are, to coin a phrase, just tools.'

Jason sniggered. David, wearing a smile of surpassing innocence, carried on.

'The important relationship is between you and the book. I am interested in what you truly think, not in what someone else thought, nor in what you think I want to hear. I have perhaps an intimidating manner, but I tell you this, I will never think less of you for voicing an opinion, no matter how much I disagree with it, as long as it's your honest opinion and you have the courage to state it and defend it if necessary. You do not exhaust these works with a single truth. They can bear a great weight of conflicting opinion. We are each of us creating a fresh work as we read it into being. To read a good book well is perhaps the greatest, the richest and most rewarding thing you will ever do, short of creating a new life. On the more practical side, if any of you at any point do not have and cannot afford one of our tutorial texts for whatever reason, come to me either here or in my office and I will supply you with it. I have stacks of the cheapest possible editions of all of them, which I scatter about me like confetti anyway in my mission to bring civilisation to Europe, so think absolutely nothing of it. Neither of us is doing the other a favour. It is fair exchange. I give you the book, you read it. We are quits.

He paused. I breathed out. He glanced at me, and then away, out the window into the golden mist. I followed his glance. A bird flew past the window, too close, in a shallow dive, then flicked a wingtip and down into the mist and gone. The mist was thinning. I looked back at David.

Again, if there is anything you do not understand please ask. These books may be written in what is technically known as Modern English, but Modern English has been around quite a while now. Both the words and the world have changed considerably. Some will have been written in your lifetime, but in an England or America unfamiliar to you. Much may be obscure. You are still very young. You are not expected to know everything. That's why you are here. Do not be ashamed of, do not hide your ignorance. Ask. I may not know but I can ask in my turn. We will solve mysteries. We will lay bare truth. We will argue. We will learn. We will, I hope and believe, enjoy. For my sake, for your sake: Enjoy. That American-derived imperative form is a great addition to the English language. Ladies and gentlemen, I give you Jane Austen, PG Wodehouse, John Updike, Roddy Doyle, William Shakespeare, David Lodge, Vladimir Nabokov, Dick Francis, *Oliver Twist*, *Catch-22* and *The Great Gatsby*. Enjoy.'

He bowed. Some of us began to applaud. He sat back into his chair. The spontaneous applauders were joined by the rest, nervous and reluctant, dragging the speed down. He waved us into silence.

'Just read *Emma* for next week, OK? Now, please do ask any questions you might have.'

I slipped my hand into the air when it seemed no one else particularly wished to.

'I've heard of the others, but, um, who is Dick Francis?'

David Hennessey smiled. 'Ah. Yes. Dick Francis . . . Well some of you are bound to know Dick Francis. Anybody?'

Halfway down the table Tom Fitzmaurice, a boy with a great frizzy head of brown curls, spoke, his voice cracking high on the first couple of words.

'He, he's a writer, well, ah, he writes thrillers. About horses.'

He immediately looked as though he bitterly regretted opening his mouth.

'Yes.' David smiled again. 'Quite correct, he's a bloody fine writer of racing thrillers. My particular area of, ah, expertise, is that of genre fiction, the kind of books which are usually not considered literature at all. At this point in the century, however, you'll find some of the best and most vigorous writing is marketed as genre fiction. The literary novel is, in my opinion, suffering from a crippling self-consciousness. It has too many options. It's paralysed by freedom. After *Ulysses*, after *Lolita*, after *Gravity's Rainbow*, no subject is taboo, no style too outlandish. It's been very bad for the literary novel of course. Absolute freedom is oppressive and always leads to a dreadful conformity. Can you tell free-verse poets apart? Can you tell abstract paintings apart? Can you tell contemporary literary novels apart, with their tiresome ambiguities, their massed ranks of unreliable narrators? I mean how many of you can say in all honesty that you prefer John Banville to Stephen King?

There was a horrified pause, as though we'd been smilingly invited to grasp an exposed electric wire. Then Rachel spoke up beside me.

'But that's just populism, that's just saying it's good because it sells, it's good because it's mainstream.'

David shrugged. 'Shakespeare was mainstream. Jane Austen was mainstream. Dickens was mainstream. Modern literary fiction's gone down a dead end. By abandoning the mass audience it's cut off its own tap-root, the spring of its vitality.' He seemed to be enjoying himself now, as his unexpected attack on literature goaded the slumped students erect in their seats.

'So are you honestly saying thrillers are better than, you know,

Booker Prize winners?' said Jason, a pugnacious tough in a faded Fatima Mansions T-shirt that read 'Keep Music Evil'.

'I'm saying a good thriller can be better than a bad Booker nominee. Not just as entertainment, but as literature. Of course, good genre writers are happy to be kidnapped by the literary establishment, by us. Which maintains the status quo. When Cormac McCarthy writes a truly great western, we refuse to call it a western. When Kurt Vonnegut writes a truly great science fiction novel, we refuse to call it science fiction. *All the Pretty Horses, Slaughterhouse Five*: it must be literature really, because it's good. Circular argument. And ask any publisher' said David, 'the Booker book is as tightly defined a genre as the western . . .'

'But you're contradicting yourself, you said literary fiction has no rules and now you're saying it's tightly defined' said Rachel, exasperated.

'Well, how would you define a literary novel, a novel of literary merit?' said David.

'It's written . . . it's written . . . it's not written for money.'

David nodded encouragingly and said 'Dickens wrote for money.'

'It's not just written . . . I mean . . . it aims . . . it tries to do something new.' Rachel was struggling.

David nodded and said 'All Shakespeare's plots were stolen.'

'The style, the style is new'

'The words are more important than the story' broke in Maolissa, formerly The World's Quietest Boy.

'Interesting . . . good, Maolissa . . . this is all good . . . Seamus, you look like a man with an idea.'

'It's really that, we agree that, there's a type of book from a type of publisher and we call it literary fiction, so, it's how it's presented, it's an artificial construction, it's a social construct . . .'

David nodded. 'Good, interesting approach . . . But, well, Beckett's novels were first published by a French pornographer. Were they literature then? Or did they become literature later? Siobhán?'

'They were literature always'

'OK, good, we're getting somewhere . . . But, looked at from another angle, can a book stop being literature? Nobody reads Galsworthy now. He used to be literature. Has he stopped being literature?' Nobody wanted to go for that, it felt like a trap. We mulled it over suspiciously. David smiled and moved the argument sideways. 'Is literary value something we discover inside a work, that's intrinsic to the work, or is it a label we stick onto the work, that we can always take off again if the fashion changes? Does the writer make it literature, or the reader?'

Maolissa raised his head cautiously. 'Whether it's literature or not isn't about the reader, or the genre either, it's about the ambition of the writer.'

'Ambition, excellent point. But let's flip that on its head, to test it. Could a great work of literature be written by mistake? By an unambitious writer? Could you think you were writing a formulaic piece of junk and accidentally, for subconscious reasons, or through innate talent, write a great piece of literature by mistake?'

Yes said Siobhán and No said Maolissa, and we were off. David unobtrusively stepped back from the argument and began to act as referee. Our arguments got better, as our brains slowly warmed up with use. David held it together, kept the debate moving briskly, and subtly coaxed contributions from the mice on the margins. Even when their initial ideas were banal and, frankly, stupid, he treated them with respect and we took our cue from him and did likewise. After a while a few of them flowered into quite respectable human beings with interesting views, especially surly Jason, who turned out to have an incandescent passion for Patrick Kavanagh, the poems and the novels. David's were the only tutorials I ever attended which weren't dominated by their tutor and perhaps two or three interested students.

I don't mean to give the impression that ten lives were changed in an hour. It wasn't like that. Life isn't.

But at the end of that first Modern English tutorial there was a vigour and a pride to the air as the group dispersed, and I moved to the window and looked out to see the fog had lifted, burned off by the sun. Exultantly, I thought 'Oh no, too gross, too crude, "Look, the fog has lifted from the world." Must nature be so obvious? Where is her Art? I would have done it better' and I felt like a writer or a God, looking down on the shimmer of the river through the trees, flowing in the wrong direction to the sea.

14

The heady rush of that first tutorial carried me giddily through the scholarly day. On Tuesday morning I was astonished to find it still hadn't worn off. I awoke glowing with rude intellectual curiosity, and raced into college. I was early for my lectures, I took legible notes, and at lunchtime I read about the Famine as I ate lasagne, each putting me off the other in a grisly, and indeed gristly, feedback-loop of multi-sensory horror. That evening I stayed late in the library finishing a long-overdue essay on Aristotle's *Poetics*.

When I finally crawled home, exhausted with virtue, Juno had already gone to bed. She seemed to be sleeping uneasily, I could hear her mumbling something through the thin door of her bedroom. The air was warm but the stove was out, I touched it, cold, it hadn't been lit. A faint smell of burning in the air, though. Cigarettes? More like paper . . . both. I sniffed and shrugged. Cooker. One electric ring was on full. That was most unlike Juno. Michael must have been round, lighting cigarettes off the cooker again, and left it on. Spa. Pity I'd missed him. The downside of this newly virtuous life. I switched off the ring and stood swaying with my face in the rippling column of heat above the ring, feeling its power fade. God I was tired. My brain ached like a muscle. Bed.

In bed, I fell straight into an uneasy, unpleasant half-dream and dreamt I was trying to row to an island but the oarlocks were too loud and kept creaking and everyone was going to hear me and they wouldn't let me land, and the beach filled up with couples and they wouldn't let me land, and as the boat sank beneath me I sank into the cool silent dark and it was beautiful.

15

I walked into Juno's room the next day in my ordinary nightdress, not my night gown with the roses, and saw Michael's narrow back. His face was hidden in my sister's hair. Her back was to his chest. The tiny single duvet had slid down and half-off them as they slept. They faced the wall, the two of them forming the same curve.

I stopped before the bed and stirred their mingled clothes with my right foot. I lifted Michael's jeans a little, grasping the belt with my toes. I let it go, and drew out Juno's shoe and slid in my foot. Wrong foot. I pushed it back, under his shirt, and turned to go.

'Juliet' said Juno.

I turned again, to see her twisting in his arms to raise herself.

'Juliet, we didn't, last night, there was another letter . . .'

Michael was blinking and waking. He rolled on his back and looked past Juno at me.

'Juliet' he said, pleased and sleepy. 'Morning. Juno, Juliet, morning.'

Juno put her hand over his mouth.

'Shush. I want to talk to Juliet about the letter and everything. Stay.'

She got out of bed in her Doris Day pyjamas and pulled the duvet up over Michael.

'Hey, my arm's dead' said Michael, lifting his left arm from under the duvet with his right hand, and laying the arm across his chest. 'Look' and he lifted and dropped it a couple of times with his right hand. He attempted to swing it off his chest under its own power, to lay it by his side, but his control of the dead arm was erratic and it buckled back at the elbow and the dead hand slapped across his face.

'Ouch' he said. 'Hurts. And pins and needles.'

'Very good, Michael' said Juno. 'Now put it away before you do any more damage' and Michael laughed till he coughed.

I thought, They have private jokes.

In the living room-kitchen I sat at the table while Juno put on the kettle. 'Michael' she shouted. 'Coffee?'

'No, yes' dull through the shut door. 'Milk, one sugar.'

Juno sat across the table from me. The kettle began suddenly to rattle as the element warmed and expanded. It was the noisiest kettle I'd ever heard. I glanced up at Juno.

'I got another letter' Juno said, holding my glance. 'From the pervert. He really is a pervert. And he's definitely a he. It wasn't a nice letter. It wasn't like the last letter. It was . . . I waited a long time for you to come home.'

'I stayed late in the library, that essay on Aristotle's *Poetics*.' Juno nodded but I kept going

'. . . It was overdue, you know I had to get it done . . .'

'You couldn't have known' Juno said. 'But I got upset, alone with it, I burnt it.'

'I smelt the smoke when I came home.'

'I burnt it to stop it . . . I washed the ashes down the sink. But it was worse, remembering, and not remembering, and thinking, did he say that? Did he say that? I shouldn't have burnt it.'

'Oh Juno, I'm so sorry.'

'I got into a bit of a state. I nearly went looking for you but I was afraid to go out. And then Michael called.' She shrugged.

'He loves you' I said.

'Yes' she said. 'But we didn't do anything.'

'It's OK' I said.

'Mmm' Juno said.

'No, it's OK' I said again.

Juno stood up and walked round the table. She sat in my lap and put her arms around me like I used to do with her when we were very young and I was frightened by something on the television, or by something that I'd heard somebody say. I rested my cheek on her shoulder, I could smell my shampoo on her hair, we liked different shampoos but she'd run out a few days before and had been using mine. I breathed way in. The smell of her hair, the smell of my hair. This must be what it would be like to lie beside me.

'I would never hurt you' she said, very quietly.

'No, it's OK' I said. The kettle would boil soon. I could hear the noise changing. It was moving toward the quiet, low roar of boiling point, the tone deepening and widening.

'I don't mind' I said. 'It's good. He's nice. You like him. I'm . . . It's good.'

Juno turned her head a little toward me to kiss the top of my head. Her hair bunched and piled against my face as she turned. I inhaled again the sharp smell of the shampoo, harder.

'Thank you' said Juno. We were silent. 'I wish he didn't love me' she said.

'Mmm' I said.

'It's . . . I don't think he's used to love. Even though he's been through college and everything and travelled and done all those things . . . he doesn't seem very grown up about this. He seems too happy. Is that stupid?'

'No' I said.

'He says he's never been in love, but Michael . . . how much should I believe? I mean, he does exaggerate all the time . . . But I think he loves me. And I like him an awful lot. Do you think this is a terrible idea?'

'No' I said.

The kettle was boiling now.

'He was lovely last night' said Juno. 'About the letter. I was nearly hysterical. He was . . . considerate. I didn't think he was that nice, you know? I liked him a lot but I thought he was cold inside. Funny, but self-obsessed. Harsh. Funny but harsh. But he was crying. Shaking . . . He held me till I fell asleep. He wasn't . . . I didn't think he could be so nice . . .'

'Kettle's boiling' I said. I lifted my head from her shoulder. Juno unwrapped her arms from round me and stood up.

'Oh yes. Coffee?'

'No' I said. 'Or, I will, yes. Thanks.'

There was a tanker in the harbour, unloading oil by the huge storage tanks. Three tiny men stood on the deck, their arms in the air, waiting to receive the weight of the first of the rigid, hinged pipes that was swinging out from the dock into position over their heads, ready to be coupled to the valves through which the oil would be pumped ashore. I had watched it perhaps a dozen times before. I admired them, it seemed such real work. Some of that oil would heat buildings I passed through. They wrestled the pipe down to the big valve.

A spoon chimed off a lip as Juno made three mugs of coffee.

'They're unloading a tanker in the harbour' I said.

'Mmm?' said Juno. 'Oh. I think I made yours a little strong.'

'It's fine' I said as she put it on the table. I took a sip. 'Fine.'

16

The three of us walked to the Dramsoc auditions. Michael had painted the sets for their last production, and if they paid him for that tonight, he would be painting the sets for their next production too.

The auditions were held in the Aula Maxima, where the play was due, ultimately, to be performed. The Aula was a lovely old Gothic limestone barn of a building, straight across the Quad from the Main Arch. As we approached the Main Arch from the tennis courts we could see the front of the Aula across the grass and gravel, at the far side of the Quad, framed nicely in the archway, its massive wooden doors surrounded by reddening creeper. We entered the archway, walked through and out into the Quad and the last of the day's light, across the grass to the steps of the Aula, arguing.

'You bastard, you gave me the impression you wanted help painting a set and now you're saying we're auditioning? You've set us up for an audition? Michael, I can't act.'

'Oh, Juno said the same, and even if it's true you attach far too much weight to it. Have you ever seen student drama? None of them can act.'

'But I don't want to act.'

'Oh they won't hold that against you. You could walk in by mistake to do the dusting and you'd end up playing Hamlet. I'm afraid you're beautiful, and thus doomed to act. They'd rewrite a one-man play about a rugby-playing sperm-donor to give you a part.'

'Michael, you're not listening, I can't act, I don't want to act, I won't act, cancel the audition.'

'Ach it's nothing as formal as that.'

We were at the double doors. Michael swung the left one open and bade us enter. Juno entered, and he patted her bottom as she did so. I entered and he didn't. He entered and I slapped his bottom hard. He gave me a hurt look, I gave him a sweet smile, Juno laughed and then looked contrite as Michael switched his hurt look to her.

'Poor Michael' she said. 'Beaten and mocked. It's hard, being an artist.'

He grabbed her and growled 'A little more sympathy and understanding from the little woman, please. I fall upon the thorns of life, you know, I bleed.'

'Not as much as I do' said Juno very quietly and kissed him. They stood backlit and framed by the open door. Soft piano music played from somewhere. It looked ridiculously like a scene from a film. I felt sublimely ill.

Ironic applause came from the far end of the empty room. 'Bravo! Magnificent, magnificent, Michael.' I turned but could not see the speaker in the long gloom of the room, the stage in darkness.

'A wonderful entrance. It had everything.' A tall, thin boy with a great swag of dark brown fringe jumped down from the distant stage and walked into the light. 'Drama, passion, beauty' he continued towards us 'mystery . . . what did she say to you, to make you blush so, Michael? So this must be Juno' arriving at us, he shook her hand 'and Juliet?' he reached for mine, I grasped his, a handshake as firm and reassuring as a salesman's. 'Delighted to meet you both, I've heard so much. I'm Dominic O'Connaire. I have the honour of being Auditor of Dramsoc this year' an ironic bow.

We walked toward the stage. 'I'm not here to audition' I said.

'I'm afraid Michael may have misled you' Juno said. 'We can't act.'

'Oh, none of them can' said Dominic airily. 'We haven't had a decent actor in Dramsoc since the Emergency, isn't that right Gemma?'

I looked where he was looking and saw a girl sitting at a piano in shadow at the back of the stage. For a moment the thought, Oh there's a girl up there playing the piano, sat comfortably alongside the thought, And I must remember to ask what's that album they're playing, until with a mental double-take I realised that the music that had been playing softly since we entered wasn't a recording. Gemma looked up from the keyboard. Her face wasn't pretty, but was very alive, very strong, with high cheekbones, long dark hair, a severe spiked fringe.

'We had a good actor, but he died' she said. Nice voice, carried well. An actress?

We arrived at the stage. Dominic bounded athletically up and over the lip, avoiding the steps provided.

'A sad business' said Dominic, frowning down at us. 'Got a good review in the *Irish Times* for a thing we did at ISDA. Singled him out. "Tremendous, controlled performance. Seldom have I seen . . ." Ego burst.' He looked sorrowfully at his shoes for a moment and seemed briefly lost to melancholy. 'Seven hundred and seventy-six people signed up on Societies Day . . .' ('. . . free Murphy's . . .' explained Gemma) '. . . all pledging their immortal souls to Dramsoc, in their hearts' blood. Three have turned up for the open auditions.'

'You should have promised them free tequila slammers' said Gemma. Dominic ignored her again. I didn't like him. Then again, I didn't like anybody.

'We're waiting for the man' said Dominic to Michael.

'On the piss?' said Michael.

'Worse. On the wagon' said Dominic. 'Probably can't tie his shoes with the shock. I sent the three laddeens away for a fag, they were annoying me with their wetting themselves and their stench of fear. "But we don't smoke". Well fucking learn, I told them. Ye're actors now.'

Michael walked up the steps onto the stage with Juno, holding her hand. He nodded Dominic to one side. Dominic had a last attempt to look down my cleavage, sighed, and joined them. Juno crossed her eyes down at me as Michael and Dominic began to talk money.

I simmered gently. Gemma stood up from the piano and walked over to the stage edge. 'He's a pig, isn't he?' she said to me. Dominic, with his back to her, oinked without turning around. I nodded. 'Fag?' she said.

'Don't smoke' I said.

'Well, you can sit upwind' she said, walking down the steps and taking my elbow. 'If I stay, I'll hit him.'

'Again' said Dominic over his shoulder.

'Harder' she said, over hers.

'Juliet' I said. 'Juliet Taylor. That was lovely, the piano.' We began to walk slowly towards the door.

'Gemma Mannion. I was making mistakes all over the place, but thanks anyway.' She released my elbow to take a packet of rolling tobacco from her pocket, removed a packet of Rizlas, and began expertly to assemble a rollie. 'Are you auditioning for Dominic's mad republican version of *Cavalcade*, or the Synge?'

'I'm not auditioning for anything. I'm here with my sister and' that trip of indecision when someone has dual roles in your life 'her boyfriend.'

'Her boyfriend' didn't sound right, but neither did anything else.

'Oh, Michael.' She smiled. 'Yes. She seems to have calmed him down a lot. He was a mental bastard last year.'

We looked back to where Michael stood on stage with his arm around Juno, talking to Dominic. They must have sorted out the money. Now Michael was gesturing broadly with his free hand, all of them laughing at his description of an exhibition opening he'd attended in Dublin, I could pick out the artists' names. He'd told myself and Juno the story before, it was funny.

'Why, what did he get up to last year?' I said absently, still looking at him. We were standing just inside the doorway now, shadowed.

'Oh, you know' said Gemma, pausing to lick the Rizla. 'Every kind of mad crack' and I could tell he'd slept with her, the evasion swept around the unspoken admission like a river round an island, just helping to define it.

'Yes' I said. 'He's pretty wild alright.' I looked back at Gemma and studied her more carefully. No, not pretty. Better than pretty. Interesting. Her face was alive and her body seemed restless just standing, like a dancer waiting to go on. 'Are you auditioning?' I said.

'No' she said and lit the rollie. 'They don't bother auditioning me any more. I end up in everything anyway.'

'So that's the auditor of Dramsoc. No wonder nobody turns up for auditions.'

'In . . .' said Gemma, paused, and emitted a cloud of smoke that emerged from the shadows to blot out half the Aula '. . . deed.'

'If he's auditor, what are you?' I asked.

'His girlfriend' said Gemma drily.

'Shit, sorry . . .'

'Don't worry, I'm thinking of resigning the position. He claims he only pretends to be a sexist arsehole to wind people up, and for the laugh, like. But for the life of me I can't tell the difference between pretending to be an arsehole all the time, and actually being an arsehole. I suppose I should have done philosophy.'

I was still somewhat preoccupied with the biting of my tongue, and said nothing. From the stage, Dominic looked over at us. 'No smoking. Out' he called.

'After you, dear' said Gemma, placing a hand in the small of my back as she took a deep, deep drag and released it straight up like a steamtrain blowing off pressure. Was that an actressy 'dear' or a country 'dear'?

17

Gemma and I walked out onto the stone steps, into the low autumn sun, the enclosed Quad holding surprising warmth. An unshaven derelict was sitting on the top step, slump-shouldered, staring into space, the bottle in his right hand, the cigarette in the other. The collar of his tweed jacket was frayed. Smoke from the cigarette swirled out of his mouth and drifted round his neck like a spiderweb scarf, to reappear at the back of his head. The air behaved oddly in the Quad, enclosed, and heated, and protected from the world outside.

'Hello, Connie' said Gemma, and the derelict stood up, straightened his shoulders, and turned into a dignified man in his forties, maybe fifties, sporting a short, neat beard and wearing a favourite old jacket. I'm too quick to judge, I thought despairingly. He put his cigarette in his mouth to free his left hand, passed his bottle of Lucozade over to it from his right hand, and shook hands with Gemma, saying 'Gemma, delighted, sorry I'm late', the cigarette bouncing on his lower lip as he spoke. Smoke swirled up into his eyes, squinting them, as he looked at me.

Gemma introduced us. 'Conrad Hayes, he's writer-in-residence. Juliet . . .'

'Taylor'

'. . . Taylor, she's auditioning with her sister.'

'Oh right.'

'I'm not really.'

'Oh that's a pity, you should. It's a very good experience for anyone, I feel.'

'Connie's doing workshops with the auditioners. The basics.'

'They're usually rather enjoyable.'

'I'm not an actress.'

Perhaps I said it rather forcefully. He took a step backward, slipped on the smooth step edge, and dropped his bottle of Lucozade.

Gemma pointed out fragments ('Can't risk the fingers, got a recital Saturday . . . bit over there by the Tayto packet'), while I helped him pick up the pieces, and he was absurdly grateful and humiliated.

When I'd piled all the sticky glass into Conrad's hands, we re-entered the Aula. Conrad cautiously tipped the sharp wet heap into a bin and then looked around helplessly, arms outstretched. His hands began to flutter like butterflies. Drinker, I thought, disapprovingly. He brought his arms in to his sides and half-closed his fists, touched them to his hips, trying to stop them fluttering without being obvious. Poor sod.

'You should rinse your hands' I said. 'Slivers of glass.'

He began to walk toward a door at the back of the hall. 'Locked' said Gemma.

He made a noise of annoyance. 'I'll use my own place.' He headed toward the double doors, stopped, and turned. 'You really might like acting.'

'No' I said. 'May I wash my hands too?'

'Of course, yes' he said, flustered. I followed him outside, and diagonally across the grass of the Quad to the far right corner. 'The grass isn't too wet? Your shoes?' he said anxiously, halfway across. 'Too late now, I suppose.'

'It's fine' I said. We walked in through the open door of the tower. He hesitated. 'You have an office here?' I said, impressed.

'An office of sorts, yes.'

'Beautiful building.'

'Cold building . . . hmm, my rooms are at the top, it's easier . . .' He led us past the stairs along a corridor, a sharp right, along another longer corridor, to a toilet with a quaintly skirted female figure on the door. 'There you are' he said, and turned.

'Don't you want to wash your hands?' I said.

'Oh, no, no, no' he said, taken aback. 'This is . . . I'll wash them in my rooms . . . off my rooms, I'm used to . . . there's a washroom, in my corridor . . .'

'I shan't tell' I smiled.

He hesitated. 'Well, my generation don't . . . can't . . . I've never been in a ladies' toilet' he said.

'Oh, they're amazing' I said. 'Jacuzzis, attendants, waterbeds . . . If you're lucky a eunuch will anoint you with oils.'

'In the present, ah, political climate, I'd prefer not to risk it' he said, and smiled back.

'Save you a walk.'

'I'm old-fashioned' he said, apologetically, and bowed to me and turned away. I went in and turned on the hot tap.

'So am I' I said into the mirror. Slowly and carefully I washed the stickiness and glittering fragments from my hands. Then I had a wee and stayed in the cubicle while thinking of this and that. Then I unlocked the cubicle door, washed my right hand and returned to the Aula.

18

By the time I arrived back at the Aula, things were looking up. A good half a dozen people who couldn't act had arrived.

Conrad greeted my return warmly. 'I thought you'd gone home.' His breath smelt of whiskey.

'Dominic said you were on the wagon' I said.

'I was' he said happily, rolling a cigarette. 'I gave these up too.' His hands were rock steady.

'Can't do that in here' said Dominic. 'Fire regulations.'

Conrad licked it, stuck it, and placed it behind his ear. 'Fine Dominic, fine.'

Then the original three Dominic had told to take a fag break rolled back in singing with a bunch of new friends. They had obviously taken their break in the college bar, and recovered their spirits there.

A quiet, skinny fellow wandered in and began to rig some lights. He dimmed the hall lights to try out a new lighting board with lots of knobs and sliding switches. The walls faded, and were gone.

We were in a space.

Suddenly, all about me was theatrical life. On the stage, Dominic began auditioning those who'd acted before, Conrad began workshopping the basics of drama with the theatrical virgins, while Michael worked on the sets. You could smell the greasepaint, et cetera. It was the kind of bustling, flirtatiously theatrical atmosphere designed to seduce a young lady into giving her heart to the theatre.

I hated it.

I had always hated actors and acting. I had disliked very much the experience of acting in our school plays. Acting is a kind of lying with your whole self and it can infect the self. I could neither understand nor share in the enjoyment of acting that many of the other girls felt. They had frightened me a little with their willingness to stop being themselves, with the joy they took in it. I could never lose myself. Even in the tiny parts I played, I could never stop being myself, I was afraid to stop being myself, and would stand there, stubbornly, hopelessly me, imitating something outside of me. I was scared and a little contemptuous of those of my classmates who could abandon themselves, act another part. They seemed to get drunk on it, frightening me more, level after level of loss of control. For weeks after, they would seem to be acting their own lives.

Lurking in the dim light of the Aula then, I hated it but I couldn't bring myself to leave. I hung around, without really joining in. When Juno was free I chatted with her. I helped Michael build sets till I hit his thumb with a hammer. I chatted with Gemma a bit. Mainly I watched Juno, as she chatted, as she acted, as she lived. I saw her as though through the eyes of the others, I imagined what they saw when they looked at Juno.

Very beautiful.

Very still.

You could see anything you wanted in her.

I would look at her when we were fourteen and I would see myself. She looked more real to me than I did. Our faces identical, our hair the same then, long and blonde, I would hold her by the shoulders in our room and look at her as in a mirror. She joined in the game. I would stick out my tongue at her and she would stick out hers at me. We would blink together, and rock our heads from side to side in unison. She was very quick. I'd try to catch her out, and fail. Then she'd smile and I wouldn't and the illusion would be gone. I'd look into her smiling face, no longer my face, and think, She's nothing like me, and feel desperately alone. Happiest days of your life.

I looked at her laughing across the hall. And felt desperately alone. How I hated her. How I loved her. It hurt.

Dominic stuck two fingers in his mouth and whistled, a shriek like a rabbit in a snare. 'Everybody in the centre for this one. Chop-chop.' As a dozen or so boys and girls assembled in the middle of the room, and I found a shadow and glued my backside to the wall, Dominic dragged two plastic chairs out onto the sprung wooden floor and placed them back to back, about ten feet apart, either side of the door. He walked back toward the stage, did the same with two more plastic chairs at that end, and returned to the centre of the wooden floor.

'Goalposts: we're going to play football. This is the football.' He held up nothing. 'There's no offside, no referee, I trust you to keep it clean and not to cheat. First to three wins.'

He divided them into boys and girls. My heart shrank. 'Boys versus girls . . . in the World Series . . . of Lurve' said one spotted dick. Dominic tried to steer me onto the floor. I was stuck to the wall like a suction cup.

'I'm not an actor' I said, again, exhausted from saying it.

'It's just a game' he said

'I don't play games' I said

He left me.

The boys kicked off. I hated it. They passed the imaginary ball from wing to wing, balanced it on their heads, flicked it from foot to foot, danced past the tackles of the girls. There was some uncertainty and giggling at first but the boys very soon got serious. The spotted dick scored, a hotly-disputed header from a tight angle.

'I was right in front of you!' said Gemma. 'How's that a goal? I was right between you and the goal.' The boys shouted her down. The girls muttered among themselves, put Juno in goal, and kicked off from the centre circle. Michael tackled a shy and retiring pre-Raphaelite and won the imaginary ball, took it with him along the wing nearest me. Juno came out to meet him. Michael slowed, feinted left. Juno took the ball cleanly from Michael's toe, but he refused to acknowledge it and kept going, the imaginary ball tight to his feet, leaving Juno standing there, staring after him.

'Goal!' he said, dribbling it through the chairs.

'I can play this game' I said, and walked onto the pitch.

'What?' said Dominic. He and Conrad had been standing on the sidelines, unobtrusively talking, observing, and taking notes.

'I can play. This' I said. (As I had a sudden flash of memory. Watching *Match of the Day* with Paul and Aengus, them arguing about offside decisions while I prayed for Gary Lineker to score, so that I could watch him getting kissed, hugged and fondled, in close-up and slow motion, by the rest of the team, again and again.)

I picked the ball out of the back of the net and walked to the centre circle, put it down, and walked forward. 'Kick it to me for fuck's sake' I said to the long drink of water nearest it. She feebly poked at air. The ball came to me, I cut straight into the box and slammed it sidefoot across the body of the keeper, who went the wrong way.

I picked it out of their net, walked back to the centre circle and threw the ball at the chest of their least effective-looking player. He dropped it, tapped at it, back vaguely toward his keeper. Michael ran across and intercepted it, tried to go by me. I stood straight in front of him. He went into me, and was so surprised he stopped playing for a moment and didn't even try to recover the ball. I put my foot on it, made to go right, went left with the ball, left him standing. A huge red-haired ox of an engineer tackled me and there was a moment of confusion as we both came out of the tackle with the ball.

I believed in mine more. I scored from the centre circle.

It got a bit heated and personal. 'They've got more players!' the boys complained to Dominic. 'Either she goes off or one of you comes on.'

'Why don't you both join in' I said, 'they need all the help they can get.'

'Fair enough' said Dominic, and he and Conrad came on for the boys for the restart.

'Now they've got more' objected the long drink of water in my general direction.

'So what' I said.

Dominic tried to go past me on the wing, I tackled, took the ball, but he'd done this before, knew the tricks, saw through me, kept going, and all the eyes and players followed him.

I went after him and I kicked the fucking legs from under him, from behind. 'Foul!' 'Card!' 'Ref!' shouted the boys.

'There's no referee' I said. 'Dominic trusts us.' I turned the ball around the spotted dick and drove a rising shot into the roof of the net. 'Three. We win.'

I walked out of the Aula, and went home.

19

Juno and I had been in the library every night for a week. We arrived early enough to get seats opposite each other, at the same table, and we stayed till it closed at eleven at night. All our books and notes in a great pile between us.

Juno was studying history carefully and well, highlighting the key points as she slowly read a paperback on the Reformation, taking notes at the end of each chapter to summarise the argument.

I was studying her.

The familiar despair and paralysis had me. I would never get it done. I couldn't hold my attention to the page. What blocked me from doing what I had to do, what I even wanted to do? How could Juno find it so easy? I had my lecture notes on Yeats open in front of me, but I'd only read through two pages in an hour. Every change in the hum of the fluorescent lights, every crack of a fresh page turning, every whisper between distant friends ten tables away whipped my attention into a towering, helpless foam. The door to the stairs banged, and my thoughts jangled like cutlery dropped on concrete. Just another week to go, nothing done. When would I learn? Where would I find the discipline? And: Why was I, why was I, why was I wasting so much time in fruitless self-reproach when all I had to do was *start*. Start *now*. Eyes down. Pick up the pen. Read the words. Study.

Yeats' love poetry. Realistic, personal. 1903 Maud Gonne marries John MacBride.
Disillusion?
He celebrates his loss. <u>*Helen of Troy*</u>*. She is beyond blame or comment. Complete change of style: topical, specific, prosaic, yet poetic and universal. Like the Greek Myths. Deliberate parallels.*
Yeats, Joyce: new mythologies.

Just words to me, no sense. I threw down the pen and pushed away the foolscap notes. All just words to me. I rested my chin on my forearm and watched Juno over the low wall of books, watched her eyes darting back and forth, back and forth along the long lines of the Reformation text, taking it all in. How could she do that? To the bottom of the page, turn over. Scanning it in. Stop. Highlight a line in yellow. Move on. Her hair about her shoulders waved a moment, the long blonde ends drifting a lazy inch, and then back, above the black table in the brief breeze as the door to the stairs opened. Slam. She read on, impervious to disorder, immune, blessed.

I couldn't bear it, looked away. Why weren't we the same? I glanced about me, countless heads, all lost in learning, or seeming so. Far down and to the right another head looked up, a boy, dark hair, goldframed glasses, handsome. He yawned and stretched his head back and closed his eyes a moment. Oh look at me, I thought, startling myself. He took off his glasses right-handed and rubbed his eyes with the knuckles of the left. Replaced them, returned to work. Disappeared among the rows of heads, studying.

My eyes filled with tears. Juno, with the usual casual intuition, looked up. Leaned over, whispered

'Are you OK? Want to talk? What's wrong?'

Infuriating, infuriating. I blinked them back and wiped them away with a sleeve and said 'Nothing. Headache' and she said

'I think I've two Paracetamol in my bag downstairs' and went to stand and I said

'No', rather too loud, and 'no' again, 'I can't concentrate . . . I'm going to go clear my head' and I walked to the door and through, slam, and ran down the stairs making a hell of a clatter and out of the library, picked up my coat and bag from the heap in the foyer and out into the drizzle and cold air. Oh, lovely. She'd bring my notes home when she left.

I walked home by the canals, but there was no heron at the little weir.

When I exploded into the living room I startled Michael, who was rummaging in the drawer by the sink.

'You're early' he said. 'Where's Juno?'

'Still studying' I said, disappearing into my room and shutting the door. Well, no, slamming the door.

I threw my bag into the corner and dropped full length on the bed. Face into the pillow.

A tentative knock at my door. Slowly it opened enough to let Michael peep round it.

'Er, Juliet . . .'

'*Yes?*' through the pillow.

'I thought maybe, ah . . . you knew where the can-opener might be.'

20

I helped him find the can-opener, I helped him find the saucepan.

In my best Australian soap opera accent I said 'You're a *moron*, Michael.'

'I can do it, I can do it. Once I'm past the tricky early stages it's a breeze. Opening the can, that's where a lot of people lose it completely. They fail to grasp that opening the can is possibly the most important step of the entire process.'

He clamped the opener to the can.

'Too many people are dazzled by the details, lose sight of the basics.'

He slowly ran the opener round the rim.

'This is where the war is won or lost. I've seen it so often, perfectly intelligent people, lawyers, doctors, hereditary peers, could buy and sell you, thinking "No, not the Ritz tonight, I think I'll stay in and have some baked beans" and two hours later there they are with their parsley sage rosemary and thyme, but they've neglected the *basics.*'

He tipped the beans into the saucepan, pushed the flap of lid down into the can, put the can on its side on the floor, crushed it flat with his heel, picked it up and slid it into the small, almost full plastic rubbish bag hanging by the sink.

'And where are they then, Juliet, for all their wealth and intelligence and the perfect toast and every sauce known to man? *Fucked*, that's where.'

He turned on the heat and sat in the green armchair, across the table from me.

'See? The rest's a formality, a child could do it.'

'Describe Juno' I said.

He blinked. 'What, physically?'

'No, the things you like about her. Why you like her.'

'Whooo.' He ran his palm across his chin. Stubbly noise. I liked

it. We used to do that to our father when I was very young.
'Tricky . . . where to start? . . . well, first of all, she *is* very beautiful'
a nod in my direction 'as you well know, but it isn't that or not
just that, of course not. Lots of beautiful women in the world.
She's . . . strong.'

He was struggling, moving his hands about, trying to pick the
right words. Taking the question seriously.

'She's very strong, I mean, ah, morally, she's a good person. I
can trust her. And she's worth trusting . . . This doesn't sound
very appealing, does it? Sounds like I'm going out with a nun.
Intelligent . . . Christ, I don't know why I like her so much. She's
just not like anybody else. She's beautiful, she's tough as nails, she
wouldn't have obeyed orders at Auschwitz. And she's an incredible
fuck, I mean I don't know, sorry Juliet, I can't explain it. I didn't
want to love her but I do and I can't explain why.'

He got up to stir the beans and add some black pepper.

'Is she . . .' I changed tack. 'What do you think she sees in
you?'

He looked over at me. 'Why on earth are you asking these
questions? Got a sociology essay to do on human bonding?'

I shrugged and smiled a none-too-impressive smile.

'Interested' I said.

I felt like an old wooden dam with too great a head of water
backed up behind it. I felt an extraordinary, almost unbearable
pressure, as though I would crack or split or burst if any part
of me began to weaken. The smile was a risk. I held myself
still.

He could tell I was serious.

'You're studying too much' he said. 'You need a break.'

'Tell me' I said.

He shrugged. Lot of shrugging going on. Happy Italian family.
My eyes were hot in my head but I held myself still. He was
wearing black jeans and a T-shirt he'd made himself, white print
on black cotton, a still from a film of the Nuremberg rallies, a
night shot of the great searchlights roaring straight up into the
black sky above the stadium. Under it a simple mathematical for-
mula, a refutation of Keats: 'Truth $\neq$ Beauty'. Truth not equal to
beauty.

'Tell.'

He put two slices of bread in the toaster.

'My dog-like devotion' he said.

'No' I said.

He looked at me again. 'You're right, it pisses her off. I can't help it. I try not to smother her. I know . . .'

Long pause.

'I realise that she . . . doesn't feel as strongly about me as I do about her. Hard, that. But I'm older, had never loved. Had further to fall. I try to keep it in check. Then the danger's swinging the other way.'

Sharp look at me.

'I try . . . this sounds ridiculous . . . I try to love her less. And then of course . . . you're on word of honour, girl. This is not for broadcast.'

I nodded.

'Between us? Because it's difficult, not speaking . . .'

I nodded.

'All bastards love good women, helplessly. But it doesn't stop them being bastards. The love is real, but so's the bastardry. I feel so helpless when I'm away from her, in Dublin or in London. I hate how much I need her, really rage against it.'

He was talking down into the saucepan now, stirring. Choosing his words more carefully than usual. He reminded me suddenly of David Hennessey, that high seriousness. Oh Michael you're deep after all I thought, only half mocking.

'So short a time, and I've been away a lot already, and that's going to get worse . . . Did I tell you they might want me in London, set design on a Pop-Art musical, Roy Lichtenstein back-drops and cartoon characters?'

I shook my head.

'They saw the Dramsoc show that made it to the Fringe, shit show, good sets. Rang me out of the blue on Tuesday. Afraid to mention it in case it doesn't happen.'

He brooded till the toast popped. I wasn't sure if he was going to go on. He was giving me an answer to a question I hadn't asked. He seemed to wish to justify himself, though I'd accused him of nothing. I had that in common with Juno. Our silences drew confidences, and confessions. Again though, Juno more than me. The sticks and the stones by the side of the road would tell her their stories if she stopped for a moment, and cry for Cyclops and Goliath at the end of it. What a talent for inducing guilt we had. What reproach in our silence. What a terrible gift.

I watched him as he found a plate, buttered the toast, poured the beans on, left the saucepan in the sink to soak. These banal and domestic actions didn't lessen him or make him absurd and again I was reminded, strangely, of David in the tutorials.

Michael put the plate on the table, but remained standing. Clasped his hands behind his back.

'When I try to love her less, because she's not around and I know she loves me less than I love her and it's too painful . . . other women offer me comfort. Women from my past, and new women. *But I don't fuck them.* Already I've ended up in . . . in the arms of one or two. But I didn't fuck them.' He walked around the table and crouched by my chair, and I looked straight down into his face, my eyes darting from his mouth to his eyes and back, and I thought 'My God, what question did I ask?'

He held the arm of my chair, head not much below mine, weight forward, on the ball of the foot. 'And I wanted to. But I love her, helplessly and stupidly and probably too much. I've ended up in bed with women I've liked very much, but I haven't fucked them. I've been pushed into bedrooms at parties, I've had to tuck my cock back into my pants, I've lain awake beside women I've wanted, with a short bar of iron between my thighs, but I haven't fucked them. I've ended up in these situations because I hate the stupid lovesick puppy I've turned into, I *want* to prove I'm free, and I'm still me, and I'm still a bit of the old bastard. But I can't do it. I kiss them a lot and talk about Juno.'

My face was burning. I opened my mouth slightly to get more air.

'Sometimes I'm attractive and sometimes I'm not. I don't know what controls it, but since Juno I've been radiating something, you know it's true, I won't fake modesty with you. When myself and Juno went down to Tipperary for the weekend even her friends were coming on to me. And it's very difficult and it's going to get worse.'

His face seemed closer to me.

'When I love her too much, she retreats. When I love her too little I risk ruining everything. Some day I'll slip, and I'll resent

65

Juno for my own infidelity and I'll resent the girl I've fucked and it'll be very bad for everybody.'

I realised my face had been drifting closer to his and I jerked back. He stood up.

'Thank you' I said very formally. My face was so hot. I could feel sweat at the roots of my hair, at the back of my neck, at the base of my spine, between my breasts.

'Ach' he returned to his side of the table 'it's a relief to talk. I have to be so careful with her lately.'

'I think it will be alright' I said, still formal.

'Hmm' he said and sat down to his meal. 'Let's change the subject.'

We changed the subject, and Michael was funny and kind, and the bleakness slowly lifted and dispersed.

By the time Juno arrived home we were laughing ourselves sick remembering the best bits out of Billy Wilder films.

'Juno! Good to see you! Do you remember the bit in *The Apartment* where Jack Lemmon's draining the spaghetti with a tennis racquet?'

I objected 'Billy Wilder didn't make *The Apartment*.'

'Come on' said Michael. 'Of course he did. What's black and white and still funny? A Billy Wilder film.'

'Your headache's better then' said Juno.

'Oh yes' I said.

'What headache?' said Michael.

'I wasn't feeling well earlier' I said.

Juno said nothing. Oh God, I thought.

'It wasn't really a headache' I said. 'I just felt terrible and I couldn't concentrate so I left the library and I couldn't bring myself to go back.'

'I brought your notes' Juno said.

'Oh, thanks.'

She put them in the middle of the table. Michael stood.

'Coffee?'

Juno nodded yes, I said yes.

They went to bed early, after the coffee, and I put on music and danced round the living room, on my own. I danced thoughtfully rather than ecstatically, but I danced.

21

In the last Modern English tutorial of the year we pestered David
Hennessey with questions and complaints about the exams.

Both questions and complaints were greeted with sighs. He
seemed to have a lot on his mind, was almost snappy, appearing
preoccupied sometimes with something that was none of our
business. It was unsettling.

'Children, children, you are here to do exams, it's the point of
the exercise. Don't *wince* Siobhán, I shall continue to call you
children for as long as you continue to be childish. When the
English exams were immediately *after* Christmas students complained that the study spoiled their Christmas. Now they are
immediately *before* Christmas and students complain that they have
no time to study. Personally I think the lot of you should be
herded into the basement and executed, and that we should start
again with candidates who actually wish to learn, if any such can
be found, but of course the department won't listen to me, so
I'm stuck with you.'

The levity seemed forced, masking a genuine annoyance with
us. Several times over the course of the tutorial he spoke with an
unusual sharpness and then expanded and exaggerated his ill
humour till it became self-mocking and the sting was removed
from the initial remark. But it made for an uncomfortable hour
and by the end of it we were unusually subdued. He was enough
his old self to seem to notice this and regret it. As we gathered our
books and notes he gestured the rising end-of-class conversational
mumble back down to silence and said

'Before you go, I'm sorry if I wasn't entirely . . . supportive
today. Events in my own life are occupying much of my attention
at the moment and I'm afraid I was a little bit, ah, brusque with
some of you. Please accept my apologies. I was entirely at fault
there.'

He coloured a little, paused, and pressed on.

'As this is our last tutorial of the calendar year, I'd like to say one or two, ah, embarrassing things which we can all forget over the holidays. Firstly, it's been a great pleasure teaching you this year, and in the case of *The Great Hunger*, a great pleasure being taught.'

This was a tutorial in-joke too complicated to explain, at which we all gratefully laughed as a way of shyly avoiding the compliment.

'Secondly, none of you need fear these exams. You've fine minds and a fine understanding of what literature is and how it works. Believe me, many of you will be surprised at how well you do. I have great confidence in you.'

A brief, pleased and embarrassed silence.

'Thirdly, may I wish you a Merry Christmas and a Happy New Year? And read *Heart of Darkness* and *The Great Gatsby* over the holiday, they're not long.'

A chorus of mock indignation and some 'Merry Christmases', and the group dispersed.

I found myself beside him in the crush for the lift.

'Could I buy a *Heart of Darkness* off you, sir?' I said.

'Oh lord, Juliet, don't call me sir, it makes me feel hideously old. If you're stuck for one I'll give you one, of course.' The lift arrived and he stepped back politely to allow the others in first.

'Oh no, I don't mind paying, it's just that they'd sold out yesterday in the college bookshop and rather than traipse around town looking or maybe forget, I thought I'd ask you now and save time.' I was overexplaining, and stopped myself, blushing crazily and feeling like a perfect idiot. The lift, full, descended, leaving us alone by the silver doors.

'Well, certainly, yes.' He hit the button to summon it back up again. 'I've a stack in my office, nice cheap Wordsworth Classic edition, nothing wrong with it. So you'd like a copy now?'

I nodded. 'Unless you're in a hurry.'

'Oh no, not at all.'

We stood in silence. The floor indicators showed the lift approaching us. I cleared my throat.

The up-light went off and the doors clattered open. We each waited for the other to move. David waved me forward and I entered the lift.

We ascended to the top floor of the tower and stepped out into the corridor of the English Department. I followed David around two corners, to his door.

He opened the door, which hadn't been locked, waved me in. Leaving the door ajar, he began looking.

'*Heart of Darkness* . . .'

Absent-mindedly he indicated a chair, and I sat. The office resembled a large library in a small telephone booth. The computer was buried in books. The bookshelves round the walls were jammed to capacity, and tall piles of paperbacks occupied the corners of the room. From a stack of new books in the far corner, which wasn't very far at all, he extracted a copy of Joseph Conrad's *Heart of Darkness*.

'Here, yes.'

He stepped back and gave it to me. I stood, took a note from the money-pocket of my bag and made to pay him.

'God, no, don't be ridiculous. Take it. I've no change and they're so cheap, it's nothing.'

'No, I must pay for it.'

'Look, really, it's nothing. Buy me a coffee sometime.'

'Now' I said.

'Pardon?' he said.

I stuttered slightly in my eagerness not to be misunderstood. 'I'll buy you a coffee now, if you're not busy. It's not a, I'm not, it's, you look like you need one and you gave me this, so . . .' I shrugged. Thank God for the shrug.

He looked at me thoughtfully.

'Well, that's very kind of you Juliet. Thank you. I'm afraid I'm being collected by a friend in' he checked his watch 'twenty minutes, but I'd be glad of a quick cup of coffee first, thank you. The canteen, I suppose?'

We left his office and made our way down to the canteen. He loosened up, unbent as we walked, began to seem younger than in the tutorials. By the time we sat with our coffees at an empty table in the large and, this early, only half-full canteen, I was almost at ease with him. Almost. I even dared to ask him what had been on his mind during the tutorial.

'My father is dying' he said, which rather put me back to square one, blushing and apologising and wishing I'd kept my mouth shut, or better yet, not gotten out of bed at all. He brushed it off.

'We've both known for some considerable time that he was dying, it's not a great shock, but the results of two tests came through yesterday and they're both bad. He has less time than we thought. I'm very close to him, I took it rather badly. Rather worse than he did, in fact. I shouldn't have taken it out on the class today, but their complaints seemed unusually petty, I was a little disappointed in them, and that didn't combine at all well with the mood I was already in. I wanted to get stuck into *Murphy*, and they wanted hints on the Middle English paper.'

I apologised on behalf of the class, sounding depressingly pompous in my own ears.

'Oh, not your fault, and at least we got some discussion of the book in towards the end. Besides, it's understandable that you're worried. You're a conscientious lot, by and large. I should have been pleased you cared about the exams at all. Half of this year's take are probably going to fail at least one paper. None of you will, or not the regular attenders anyway.'

I didn't particularly want to talk about the exams, and changed the subject. 'Could you have had an office in the Quad if you'd wanted?'

He seemed amused. 'Not since about 1969. Rather before my time.'

'But people do have offices there.'

'Oh, accounts, admissions, the building department. Only useful people, not us flighty academics.'

'But Conrad Hayes has an office in the Quad, and he's in the English Department' I said.

'Conrad Hayes is a special case. He was appointed as a kind of writer-in-residence and as such has a special status, and quarters in the Old Quad.'

'Alcoholic-in-residence' I said involuntarily, a phrase Gemma Mannion had used in the Aula.

He looked startled. 'Well, yes, ah, he does . . . well, yes, he is an alcoholic. He used to be quite a fine dramatist though. Marvellous first play. Dreadful second play, but marvellous first play. *The Living*. I saw it revived in the Royal Court when I was even younger than I am now, I found it most affecting. It was quite a talent he ruined.'

'What's it about?'

'Oh, sons and mothers. An uptight father. Everybody eloquently unable to communicate. The guilty secret, the usual. It's the same play Druid have been putting on under different titles for twenty years. A repressed rural family bottling everything up, all the better to uncork it in the third act. Heritage theatre, for the tourist crowd. They had a big success with it when they were starting off. Of course it's yet another rewrite of *The Playboy of the Western World*, like all Druid's stuff, but good of its kind, confident. He did it very well. He had a strong, clear, funny, original voice in that play. It says nothing but it plays like a dream. If only he'd found something worth saying in the subsequent twenty years.'

'Has he written much since then? I mean, I'd never heard of him before I came to Galway. I've never seen anything by him.'

'Oh he's written the odd thing. There's the second play, which is just shockingly bad, and a novel, God, the novel, it's named after his ex-wife I think, *Sarah*, or no *Sandra*, no, it is *Sarah*. My memory revolts against containing such information. Awful "experimental" nonsense, quite unreadable. Worse than *Lost In The Funhouse*.'

'That's his second play?' I said.

'Bless your ignorance, no. *Lost In The Funhouse* is a novel, and another man's drivel entirely, John Barth. Continue in ignorance of John Barth's *Lost In The Funhouse* and you will lead a long and happy life.'

I had, literally, kicked myself for making the mistake, not too hard a kick, but he seemed actually pleased I hadn't heard of it.

'The technical term for books like *Sarah* and *Lost In The Funhouse* is "utter crap".'

'So why's he writer-in-residence then?' I asked.

'Ah. Brilliant question. You could baffle a finer mind than my own with a question like that. I'll attempt to guide you toward the truth, though.'

He paused and steepled his forefingers and looked comically stern and professorial for a moment, and I felt a surge of warmth towards him as I thought of how often I'd seen him look like that in the tutorials and not thought to think he might be born of mortal man and have a father he was fond of, private worries, private grief. He'd always looked so composed, so controlled, like this: gathering his thoughts, answering my questions, telling me things I didn't know. I felt absurdly like a schoolgirl with a crush and I laughed at myself, don't be silly, Juliet. But there was such a lot I didn't know, and I could feel the world expand as I listened to him. He seemed to have such a firm grasp of the goings-on of the whole, great, gaudy globe. I was only eighteen.

'Hayes . . . Do you really want to know all this about Hayes?'

I nodded yes.

'Conrad Hayes.' Pause. 'Writer-in-residence.' Another pause. 'God help us. You've got to understand that the universities of this world are as brutally exposed to the fickle winds of fashion as are the catwalks of Paris and Milan. Or perhaps a better comparison is with the stock market. Yes . . . The university system is a vast, sluggish stock market of ideas, with various major centres of trade, Yale, Harvard, Columbia, Oxford and Cambridge of course, the Sorbonne. All the minor universities of the world take their cue from the great markets. If, and I'll speak of the wonderful world of English literary criticism here, Dickens' stock begins to rise in Yale, the other markets will follow suit. Dickens will return to the core curriculum, Dickens Studies will be offered in a dozen centres throughout the world, a Dickens Chair may well be instituted in the neobrutalist gold-glass-and-steel university of some nouveau riche American oil town, and for a vast fee the board of governors of Hickslick Illinois will manage to poach from Yale the very man who started the whole Dickensian gold rush with his startlingly fresh approach to *Oliver Twist*. His reputation secured by the amount of money he's being paid to take two classes every six months in what might as well be the wilds of Borneo, he can now relax. He need never make a fresh approach again, unless perhaps his eye is caught by some pretty girl or boy in the front row and even then his approach is unlikely to be, and doesn't have to be, original. He can stop publishing. He can grow fat. That round of the game is over. Already some fiery-eyed revolutionary is riding into town, Cambridge perhaps, from, say, Italy, bearing aloft the strange device post-structuralism. Dickens ceases to exist. The word goes out from the markets: ditch the author, invest in revolution. The academic hem shoots up six inches.'

He took a sip of black coffee, and raised an am-I-boring-you eyebrow. I gave a please-do-go-on nod. He continued.

'Sometimes books are important but authors are an embarrassment to be hidden in the attic when visitors call. Sometimes authors are so important there's no time left over for reading the books. Sometimes books are texts and you can be hauled in front of a disciplinary committee for calling them books. Sometimes semiotics takes over completely and the English language in its entirety vanishes. Frequently the novel is dead. Shakespeare is sometimes dead and sometimes God, but across the corridor in the Philosophy Department God is sometimes dead too, so Shakespeare watches his back at all times and gets Marlowe to taste his food for him. And every academic finds his career rising and falling in the wake of these great movements. The greatest living authority on *The Ancient Mariner* is destroyed by the collapse of Coleridge Preferred. A bullish run on the Beats pushes a previously obscure Milwaukee professor to giddy heights. It's a marvellous game. Of course I'm speeding it up to make it interesting, most of these shifts take years. But back a decade or so there was a brief boom in utter crap. The utter crap market just exploded overnight, if you'll forgive the image. Certainly it boomed very quickly, over a period of only two or three years. If it was pretentious and written on drugs, you could name your metaphorical price. There was a particularly virulent form of structuralism floating around at the time which worked brilliantly on plays and novels that had no plot and no character development. It was a bit of a write-off when applied to Jane Austen or Shakespeare or Henry James but a lot of universities had invested heavily in this brand of structuralism and they had to use it on *something*. Negative reports were beginning to come in from the provinces. "We have applied your theory to *Huckleberry Finn*, comma, and it appears to be nonsense, full stop. What should we do, query? Message ends." Well, it was a full-scale crisis. The beast of theory has to be fed. If it wouldn't eat steak there was obviously something wrong with the steak. Luckily, the solution was simple. Throw out the steak, and find it something it *could* chew.'

He sipped his coffee again and I thought about how sad he looked when he was being funny, and did he do that deliberately to make the funny bits funnier by contrast, or was he really sad?

I didn't know, I didn't know him at all. He put the mug down and looked past me.

'After a little trial and error, someone in Harvard came up with a strain of experimental literature running from about 1956 to the mid-1980s that kept the theory purring like a cat, and the word spread like wildfire. Across every campus in North America, coast to coast and right up to Quebec, you could hear full professors on the phone to their Utter Crap brokers, screaming "Buy! Buy! Buy!" It was a good boom while it lasted. And it lifted Conrad Hayes to giddy heights. Both his second play and *Sarah* fitted the requirements of the age. Here was a man who could write Utter Crap for both page and stage! Academia wet itself. Some students revived his second play in Prague, and it proved so obscure that they were all arrested on suspicion of attempting to bring down the government. Huge kudos for Conrad! He was suddenly the fairy on the Christmas tree of fashion.'

He waved at the illustrative reality, standing in a tub off to my left and shedding its needles already in the artificial December heat of the canteen.

'Prestigious reprints of *Sarah* and the second play ensued. Ironically, his good play was legally tangled up with a bad Irish publisher and didn't get reprinted. Nobody wanted it anyhow, it made sense. Anyway, offers of posts followed high profile reviews of the reissues. Half a dozen writers were raised from the dead in this fashion, including a couple who'd actually been buried and who therefore weren't in the best position to take advantage of this upturn in their fortunes. Conrad Hayes, though, through the lucky circumstance of an expensive English divorce and an inadequate salary as a junior lecturer in Trinity, hadn't had the financial wherewithal to drink himself to death since *Sarah*, and so was alive to receive a generous offer from the University of Texas which he accepted with a speediness that would have put men half his age to shame.'

He paused.

'Am I boring you to tears with this? Conrad's life is a great source of departmental fascination and gossip but I can't imagine it being of any great interest to anyone living a real life outside these walls.'

'No, go on, I really am interested. It's like a soap opera with a real person, alcohol and America and everything. Failure and success. I'm interested in other people's lives.' I felt so stupid. 'I mean, everyone is.'

'Alright. The story continues. Conrad . . . did you know that Conrad's not in fact his name? He was christened Conor Hayes, was always known as Con, changed his name to Conrad for the first book and later changed it officially, by deed poll?'

'You know a lot about him' I said.

'Conrad Hayes . . . Conrad Hayes fascinates me . . .'

'But you don't like him.'

'No. He . . . disgusts me is a bit strong. I haven't been in UCG long but I've learned a lot about him. I do not like the man at all. I shouldn't' he smiled 'speak about another member of the department like that in front of a student but I feel rather strongly about Conrad Hayes.'

'What did he do that was so terrible?' I said.

David said nothing.

'You don't have to tell me' I said.

David sighed, looked at his watch, gulped down some coffee.

'I should feel sorry for him. He achieved recognition too late, for the wrong thing. For the wrong reasons. When he got a good post it was under false pretences, writer-in-residence in Austin, Texas. He'd been talking for years about his great unfinished work, sometimes a novel, sometimes a play, but it never existed. They found him out in Austin, saw through him very quickly. After a couple of classes they didn't even let him take classes. He was a wreck. He was kept on the payroll for a couple of years out of pity and because it would have been too cruel and embarrassing to make him face the fact that he wasn't writing and he wasn't capable any more of writing. Then UCG got a vast European grant and in a fit of hubris somebody decided we should have a writer-in-residence and Conrad heard about it and the University of Texas colluded with him to win the post and get him off their hands, played a very sly game pretending to try and hold on to him, and UCG got stuck with an expensive turkey. No one has the guts to admit they made a terrible mistake, so they stick him in the Quad well out of everybody's way and pretend to believe in his impending masterpiece and hope he'll drink himself to death. It's a mess.'

He looked at his watch again.

'Probably best if you treat this chat as confidential. They get very touchy on the subject and I'd find myself fielding self-important little memos from Flannery Ryan if he heard I was speaking ill of other members of staff, especially one he helped to appoint.'

'You can trust me' I said.

He gave me a huge smile, much wider than the usual tight, controlled smiles I'd got used to. He seemed to have surprised himself with it. 'Of course I can. Sorry.'

I smiled and shook my head at the apology. 'Why do you dislike him so much?'

He paused again. 'He betrayed his talent. He betrayed himself. He didn't have to turn out like that.'

'But you can't hate someone for hurting himself.'

'Mmm. He named himself after Joseph Conrad you know' and he pointed at my book.

'Really?'

'Yes. Did you have any Joseph Conrad on your Leaving Cert course?'

'No, not my year. *Typhoon* was optional.'

'Pity. He's good. Terribly serious, but good.'

I grinned against my will. He raised an eyebrow and I shook my head.

'Well. Thank you very much for the coffee, Miss Taylor, and now I must leave you, my friend is probably waiting.' He rose to his feet. 'Enjoy your Christmas, and I'll see you in class on January . . . twelfth?'

I didn't know. 'See you then, sir.' He winced. 'And Happy Christmas too.'

He gave a funny little bow and left.

I finished the last of my coffee, cold now at the bottom of the white mug, and sat a little longer looking at the cover of *Heart of Darkness*, a beaten up African steamship chugging away up-river, into a bank of fog.

22

The day before the first exam I went to a film. Not to the cinema, but to a College Film Society showing of *Wuthering Heights*, in a lecture theatre. 'Revise Without Studying!' said the posters. The moribund Film Society had been taken over that September by a group of high-spirited first-year English students, and in the week before the exams they had been running a successful and well attended mock-educational Seven Day Season of vaguely course-related films. I'd seen Kenneth Branagh's *Henry V* at the start of the season, instead of studying *Henry IV Part One* as I should have done, a typically guilt-inducing evasion of my proper work. Even as I'd sat there I'd known that, had it been on my course, as it would be in a year's time, I probably would not have attended. For the subsequent five days I'd avoided study a little more subtly, with the books open in front of me, but now it was Sunday evening in the library, the first English exam was at nine the next morning, my other three first-year subjects filled out the following days of the week to the full and if I was unprepared in English I was even less prepared in them. My head was throbbing and booming, on the verge of migraine, and my mouth tasted of metal. I stood and when Juno looked up I said quietly 'I'm going to see *Wuthering Heights*.' She nodded, and apologetically indicated the neat stacks of notes in front of her. I shook my head, it's fine, and left.

On the concourse I queued between rowdy groups of engineering students who didn't have exams. The boys made crude remarks about Juliette Binoche and the girls made crude remarks about Ralph Fiennes.

I recognised some other first-year English students in the queue and was relieved to see that most of them looked anxious and depressed.

Then I'd paid and was in the theatre. I walked down toward the front and was hailed by Dominic O'Connaire.

'Juliet! Here!'

I turned to see him sitting with Gemma and Conrad, a dozen rows from the front. Oh shit. But Dominic seemed pleased to see me. Extraordinarily pleased, given that I'd nearly broken his ankle from behind the last time we'd met. He and Gemma indicated the empty seats beside them. Double shitty shit shit. Oh well. I edged in, and Dominic bade me sit beside him. I could smell the drink coming off all of them. Ah.

'Revision or relaxation?' he said expansively. Of course, he was in science.

'Both' I said. Gemma said hello, and Conrad reached across both her and Dominic to shake my hand. He had a firm handshake and my hand jerked in his as I remembered why we'd had no chance to shake hands before. Our hands had been coated in Lucozade and broken glass. Oh lord.

'Good to see you again' he said. 'Pleasant surprise. I won't ask you, don't worry.'

'What?'

'Have you changed your mind about acting?'

'I'm afraid I haven't' I said and returned my attention to Gemma and Dominic as Gemma said 'How's the study going?' and Dominic made a horrified face and said 'What a *question*, we'll be talking about the weather next.'

'It's going OK, I suppose' I said. 'I feel I've left everything too late and I'm going to fail everything, but . . .'

'Yeah, same here, and you never do. It's always the way. I suppose if we didn't panic we'd never get anything done. Have you read this?' she said, meaning *Wuthering Heights*.

'Oh yes' I said. 'Three or four times. It was on for my Leaving Cert. I loved it.'

'Ah yeah, it's great. My sister's class did it last year, they all fell in love with Heathcliff. I've told them they wouldn't like him half so much in real life but they just squeal "No! No! He's lovely!" and fight over who should've played him in the film. Daniel Day Lewis always gets a big vote.'

I felt a pang as I realised I must be the same age as the young sister Gemma spoke so indulgently of, and a further pang when I remembered Juno and I having exactly that argument in our room. I was too embarrassed to tell Gemma.

'Are you in second or third year?' I said.

'Third. Final. I suppose I should be taking them more seriously, but I reckon the damage is done now. A bit late to be panicking. I decided I might as well take the evening off and relax. I'll give everything a last look-over when I get home.'

I envied her calm. 'And you're doing the play too?'

'Hah. Maybe. I must have been mad to say yes.' Dominic gave a 'Hey!' of protest which Gemma blithely ignored. 'Mind, it's shedding cast members like slates in a high wind. They all think Dominic's a lunatic. If any more go I'd say he'll have to abandon it, so I might get out of it yet.'

'Don't listen to her! They love me!' said Dominic. 'Anyway, we can replace the bastards with more slave-workers from First Arts after Christmas . . . I hope . . . shite on them, anyhow.'

Gemma leaned over him towards me, putting her hand over his protesting mouth, to say in a mock-whisper 'I can't see him pulling it off. You can see what he's getting at, but it's way too ambitious, as usual. He wanted to put on *Nixon In China* in the college bar last year, but only three people turned up for the audition, and they all thought it was some sort of one-man lunchtime comedy.'

'I'm too good for this world' sighed Dominic's muffled voice. 'Far too good. Wretched philistines.'

Gemma removed her hand from his mouth and gave him a consoling pat on the head. The lights began to dim in the lecture theatre. I whispered 'Good luck tomorrow' to Gemma and she grinned at me, 'And you.' Dominic ostentatiously shushed us and we sat back into our seats. Conrad hadn't joined in the conversation and I'd been uncomfortably aware of his gaze all the way through it.

The film began.

It seemed very distant, quite lacking in passion, but I wasn't sure if that was the film's fault or mine. The characters distracted me by not being how I'd imagined them. My attention began to wander. The colour and light on the great screen began to seem abstract. A tiny moth in the projector's beam almost directly above me caught my eye and held it as he danced in and out of the light, too tiny and too far from the narrow source of the beam to interfere with the images on the screen. The moth swept into the beam again and again, in search of something. My head rested on the back of my seat as I looked up at him, whirling frantically into the light, spinning free into the cool dark, and returning. Slowly he worked his way along up the beam, higher, tighter, brighter. Soon he'd be blocking enough of the light to be seen. It must be hot up there, in the first and brightest stretch of the beam, raw light from the hot projector's lens. If the film caught for a moment it would catch fire. All a moth could find at the heart of the light was death. Why did it love the light? Why did it seek out flame and death? What did it think it had found? I closed my eyes against the light.

Stupid with half-remembered philosophy and too many nights of tension and study, I fell asleep.

23

They woke me up when it was over, and offered to walk me home.

'No, thanks, I'll be grand.'

'It's no bother, we're going that way near enough' said Dominic.

'Meeting up with some friends down from Dublin, for the last pint' said Gemma. 'Are you with us, or a Guinness?'

'No' I said. 'Exam in the morning.' I collapsed inside. Jesus. I'd forgotten.

They walked me home, the two men arguing all the way. Dominic seemed to be deliberately ignoring Gemma for some reason. A spiky trio. Gemma let me lean against her as we walked. I was so tired I hardly spoke, I hardly listened. Soon I walked with my head on Gemma's shoulder, my eyes half-closed, in a lovely, dreamy rhythm over the bridges, the canal and the river. Gemma hardly spoke either. Both of us must have half nodded off, or have thought the other was leading, because we almost walked into a street lamp. We both stopped, abruptly, a foot short of it, and I woke and looked sleepily about me.

We'd all stopped.

'Gemma doesn't want to talk about girls and football' said Dominic sulkily. 'I want to talk about girls and football. Is there anyone who understands me?'

'I think we've covered girls and football' said Conrad. 'What remains to be said?'

Dominic howled at the moon. 'Everything' he said. 'We haven't begun.' He threw his arms round me and Gemma. Gemma sighed. Avoiding the lamp post, we moved on.

'Gemma doesn't believe in love' Dominic said, looking at me mournfully.

'I don't believe in football' I said back to him.

He turned to Gemma and said mournfully 'Juliet doesn't believe in football.' He pondered this, and sighed. 'Will I ever be wed?' he said.

'I wouldn't recommend it' said Conrad, calmly walking alongside us.

'Ah, shut up you' said Dominic. 'Sure what do you know about women? You're just a bloody . . . worshipper.'

'I did marry one' said Conrad mildly.

Dominic shook his head. 'And you even worshipped her. Your wife, for Christ's sake. Now that's shite, Connie. You haven't a bull's notion about women. I don't care how many of them you've married. Sure nobody wants to be worshipped, Connie. Even Christ used to get a bit edgy after a long day of it. How can a woman fart or scratch her snatch in peace with you sitting around worshipping her all day? Sure no wonder Sarah had trouble with her nerves.'

'But Dominic, I didn't worship Sarah. I'm not even sure if I liked Sarah.'

'Ah, that's all part of the same game, Connie. That's nothing to do with it, that's . . . thu . . . fff.' Dominic took his arms from around our shoulders to gesture wildly, trying to get his point across. He spluttered and laughed as his tongue blundered. They hadn't sobered up noticeably during the course of the film. If anything, going back out into the cold air had kicked the drink back in. Or had they continued to drink as I slept in the flickering light?

Dominic was very obviously drunk, while Conrad gave the impression of being full to the lid with alcohol yet not really drunk, as though his metabolism had adjusted to a new normality. They were both quite obviously sliding along the well-oiled grooves of a familiar argument now.

'You'd worship anything Connie. Marx. Bob fecking Dylan. James double fecking bastard Joyce. You're always on the lookout for someone to let you down. I'd say the fall of the Wall had you dancing. You're the man with the portable pedestal Connie.' Dominic seemed almost serious now 'And you'd put anything up on it. Sure you'd worship God if you were stuck. And what harm, what harm, what harm. You like putting them up there because you love seeing them fall off. Fair enough. Whatever. Everything lets you down in the end because you want it to, cause it proves

your shagging theory that the world is shit . . . which is bollocks
. . . sorry, Gemma. Juliet.'

Conrad was smiling and shaking his head.

Dominic waved a spare hand and continued. 'But the worship
of women, now, there's a thing that makes no sense. It's even
more stupid than worshipping Marx, because at least Marx doesn't
get pissed off with you and tell you to fuck off. Women don't
want to be worshipped, Connie. And they're right.'

We were almost at my door now. Gemma was resting her head
on my shoulder. She groaned into my ear.

'No, no, no' interrupted Conrad. 'You don't understand me at
all. You're saying worship all the time. That's not it at all. You're
too young to understand the tradition I'm coming from. I think
I understand you . . . but I don't think you understand me. I treat
women with respect because I come from a very solid, traditional,
working-class background.' (Why, I thought to myself dreamily,
are writers always bursting to be working-class? Nobody else is,
not even the workers. They're all dying to win the Lotto and soar
free on wings of gold.)

'Working-class my arse' said Dominic, toning up the muscle of
my suspicion.

'My father worked' said Conrad. 'My mother had to too sometimes. We certainly weren't . . . well off. And I was brought up to
respect women. To hold doors open for them. To think of them
as ladies. To protect them. It was a culture, a decent and just one,
that is now spat on by the likes of you.' He seemed genuinely
angry.

Dominic shook his head. 'Opening doors and saying "ladies"
isn't a culture.'

'I have heard this so often' murmured Gemma in my ear, 'Save
me.'

'No? No?' said Conrad. 'A culture's a set of shared assumptions,
of attitudes, and we used to have one in Ireland, a decent, hard-
working culture and I didn't agree with all of it, but it had a lot
to be said for it, a lot, and now we have a generation of young
bucks who have respect for the culture of Muslims, or the culture
of blacks, or the culture of gays, but have no respect for the culture
of their parents.' I winced a little, the words struck a faint chord.
Dominic tried to interrupt but Conrad waved a hand at him, one

moment. 'The young, they're concerned at the way the culture of the travellers is dying, or the culture of Polynesia, oh they're all rich, traditional ways of life. But they laugh at their parents and they've no time for their grandparents, because their attitudes and beliefs aren't a culture, a tradition, oh no, they're just sexist, racist, stupid, old-fashioned. Am I wrong? Am I wrong?'

'You are wrong' said Dominic.

'And how am I wrong?' said Conrad. We had arrived at my door. I gave it a push, in case one of the mouse-people from downstairs had left it on the latch again, as was their wont, but they hadn't. I looked for my keys.

Dominic was fading. I'd seen the tiredness piling on as Conrad made his speech. 'Oh Connie' he said sadly. 'You make it sound like there's a shagging war on and we'll have you out into the street. You make it sound like we're breaking up the pianos for firewood. We're alright, Connie. We're alright. There's no harm in us, Connie. There's nothing to be afraid of at all.'

'Thanks for walking me home' I said. 'I'd invite ye in but I'm knackered.'

'Oh, that's alright' said Conrad.

'Are you sure you won't join us?' said Gemma.

'Thanks. Thanks. No.'

In bed, I was asleep before the after-image of the light bulb had faded from my retina.

24

I entered the underworld of the exams and lived in the half-light of them for a week and a day.

The world seemed curiously far away for much of the time. I was aware of a light tension, not quite a headache, that defined my skull, and I was aware of the skin that wrapped my body. I felt very much inside my skull, inside my skin. The world seemed very separate from me.

I walked in each morning after a last burst of dawn study in the relevant subject, jacked up on caffeine, my blood tapping lightly at the back of my eyes every time my heels hit the ground, little pressure waves. Everything sounded further away than it was. A piledriver on the river behind the university drove huge concrete rods down into the river bed as part of some European-funded university expansion programme all through the first two days, and as the resentment and subvocalised complaints mounted into audible murmurs around me I wrote serenely on. It was too far away to affect me. I was living behind my eyes. Everything I needed was there, or was of no use to me. I only vaguely realised that I wasn't usually like this, that this wasn't perhaps healthy. It was how I dealt with pressure and if it wasn't the best way, well, there was nothing I could do about it now. The fact that much of the pressure I was enduring I had generated myself did not occur to me, as it never did occur to me.

Conversations with Juno for that week were strange, through fog. I sat exams, I studied, and I slept. Being spoken to felt like being woken up, forced to do something difficult. Michael gave up talking to me and walked around me carefully when he was there. Juno spoke sometimes but didn't expect answers, and that was alright. Only at the weekend, before the final day's exams, English again on a second Monday, was there a break long enough for me to emerge a little from myself into the world. Even then,

I was only half out of the underworld. I was snappy and abstracted. Juno laid a trail of inconsequential conversational crumbs. I followed it, roughly, unhelpfully, like a hungry bear woken in winter. Poor Juno.

'The Philosophy seems to have gone OK then. People seemed happy enough.'

'Mmm. Yeah.'

'You were worried about the Philosophy of Art, did he try anything tricky?'

'No.' More seemed called for. 'Easy enough.'

'My second History paper was fine.'

'Mm.'

'Do you want a look at my Chaucer notes for Monday? You were saying you couldn't read yours.'

The day I'd said that, at the height of my study-panic ten days before, I couldn't have read my own name in lights.

'No. Mine're fine.' I was forgetting something, what? 'Thanks.'

I had just spent two hours studying Middle English and if I felt anything it certainly wasn't a desire to read any more about how funny, witty and sharp Chaucer's dull, crude, long-winded *Canterbury Tales* were. Mainly I felt slightly nauseous, slightly hungry (not a good combination), and more than slightly impatient to get my period, which the stress of not studying followed immediately by the stress of studying seemed to be delaying an unconscionable length of time. I was now out of sync with Juno for the first time since the Leaving Cert, when exactly this had happened. Usually we were as regular and synchronised as two lifers in the same cell.

I bent over a little in my chair. The occasional gentle cramp went well with the permanent light stress headache. It was a small miracle I bothered answering her at all.

25

And then they were over. After Monday's Middle English paper I walked home without waiting for Juno to finish, and let myself into the building and climbed the stairs and let myself into the flat. Without bothering to get a towel from my room I put on the bathroom heater, pumped all my change into the meter for the shower, and stripped and stood under the warm, civilised water, my forehead against the cool tiles. I softened and loosened under the water, felt I was melting. With my eyes closed, I thought about nothing. Gradually my breasts ceased to feel as though they'd been stuffed with rocks.

I opened my eyes and tilted my head back into the path of the water and opened my mouth till it was filled with water and I was deaf, dumb and blind. I closed my eyes and mouth and let the water jet from my mouth against the tiles. Suddenly and effortlessly the tension and the blood began to leave me and drain away under the coaxing of the warm water. Baptism, I thought. I stood there a while longer.

When I walked through the living room to my room, carrying the old clothes I'd used to dry myself, Juno was there.

'Hello' I said, disappearing into my room to get something clean to wear, 'I didn't hear you come in.'

Juno spoke from the living room 'Nice shower?'

'God yes. How did you find the paper?'

'Fine. No surprises. Are you back among the living, then?'

'What do you mean?'

'Talking, asking questions. Smiling, unless my eyes deceived me just there.' She stuck her head round the door.

'Come in, come in, sit down.' I knocked the damp clothes off the chair and continued to dress. 'Was I bad?'

'World of your own. You had Michael frightened to speak to you. He'd put the kettle on and offer to make you coffee and you'd give him the strangest look and not answer. He's been hiding in my room or staying well out of the way at his place for most of the week, not that I expect you noticed. Poor thing, try and put him at his ease when he calls round. Tell him you're back to normal and he's perfectly safe.'

I'd been 'Oh God'-ing and groaning for this. 'Was I really dreadful?'

'Mm, yes, a bit. I'm well enough used to it, though. It unsettled the visitors mainly. Conrad and Dominic and Gemma all made *very* brief visits which you've probably forgotten, but I'd bet they haven't. Tourist figures are *down* for the flat.'

'Was it worse than the Leaving?'

'Near enough. About the same.'

'Oh God. Sorry. I'm better now.'

'Yes, I noticed. Don't worry about it. It's Christmas, home to good old Tipperary tomorrow.'

I gave a theatrical shudder but I didn't mean it. It would be good to see our mother and I felt confident I could get through a Christmas without fighting with our father if I really put my mind to it, especially if I avoided talking to him. And there was the possibility that Paul might come home.

'Did you ring home?' I asked Juno. 'Will Paul be coming?'

'No word last time I rang. Paul . . . who knows?'

We hardly knew Paul really, he was so much older and he'd left home so young. I hadn't seen him for two years, the last time he'd returned for Christmas. It hadn't been a great success. He still hated Tipperary, and showed it. Our father took it personally. A couple of stupid arguments, an uneasy peace on Christmas Day, I'd spent most of the holiday in our room listening to the albums Paul had brought me. It was Paul who'd got me listening to Kate Bush, and to classical music. Sometimes an album or a book would arrive in the post from London and, later, San Francisco, often without the excuse of a birthday or Christmas, sometimes without even a note. He knew me well enough to know what I'd like, which can be hard enough when you live in the same house, but which shows real sensitivity and intelligence when you're guessing from an ocean away, and from memories of what someone was like when they were a child. Paul's presents to me kept pace with me as I grew older in a way that even my parents' presents to me didn't always. I liked Paul very much, in the distracted and casually intense way you can like an older brother, perhaps love him, without even thinking of him that often. I don't think I wrote even once to thank him for the albums and the books. Another nag of guilt every Christmas. I wanted to see him this year to say thank you because I knew I'd love his present and that I'd never write to say so.

Part Two

TIPPERARY

26

We caught a Ryan's bus home. It was packed with people that I half knew, students, secretaries and civil servants, girls who would have been ahead of me in school and boys I'd last seen hanging out at the Market Cross when I was fifteen, four or five of them sharing a cigarette and sniggering as Juno and I passed them on our way home from school. The secretaries had had their hair done too often, until it looked as artificially over-alive as a snarling stuffed fox. The boy civil servants and insurance salesmen looked uncomfortable in tight shirt collars that rubbed raw the obligatory single boil on the back of each neck, the brave but feeble crusted remnants of their gloriously inflamed and eruptive youths. The students of both sexes just looked like students. Some of the girls said hello to me and Juno as we got on and walked halfway down the bus to find seats. The boys failed to catch our eyes, but I was very aware of the surreptitious glances. Pure, helpless hate boiled up in me and when we sat down to wait for the bus to pull out I couldn't read. Why did Paul have to leave when these creatures stayed? But I looked at them again and slowly calmed down. Their lives were punishment enough. They were going home for Christmas with their laundry and their suits and they looked terrible, sad and lost. Our brother was thousands of miles away because he wanted to be, and he was happy there and I should be happy for him, I was. He'd won. It was OK.

I hadn't been home once since coming up to Galway. Juno had been home twice, on her own and with Michael, but I'd found excuses, essay deadlines, the library, and it had been quite easy not to go. Juno had brought home my summer clothes and brought back my winter ones, all listed out for her on a sheet torn from my philosophy notes.

I swopped places with Juno, who was reading history for pleasure, to look out the bus window as we drove through the darkening countryside. How bleak the fields were. The Galway fields, all stones and little blackthorn bushes growing sideways in the wind off the Atlantic, were bleak enough but had reason to be. They looked like a desert was taking them slowly, under a sky full of inexplicable clouds. Then the fields grew greener and richer and the soil covered the rock and we came over Portumna Bridge into Tipperary. Thick bushy hedges now, instead of dry-stone walls. Lush, fallow winter pasture, instead of tilted slabs of rock with a little harsh grass on them.

But as the fields became larger, greener and more prosperous, they remained empty and silent. The cattle all in winter quarters and no corn for the wind to send waves through. Big empty fields and the occasional farmhouse, curtains closed. Nobody walking or working those fields. Nobody with a gun, and dogs at his heel. Just the night falling on big empty fields. December.

The moon and the dark blue sky and the dark grey clouds low to the pink horizon flickered and dimmed and were buried under my sudden reflection as the lights shuddered on in a ripple down the length of the bus. A song I liked came on the crackling radio and the driver retuned to a different station, very muffled and fading in and out as the bus revved to climb the low hills surrounding the town I was born in. It didn't feel like Christmas.

27

We stepped off the bus outside Kavanagh's Hotel. The street was crossed by a couple of dozen thin strands of Christmas lights. The Christmases of one's childhood are traditionally bigger and brighter than whatever Christmas you're enduring as an adult, but in my case I could quantify the decline. I remembered the Christmas the town council first hung Christmas lights across O'Connell Street, our imaginatively named main thoroughfare. I was five, and there were thirty strands, of mixed red, yellow, green and blue bulbs. I counted them every time I walked down the street with my mother and Juno that Christmas, walking with my head back and our mother scolding me for not looking where I was going, and me not answering for fear I'd forget the number. Thirty strands, with forty and sometimes forty-one bulbs in each strand. As the years went by, bulbs broke or failed and went unreplaced, and entire strands would suffer mysterious disasters and go dead, not to reappear the next year. Now there were twenty-three strands, all with an assortment of bulbs missing and others gone, for some reason, dim. I counted the strands as we walked to the top of O'Connell Street before turning right, into the narrower Well Street at the end of which lay our family's home. Well Street was dark, with few streetlights, and our bags were heavy and it was cold. We didn't talk till we reached the front door, when Juno said abruptly 'We'll have to get presents tomorrow.' I put down my bag and found my key. 'Oh my God, yes. Never entered my head.'

The door swung open as my key approached the lock.

'Paul!' we said and embraced him enthusiastically.

'My beautiful sisters' he said. 'My God, you look wonderful. You're not little girls any more. I'll have to burn the Barbie dolls I brought you.'

We laughed and jumped around him and pretended to be babies

while he picked up our bags with exaggerated groans and carried them into the living room.

'Look what I found' he said.

Our father grunted from his armchair. 'Oh, more mouths to feed. I thought we were rid of ye.'

I gritted my teeth a little but I was too pleased at seeing Paul to let my father spoil it.

'Paul, Paul, give me my present, I want to weigh it', a reference to an old family joke about the value of presents, dating from when Juno and I used to weigh each other's presents on the kitchen scales as they arrived in the week before Christmas, as a poor substitute for opening them, which was forbidden until after dinner on Christmas Day. Whoever had the lightest presents would often end up in tears. One year my father gave Juno two bricks among her other presents, to annoy me. I cried when she weighed them on Christmas Eve, but Juno cried when she opened them on Christmas Day, and our mother stood up and swore at him in front of us all, which was very unusual and silenced everyone for hours after.

Paul lifted me up in the air and then lifted Juno up in the air.

'Presents of great worth' he said. 'Oh, valuable presents these two. Who are they for?'

'No one' I said, blushing.

'Ah! You're blushing! You are somebody's present!' But he saw I wasn't enjoying the game and didn't pursue it.

'Where's Mum?' I said.

'She's gone out' said my father.

'I know she's out, where's she gone to?'

'She's out visiting the Brownes and trying not to get given one of their terrible cakes.'

The Brownes were friends of our mother. Mrs Browne had a love affair with cookery that wasn't reciprocated, and a number of distant, half-remembered Christmases had run aground on the rock of Mrs Browne's Christmas cake. Eventually a rebellion led by Paul had brought about a compromise, and ended the tyranny. Now every year Mrs Browne gave our mother a Christmas cake as a present, and every year our mother brought the cake home and put it in the dustbin with much swearing of the family to secrecy, and everyone was happy. I liked all these rituals.

Juno went to put on the kettle. There was a turf fire in the living room, and a small, real tree with the familiar decorations, dented silver balls with frosted top halves, and silver and red streamers of tinsel, moulted in places till you could see the string. The fairy on the top of the tree, a baby-doll in a white dress our mother had made out of cardboard and a strip of net curtain, sat at the familiar uncomfortable angle, the glue that held on her head old and yellow and visible through the mesh of her net ruff.

Juno swung open the kitchen door to ask who wanted tea and a small gust of turf-smoke came into the room and suddenly, and just in time, it felt like Christmas.

28

That night Paul, Juno and I went to Connollys Hotel, Bar and Disco.

'Let's take in the best Tipperary has to offer' said Paul, and off we went.

It had been Connollys unfortunate slogan on their local radio ad for years, dating back to the days of the pirates, and a source of unending joy and sarcasm to Paul and his friend Aengus Cleary. They used to roar it, rolling home drunk together at half two in the morning after an evening in Connollys Bar, followed by a night in Connollys Disco, and a shared bag of chips from Connollys Illegal Chip-Van in Connollys Famous Car Park, the Biggest in the South. You'd never catch an apostrophe off a Connolly. A good Tipp hurling family, no time for soccer, the Devil, the Brits or punctuation.

'The best' Paul and Aengus would bellow, 'the BEST Tipperary has to offer . . . take in the fucking BEST . . .' The drunker they got, the broader their brogue, till they were singing in pure Tipperary 'deh BESHT'.

I'd hear them shushing each other below at the front door, dropping the key, entering the house with elaborate care, closing the door as quietly as they could, going into the living room and turning on the radio full blast for thirty seconds before they could get it together to find the volume control and turn it down, 'Shush!' 'SHUSH!' 'Jesus, the parents . . .'

If our parents woke, they never did anything about it. I don't think Juno ever heard the boys come home. She slept a lot deeper than I did, but I was sensitive to their coming home, I liked to hear it, I wanted it to wake me, so it did. Once or twice, careful not to wake Juno, I snuck downstairs to join them. They were pleased to see me, in an absent-minded sort of way. They asked me about school and my friends and my hated dance classes in a way that they never bothered to in our everyday encounters at breakfast and dinner and in front of the TV. It was as though we were all part of some underground community, meeting in the hush of the night, speaking in low voices, the last cigarette of the night going round, casually equal. It was only years later that I realised they were probably stoned out of their heads as they focused intently on my banal answers to their polite questions.

I loved it but I felt so dumb, in both senses, and young, in my stupid little pink going-to-the-bathroom socks which I tried to hide under myself as I sat on the sofa. When I did say anything the sentence would just come out so helplessly, hopelessly wrong that I could practically see it stranded in mid-air in front of me, dying in the silence. Eventually I would mumble something that sounded like an explanation or an apology or a straightforward goodnight but which didn't have any actual words in it and wasn't properly any of them, and I would sneak back to the cowardly safety of my room, my awful mumble ringing like a persistent tuning fork tone in my ear, a blaze of embarrassment consuming me as I climbed the stairs in a rage of self-pity and fury at my youth and immaturity and stupidity, stupidity. Yet I still liked to hear them below me, murmuring, even after I gave up trying to join them.

As Juno and I accompanied Paul to Connollys then, I found myself almost giddy with excitement. I'd been to Connollys a billion times with Juno but this was different. Look at me, going out on the town with Paul! I felt like singing, so I did.

'I could have danced all night, I could have danced all night . . .'

I didn't know enough words, it was one of my father's favourites and I'd never really listened to it closely.

'You're in flying form' said Paul.

'Mm, yup.'

And I was. All my melancholy had vanished, ping! as the front door closed behind us. I did a giddy little dance and nearly tripped on the cracked pavement. I felt quite drunk and we hadn't even arrived at the pub yet.

Paul pushed Connollys door open and waved us in. It was like putting your head in a kettle. The heat and steam and noise were overwhelming. I was, what's the word? Overwhelmed. Every exile on earth seemed to have arranged to meet here, just inside the door, tonight, and most of them would appear to have arrived in the previous sixty seconds. The air juddered with backslaps, roared greetings, howls of recognition and delight. Seamus! Jaysus! How'r ya! Moira! Feckit! Odysseus! C'mere t'me! Is it Napoleon is it! Shake, man! Cain, begod! How's the brother?

All the Christmas returnees met up and exchanged histories in Connollys at Christmas and now to my shock I found I was a returnee. People greeted me, greeted Juno, greeted Paul, shook hands, offered drinks, refused money, piled coats, pushed over, and in a dizzy minute I was sitting at a table with a bunch of semi-strangers, a glass of Harp in front of me and another on the way. My protestation that I didn't like Harp, or glasses, had been as benignly overlooked as my proffered ten pound note and my request for a pint of Guinness. Paul leaned over to calm me as steam leaked from my ears to aid the general smog. 'They mean well' he said softly. 'They're idiots but they mean well. They probably don't even remember beating the shit out of me in the Christian Brothers. If I can forgive them that, you can forgive them buying you Harp. I'll get you a Guinness later. Sit back and enjoy the comedy. It's Christmas.'

So I sat back and calmed down and even drank some of one of my Harps before the flailing elbow of a new arrival swept them both into Paul's lap.

'Oh Jesus, Paul, I'm sorry, buy you another, what was it.'

'Harp, but don't worry.'

'Shit no, I'm not buying you that piss, Guinness is it, and what're your sisters having?'

'Hello Aengus, I'm grand.'

'Hello Aengus, they were both mine and I'd have paid you to get rid of them, don't worry about it.'

Aengus settled in among us and the night began.

'God you're looking lovely, are you old enough for Guinness? Grand, three then, I'm shagging loaded don't touch that, oh fuck it's murder at that bar let me get a breather first, is it English Paul tells me you're learning, well that'll come in handy if you ever visit me in London, not that any fucker speaks it there any more, did you hear the streets are paved with gold there, shagging right they are, but it's like lead, sure it causes terrible deformities, the people there have hearts the size of gooseberries and fierce short arms, every bastard in Soho must owe me a pint.'

And having had his breather he leaped up and squeezed through the scrum towards the bar.

'He's a dote' said Juno.

'He's a sexy dote' said I.

'Jesus, hands off Aengus, he's a friend' said Paul, alarmed, 'And if I hear he's laid a hand on you I'll kill him.'

'OK no hands' I said.

'Jesus' said Paul mopping his brow. 'You are joking, aren't you? Don't answer.'

The night grew increasingly ribald, energetic, and drunken. Paul and Aengus vied to ply Juno and myself with pints. Juno found herself at the eye of a hurricane of male attention and as I grew increasingly relaxed and less inclined to scowl at rubbernecked passers-by, so did I. I almost began to enjoy the attention, a very rare feeling for me. When James Power fondled my upper arm and playfully tousled my hair in his familiar creepy way I told him to piss off rather than fuck off and didn't even stop smiling. Of course he took that as a come-on and did it again, brushing his forearm 'accidentally' against my breast as he did so, and then I had to say 'Fuck right off James, I mean it' and tread very hard on his instep to make absolutely sure he understood I meant it, but all in all it was a lovely, relaxed evening. By closing time I was pissed as a coot and up for divilment.

29

We swayed the very short walk from Connollys Bar to Connollys Disco, out the pub door and in a door six yards away, paid our money, found a table on the edge of the dancefloor and the night roared on. I leaned against Aengus.

'Tell me more about advertising' I said.

'I'm boring you' he said.

'No, tell me more. I love your voice . . . it's all mixed up, all London and Tipperary.' Either Aengus went red or the disco lights did, I wasn't sure and didn't care.

'Ah, they love me Irish accent over there' he said. 'It's worth an extra ten K to me no bother. They think I have a fiery Celtic creative soul. They know I can't be as thick as I sound so they mistake their estimations in the other direction.'

He said 'thick' as 'tick'. And 'mistake' as 'mishtayk'.

'What's kay?' I said. He had to think back.

'K. A thousand. Thousand pounds. Forty K. Ninety K. It's a stupid way of talking about money, real casual. Came from the City. I don't even know where the fuck I got it. I don't even know if it's fashionable any more. It just slipped out cause I was drunk.'

Thrunk. I wuz thrunk. I thought of saying something and thought better of it. 'Let's dance' I said.

He hesitated for a moment, not sure if I wanted to dance or if I was merely identifying the tune. 'Let's Dance' by David Bowie throbbed from the speakers. Someone should have slapped a preservation order on the DJ box as a Site of Special Historic Interest. Someone probably had. Was this DJ stored in one of the hotel freezers and only thawed out at Christmas? 'Let's Dance' segued jarringly into 'New Year's Day' by U2. Mother of God. It was a fucking museum with a mirrorball. We danced. I was having a great time.

Suddenly I felt a hand on my knee. On my *knee*? As I was *dancing*? I looked down to see one of the Gleeson twins grinning up at me, fag in mouth, head shaved to stubble, denim shirt, jacket and jeans. They hadn't changed since they were ten. Chainsmoking their way through primary school, secondary school, reform school and prison (rumour had it they lied about their age to get in), they had perfectly preserved their youthful figures, yellowed fingers and, unfortunately, heights. Frankly, the two of them hadn't a height between them. It had been a very long time since they'd been able to headbutt anyone their own age in the face without the assistance of a stepladder, but they were still tiny objects of fear in the town, on the rare occasions they weren't in prison.

'Jimmy?' I said. 'Johnny?'

'Johnny' said Johnny Gleeson. 'Jimmy's gone for a slash. They let us out for Christmas.' He leered up my skirt.

Juno and I had always had a soft spot for the Gleeson twins, partly because they were twins of roughly our own age and therefore somehow kindred spirits, and partly because they would steal things and give them to us when we were of an age to find that rather romantic. At ten they were giving us Toblerone, at fifteen they were giving us earrings and on one memorable occasion they gave us a video recorder which we made them promise to give back. They got caught giving it back and were given another go in reform school. We felt terribly guilty. They were one year older than us and neither had half an ounce of sense. It was about the only thing they didn't have half an ounce of, mind you.

'Oh it's lovely to see you, Johnny' I said. I could never tell them apart, they were always wearing each other's clothes and they had identical prison tattoos on their knuckles.

'Where's Juno?' said Johnny.

'Over there, at the table by the pillar' I said. 'Johnny, do you know Aengus Cleary . . .' but Johnny had already vanished among the dancing knees.

Aengus looked at me, faintly appalled. 'You know Johnny Gleeson?' he said.

'Oh, Johnny and Jimmy are lovely' I said.

'They're fucking *psychopaths*' Aengus said.

I stopped dancing and began assembling furious words towards a reply.

'We'll agree to differ' he added in haste, hands raised in sur-render.

I restarted dancing but at a much slower pace than before, and wearing a pout that could knock out a pack mule. It took him till halfway through the Bryan Adams set to disarm the facial expression and bring me back up to speed. Then we realised what we were dancing to and returned to our seats.

'Oh Joolz' said Juno, 'You'll never guess.' She was holding what could only be a Christmas present from the Gleeson twins.

'The Gleeson twins have given us a Christmas present' I guessed.

'Well, yes' said Juno. 'They said we should open it together.' She frowned. 'In fact they said we shouldn't open it here . . . they wouldn't tell me why.'

'Because it's stolen' said Aengus and I simultaneously.

I gave Aengus a startled look before realising that he didn't actually know anything about our relationship with the Gleesons, he just knew a lot about the Gleesons.

'No' said Paul. 'That's what Juno thought.'

'Jimmy swore it wasn't stolen. Although I suppose buying it with their money is only one step away from theft, really . . .'

'Ah sure, we ate the Toblerone' I said gaily, to the puzzlement of Paul and Aengus. 'Open it.'

Juno hesitated. The small, flat, extraordinarily badly wrapped present lay on the palm of her right hand. Juno lofted it slightly a few times as though weighing it. The wrinkled wrapping paper, striped with bands of crumpled sellotape, much of it (by the fluff on it) sticky-side out, sat enigmatic on the palm, its white ribbon, oily with thumbprints, tied in no knot known to Scout, Cub, Guide or Brownie.

Jimmy, or Johnny, whizzed by, seeming to my startled eye to pass beneath our table without stooping as he did so. I blinked.

'Hope you like your present' he Cagney'd from a mouth-corner as he orbited me. 'Don't open it here.'

And he was gone. They had always been shy.

30

Giggling like schoolgirls, Juno and I raced across the dancefloor to the toilets to open our present. Giggling like a schoolgirl is never more *satisfying* than in the year after you've left school. The knowledge that no nun will ever again have the right to say 'Stop that sniggering, girls' seems to triple the pleasure somehow. Actually that's probably just true for me, rather than a universal rule of iron, but for months after my Leaving Cert I couldn't pass a nun without giggling ostentatiously.

Anyway, still giggling, we entered the toilets. Every cubicle occupied, every mirror besieged. The air was beige with foundation as girls I half recognised tried frantically to deal with the sweat-damage sustained during 'Summer of '69' in time to get back out for 'Everything I Do (I Do It For You)'. We were greeted distractedly by a couple of old classmates, one reapplying lipstick, one standing on one leg with a hairpin in her mouth.

'Mmm, m'no, mmm m'l't.' She risked a smile at Juno and the hairpin fell to the filthy floor. She glared at us. Obviously hadn't been a close friend.

The other girl gave a theatrical wave from about a yard away, and greeted us warmly without bothering to stop touching up her lipstick. 'Juno! Just a . . . there . . . ? . . . yes . . . and Juliet, how are you?'

Juno told her. I couldn't be arsed, she'd never liked me anyway and I'd always found her as brittle as our grandmother's right hip and as artificial as its replacement. She was one of the ones who'd acted in a school play and never bothered getting out of character. My memory refused to supply me with the part or the play. Julie Bleeding Andrews in *The Sound Of Bleeding Music* no doubt. I bared my teeth as she passed me and she chose to treat it as a smile. Sensible of her. I had a mad desire to snap at her like a dog and bark lustily to see how she'd react but I fought the urge down.

It was a bit too like our old school toilets in here for my liking. Connollys doormen wouldn't ask for ID if the entire cast of *The Great Escape* turned up with the contents of a kindergarten stuffed under their greatcoats, so a good half of the girls unsteadily swigging from their smuggled naggins of Smirnoff while they waited for a free sink to spew in were still attending our old school, and thus unpleasantly familiar to me. I felt nausea rather than nostalgia. It was a bit too recent for me to have romanticised it. Spots and braces. Homework. Dress codes. Ye gods. An unfortunate called Pam whose mother was an alcoholic and who'd had to repeat fifth year came out of one of the cubicles. She'd always liked me, God knows why.

'Hello Juliet' she said shyly. Her braces shone in the fluorescent light.

'Hello Pam' I said, and it was absolutely too much for me, I hauled Juno into the vacated cubicle and slammed the door on Pam's startled orthodentistry.

'Open the present, I'm going mad' I said.

Juno opened the Gordian bow and pulled off the paper. We stared.

'It's a *stamp* album' I said. 'It's a . . . flipping stamp album. I think I'd have preferred Toblerone. And to think we made them give back that video recorder.'

Juno giggled and said 'Well it's the thought I suppose . . . and they *are* a bit dim . . .' which was a charmingly uncharitable remark from her and made me think all the more highly of her.

She flicked the tiny stamp album open and I said 'Well at least they've stuck in some stamps.'

'Oh dear . . .' said Juno, with the observational advantage of being slightly less drunk than me. 'I don't think these are stamps . . . I think they're . . .'

31

'. . . trips.'

It is a tribute to the sheltered nature of my upbringing and to the sheer breadth of my ignorance that I did not know what my sister was talking about.

'Trips?' I said, vague images of foreign travel in my head.

'Trips, tabs, acid, LSD' said Juno impatiently, sounding like an unusually specialised drug dealer offering her wares with the aid of a Thesaurus. '*Drugs*, you idiot.'

Now, I had read a lot about drugs and I'd seen *Drugstore Cowboy* three times (for Matt Dillon) and *My Own Private Idaho* six times (three times for River Phoenix and another three times for Keanu Reeves, and I still couldn't decide . . . hey, I was young) and countless TV programmes and news reports, but Tipperary and Galway were not exactly the drug capitals of Europe and I'd never actually seen a Class 'A' drug for real. I had the vague impression that 'drugs' came in whacking great kilo bags of white powder with 'DRUGS' written on them.

'They're not *drugs*' I said. 'They're *stamps*.'

I peered at the stamp album again in the bad light of the toilet cubicle. It consisted of a number of small plastic pages, each with a number of small plastic pockets for stamps. In each pocket was a small paper square. I peered even closer. They were a bit small for stamps and all the same size. And they didn't have proper perforated edges. The first row of three were white with a blue globe on them. The next row of three were white with an Arabic squiggle on them. The next row of three were white with a cartoon explosion on them. I turned the page.

'Jeeeesus' I said.

'It's a selection box' said Juno. 'They must be microdots' and she pointed at three pockets each containing what looked like a tiny ball of, well, snot.

I looked at Juno suspiciously. 'How come you know so much about it?'

'Because I didn't skip religion when Sister Imelda showed us that video on drugs.'

'Oh yeah.' I shrugged. I was still glad I'd missed it. Someone hammered on the cubicle door. 'Fuck off' I said absently. I fished a square with a heart on it from its pocket and examined it. 'Acid' I said. 'Aciiiiiiiiiieeeeeed . . .'

Now you will mock me for my innocence in what follows but I blame it firmly on National Drug Prevention Day, the Press, the Guards, the Government and Society. I had been bored to tears for years with the message that drugs, from hash and grass through acid and ecstasy to heroin and crack, were intrinsically evil and exceedingly dangerous. My experience had shown me that half the people I knew smoked marijuana in its various forms and that the message simply wasn't true. I'd smoked Satan's cigarettes a couple of times but couldn't inhale without coughing with embarrassing vigour for an impressive duration, so the full health-and-life-destroying joys of Reefer Madness had been denied to me. I'd drunk mushroom soup once at a party, too. It was meant to be magic-mushroom soup but after two hours of sitting around watching MTV we reluctantly decided that our morning on the golf-course had been wasted. So I didn't really, deep down, *believe* in 'drugs'.

Also I was a little drunk.

So I popped it on my tongue, sucked it like a sweet, and swallowed.

'Oh Juliet!' wailed Juno.

'What?' I said, a little belligerently. I was already starting to get the horrible feeling that I'd done something very silly. Juno had covered her face with her hands and was peeking at me through her fingers.

'You *absolute* idiot' she said in a muffled voice. 'Oh God, *what* am I going to tell Paul?'

'I licked a stamp' I said, facetiously. 'When will it start to work?'

I was rather disappointed the world hadn't been transformed immediately, as though a switch had been thrown. I felt exactly the same. Boo.

'Shouldn't notice anything for half an hour. Forty-five minutes.

Something like that. And it lasts for *hours*, what are we going to do with you? Is it too late to get sick?'

'I'm *not* getting sick' I said firmly. I'd done that often enough here as an under-age drinker. Reading the fine print of the Armitage Shanks logo at the back of the porcelain bowl. Indeed one of the reasons I'd cut my hair so short back in transition year was to keep my fringe out of Connollys toilets on Friday nights when I'd get sick. Not the main reason, but it had helped tilt the balance at the time. Juno, you will be unsurprised to learn, avoided throwing up on her fringe by avoiding throwing up. Hey, different strokes for different folks.

I snapped back the bolt. 'C'mon, let's get ready to rumble. We gotta fight for our right to party. I'm kool and the gang, don't worry be happy.'

She sighed but she joined in the game. 'Oh lord, please don't let me be misunderstood. Let's stick together, and every little thing's gonna be alright. Idiot.'

'Idiot's not a song' I objected.

I swung open the cubicle door and we walked past a cross-legged, bug-eyed girl with carrots in her fringe. I banged open the swing door with a nonchalant hip and we were back in the noise and the heat on the dancefloor's edge. I gave a little whoop of giddy joy and we plunged into the wash of hormones, deodorant and dancers. The air was volatile with cheap perfume and the kind of aftershave that comes free with petrol, and is almost indistinguishable from it. As we emerged on the other side to rejoin Paul and Aengus it briefly occurred to me that of all places and times to sharpen the senses and throw open the doors of perception, perhaps Connollys the night before Christmas Eve was not entirely the ideal choice, but I immediately put aside the unworthy thought. Why, Connollys was the best Tipperary had to offer, by God, and only the best was good enough for me tonight. I felt fabulously drunk, and the constant checking of my senses for signs of lysergic impact had the effect of making me feel super-alert, super-alive.

Juno was telling them what I'd just done. Paul was horrified, Aengus was amused but pretending to be horrified, I didn't give a damn.

'If you're not in, you can't win' I said.

Paul was really annoyed with me and began to say so. I stood up, walked onto the dancefloor, and lost myself.

The night had begun.

32

Juno and Aengus calmed Paul down, but I didn't care about that
either. I danced with absent-minded fury in the heart of the crowd
to half-forgotten songs half-remembered from my brother's
ancient record collection.

I'd spent most of my life in Tipperary, locked in my own head,
feeling like a visitor to a place where everybody else belonged. It
was in Galway that I felt at home, and felt it was safe to relax,
that no one would come smashing vindictively into my life if I
pulled back the bolts and let in a little light and air. It had been
so *lonely* in Tipperary, feeling like an observer, living in my mind,
feeding it books that showed me a world that felt so much more
real than my own. I looked around me at the town I'd been born
in and it seemed so thin, so poor a version of the world. It made
me sad in the way that the cheap imitations of good toys almost
made me cry when I saw them piled high in the Connollys Super-
Store toy department coming up to Christmas every year. I know
this sounds pathetic and stupid, but the thought that kids who
wanted Sindy, or Lego, or World Wrestling Federation figures, or
Power Rangers, or whatever was popular that year, were going to
wake up on Christmas morning and run down to open their presents and find sad, cheap, bad imitations of the present they'd
dreamed of for months, that their parents had bought because
they couldn't afford the real thing, or because they didn't know the
difference, its enormous, heartbreaking *importance*, the absolute
perfection of what you truly wanted and the desolation of
unwrapping a fake, that didn't move right, didn't look right, that
was nothing, worse than nothing . . . the thought of these other
kids with their wrong presents as useless as the stuff they came
wrapped in, hiding their huge, gulping disappointment, or letting
it show and tearing at their parents' hearts . . . to be honest I *did*
cry, every year.

It began to prey on my mind coming up to Christmas each year of my childhood, those great piles of cheap imitations, bad copies, with their deliberately misleading names. I would cry at night, I even cried in the aisles of the toy department itself a couple of times, feeling like a perfect fool, wiping my eyes on my coat-sleeve and trying to pretend I had a cold. But I think, now, that what I was crying for (and this is just amateur psychology at its worst, I have no way of proving this, it just feels to me to be true) wasn't really the toys and the other kids. It was my life, and me. My life was somehow tangled up in those toys, lived in the huge shadow of the special-offer stacks. I'd been given the wrong life, in the wrong town, and there was nothing I could do about it, and every single day of my life I had to hide my disappointment, because it wasn't my parents' fault, they thought I was happy here, they came from here, it was home wasn't it. But to me my home felt cheap and wrong and my life felt like an imitation of a real life and every Christmas I'd dream I was somewhere else, somewhere more real than this, living my real life.

And I would wake up just torn apart, in a thin, poor town that I hated. Cattle roaring from the abattoir. Connollys owning the town. A town without a river through it. Oh Christmas, I hated you.

And as I danced, furiously alone, in Connollys on the night before Christmas Eve, I was back in my head, locked in, sobbing silently about nothing, with no reason for it and no outward sign (because Christ you don't let them see that you're wounded). Galway had almost ceased to exist, even as a memory. I felt like I had been here forever and I'd be here forever and I'd die here if I ever died. I felt as if I'd dreamed the rest of the world. That I'd just woken up, and Galway had been a dream. All that existed was this moment in this town. Oh, this fucking town. I was in absolute, frozen despair inside as I danced and danced and danced. Juno came over and danced with me for a while and asked if I was OK and eventually went away again. The songs were taking forever to turn into other songs. I had no idea how long I'd been dancing. I looked at my watch. The song went on forever. Eventually I looked at my watch again. Less than a minute had passed. The chorus came around again and I felt a shivery feeling that I'd heard it too often, that it had come around too often, that it should be over, but I'd heard it a million times before, when I was younger, and it had always ended, so it would be OK this time too. But I always heard it again, didn't I, I'd heard it a million times when I was young and I was hearing it now and it hadn't ended, it wouldn't end.

My mind was exploding with thoughts that were moving too fast, overlapping, entangled, my mind felt shivery, I was thinking too much, it was fine. I looked at my watch again. Oh God, no time was passing. No, the second hand was moving, I could see it moving, but Christ it was slow, how could I ever get *out* of here if time moved so *slowly*, how could this night ever *end*, time had always moved faster than this hadn't it, I'd never noticed time pass so slowly, could it be slower now? It *felt* slower so it was slower, I had to trust what I felt what else have you, you have nothing, what you feel is real or nothing is but if you are mad what you feel isn't real but how can you know because you can't get outside yourself to see if what you feel is really real oh this is a new song oh thank Christ that song is over oh thank Christ I won't look at my watch but if I don't look at my watch how can I know if time is moving fast enough to ever, ever let me out of here but looking at my watch won't *help* oh God this must be the acid it has to be I don't normally feel like this do I no oh Jesus I want to go home

33

I began to try to walk back to the table. Light like liquid flooded heavily amongst the dancers so that several times I had to stop, unsure whether I could walk through the thick, viscous beams of red and orange. When a strobe came on I had to stop again and wait for it to end. The world looked like the inside of a madman's head. Arms and faces froze and disappeared and reappeared elsewhere, still frozen, but in new positions, with new expressions. Very, very fast things were happening very, very slowly and I felt a drowning sense that I had quite, quite lost my hold on time, that time had abandoned me and I could never be fixed now, that I had made a mistake that could never be fixed or made right. A big tear slowly crawled down my cheek and touched the corner of my lip and disappeared across my mouth in a burst of salt.

The tear-trail left a cool line down my cheek as it evaporated.

The strobe stopped and I walked on.

Eventually I reached the table.

'I want to go home' I said numbly to Juno.

34

Outside, in the car park, Paul decided he wanted chips. He'd left with us to look after us on the walk home, and he'd helped me into my coat when I'd had difficulty finding the armholes, but he was still pissed off with me and he was damned if I'd rob him of the pleasures of the chip queue. I didn't mind waiting, once I was away from the heat and noise and light. Out here it was cool, quiet, dark. A pleasant, fine drizzle prickled on my face. I'd retreated so far into myself by now that I didn't really feel connected to what I saw and heard at all. I'd been so overloaded in the chaos of trying to leave the building, by the impossible intricacies of answering the questions of Aengus and Juno and Paul, of stripping their voices out of the noise and taking the words out of their voices and squeezing the meaning out of their words and making some sense of the meaning of the words in the voices from the noise . . . and then trying to reply . . . that I had now shut down completely. I just heard and saw, without any attempt at comprehension.

Which was rather a pity, because the camera of my mind was running on quite an interesting scene. If you were an anthropologist. Or a zookeeper. Or a prison governor with some spare beds.

It was by now coming up to chucking-out time, you could tell because people were coming out to chuck up. My distress had cut our evening short, but not by much. Connollys Illegal Chip-Van was already busy serving the first wave of drunken clubbers, the smart ones who'd left early to beat the queue. They were all standing round in the rain feeling smug, in a huge queue. Actually, to pick nits for a moment (and you could pick nits all night in the Connollys Chip-Van queue) it wasn't really a queue at all. It was a kind of seething, low-key riot designed to deliver the minimum number of people to the van counter with the maximum discomfort, inefficiency and violence. 'Queuing' was considered an activity fit only for Brits and homosexuals. And Kilkenny hurlers. And Dubliners in general. (These categories were not rigorously exclusive. All Brits were homosexuals. Most Dubliners were Brits. Kilkenny hurlers weren't Brits but they might as well be, shaggin' homos. That was never a goal. We was robbed.)

In a peculiar kind of way, standing in the rain in the dark of the car park staring at the queue with my brain in mush was oddly soothing. I'd done this so often before. This was a familiar, reassuring childhood scene of just the sort to calm my acid-drenched mind. There was little Benny Reynolds leaning over casually to puke on the feet of the person beside him, his cousin Jacinta, who was too drunk to notice. Rumour had it that Benny was the father of Jacinta's child, but then rumour had it that I was a lesbian and that Juno had gone to England for an abortion when she was fifteen (she'd gone to the Gaeltacht for a fortnight to learn Irish from nuns, along with half her class, but why spoil a good story).

There was a Toohy picking a fight with a Sheehy over a sachet of tomato sauce. The Sheehy wouldn't give him any of his, or had squirted too much on, one or the other. The Toohy had knocked the Sheehy's chips flying anyhow, and now some older Toohys and Sheehys were intervening with confused shouts.

'We don't want any fucking trouble, now' said Billy Sheehy, smacking Sean Toohy in the face.

'Hold me back, lads, hold me back, I'll feckin' kill him' shrieked the offended Toohy, throwing himself backwards into the arms of a couple of his brothers. It was a ritual as old as time, and as soothing as a cool hand on my brow. It *was* a cool hand on my brow. Juno, checking I hadn't overheated while dancing. I had the peculiar sensation of her hand melting into my head but Juno didn't seem to notice anything strange and took her hand away satisfied.

'RUOK? Jew Lee, et? Are you OK?'

I laboriously deciphered her question and risked a nod in reply. The drizzle was falling sideways, which was worrying me a little, but I had a vague idea which I was trying to pin down that this was somehow due to the triumph of wind rather than the failure of gravity and that I had no need for concern. Then people started to fall sideways and I moaned in horror before I made the back connections necessary to interpret what I'd seen, which was a lot of people being knocked over by a small fight sprawling into them.

I closed my eyes again, and got way, way lost in the electric impacts of a billion specks of drizzle on the tight skin of my face.

35

The tap on my arm woke me back into my body. I had been someplace very, very far away, almost without ego, spread thin across a great dark space. The violence of sight when I opened my eyes frightened me. Colour and movement and noise (and I was mixing them all up by now, the light seemed to be causing the noises that I'd ceased to notice when I'd closed my eyes).

'C'mon, we're moving' said . . . I deciphered the mass of features which sat without perspective in front of me, moving under light till sound came out . . . Paul. My brother.

We moved.

Information was arriving very late.

My mind was lagging half a footstep behind what was happening, perceptions were coming in, felt early but recognised late and now cause and effect began to cross over. I felt the pavement suck at and reject my feet, again and again. We got to the start of the main street and in a peculiarly distanced, numb despair I stopped to try to count the strands of coloured bulbs that crossed it. If I could only get the right answer, the answer that I knew to be right, it would give me a fingertip ledge to cling to, a tiny proof of the existence of an objective world outside of my collapsing mind, and the knowledge that there was still an objective world out there would mean I had a fragile, impossible hope of returning to it somehow, somewhen. So it became very important to me.

And I couldn't do it. I couldn't add. Nothing would connect and stay connected. My thoughts were a babble to myself. Word and number were blurred, chopped into fragments so small they failed to form units of meaning, so charged they repulsed other fragments or snapped tight to them with no regard for meaning or truth, or with no regard for regard or regard for with or or. Thoughts spiralled out and broke apart or spiralled in tighter and tighter and vanished. The pitch of my terror grew as I tried to count the strands of light but I'd lost the words for the numbers and the words for the words and the lights were finally and forever uncountable and above me forever and I couldn't find that tiny ledge to hold me and I fell up into the light forever.

Johnny Gleeson said 'Is she alright?'

I am to some extent now depending on what Juno told me later, because though I remember every detail of the night very clearly, I remember much of it through the crystal filter of powerful acid, as sound and symbol rather than word and deed.

I stood staring up at the Christmas lights, blurred with the acid and hard, salty tears, as Juno told Johnny that no, I wasn't alright. Johnny asked her what I'd taken, brushing off Paul and Aengus who both seemed in a mood to do him injury on my behalf. Jimmy materialised to back up his brother.

Even in Juno's recollection Jimmy seems to have shimmered into existence rather than walked up to her. The drizzle made everything inconstant and tentative. Juno described the picture on the tab I had taken.

'The red one or the other one?'

The red one.

'Oh, that sheet, I don't know what they did. Half of it did nothing, we had a lot of complaints. It's not even, d'you see, not at all, at all. Very unreliable, we don't deal with them fellows at all any more. Mad London bastards. It's all Dutch we stock now. The lads in the 'Dam have the quality control.'

Johnny talked on as Jimmy reached up to grab my chin and pull my head down to his level. His eyes seemed to have a pulse in them, and the pupils seemed to shudder, to snap small and then expand slowly and I couldn't tell if that was an effect of the drug I was on or an effect of the drug he was on.

'Oh Juliet, are you hurting?' he crooned.

'The lights' I sobbed. 'Make the lights go away' and I pulled my head back up to look at the hurting lights that barred me from the sweet oblivion of the dark and the silence that lay beyond them. They burned me through my tears, as uncountable as stars.

Jimmy followed my gaze and as he put his hand on my hand I felt *understood* somehow. No less ruined, but comforted by the sure and certain knowledge that Jimmy could see what I saw.

119

And then he was gone again, grabbing Johnny by the shoulder, shouting 'I'll fix it' as they disappeared into the drizzle.

And then they reappeared after a million years of tears and Aengus and Paul and Juno looked up from their discussion of what the fuck to do with me because I wouldn't bring my eyes down from the lights and I wouldn't stop crying.

Nobody recognised them right away. They were driving an ESB maintenance lorry.

It roared with clashing gears out of Barrack Street and swerved to a halt at the top of O'Connell Street, twenty-three uncountable strands of light away. The engine bellowed again and then calmed to a mutter. Slowly the inspection platform rose above the cab like a great metal cobra's head, on its enormous hydraulic arm. The joint straightened till the platform towered above the street and the lights and the world. I saw it disappear above the foreshortened sheet of lines of light and I prayed from the heart of my terror for something I couldn't name.

The engine rose to the pitch of my terror and suddenly lurched with a howl towards me and entered the realm of light. And the great metal arm bent the first strand of light into a tight, astonished V that snapped with a noise that felt to me, as the line of light vanished, like a crisp explosion of pure silence in the heart of the great roar of light that still poured on me from the uncountable stars of light that made up the uncountable strands. And the next strand bent to a faster V and was gone, and the next. And the roar of the engine grew closer and greater as it extinguished the roar of the light until the lorry tore through the powerlines that crossed the street fifty yards from us and in a great explosion of light and sound the Gleeson twins ripped every star from the sky. The town went black and the streetlights went out. The last of the strands were torn down in darkness. Tiny sparks flared in the gutter from the severed powerlines, and then even they died.

Sirens began to go off and emergency lights flickered on in a few windows. But the huge sky above me was black and stripped of its great strands of torturing stars.

The ESB lorry braked hard in the darkness behind us. Jimmy and Johnny jumped down from the cab and ran back to join us. 'I fixed it' said Jimmy to all of us, but only I understood what he meant. 'You'll be alright now' he said to me, and touched my hand again.

Then they were gone, and I was left staring up into the night as slowly the true, tiny stars emerged here and there in the gaps in the low clouds that moved low and fast over the dark town. The drizzle swirled and cleared and for a moment I could see the moon racing across a gap in the clouds.

I could go home now. I felt everything ease and soften. I would be alright. Twenty-three, I thought. Twenty-three strands. Jimmy had cut through the knot of my problem. I would never have to count them now. Never have to count them again. Things could be changed. I wasn't doomed to repeat and repeat and repeat till I died.

I was happy as we began to walk home then in the strange, siren-filled dark. My new tears, as I walked with Juno holding my hand and with Paul's arm in mine, weren't for me at all, or not directly. They were for the knowledge that I had gained as I had looked up into the blackness after the veil of light had been torn from the face of the night.

36

I woke up with my head between somebody's legs. On either side, a warm thigh pressed against my cheek. My mouth felt filled with molten metal. Everything was warm and dark, I didn't know which way was up, and I spasmed in fright.

It woke Juno up. 'What are you doing down there?' she blurred sleepily. A grey triangle of light appeared far above me. I was in bed. I was in bed with Juno. I was in bed with Juno at home, in my old bedroom, on my side, curled up halfway down the bed, facing Juno, on her side.

Juno peered beneath the duvet at me. 'Come up, you'll smother.' The ghost of her face floated in the pale cave of moonlight. Shapes and distances reversed and rereversed. She was in a cup of light, I was in an infinite darkness. Now I was in a pool of darkness, she was in an infinite light.

I closed my eyes and pressed my face back between her thighs. 'It's nice here' I said, muffled. So to speak.

'I thought you might want company tonight' said Juno.

'Yes' I said. 'Stay, stay tonight.' I held her closer to me, drew my knees up till they touched her warm feet. She let out a harsh breath.

'Careful . . . I did my ankle carrying you' said Juno. 'Turned it.'

'Sorry' I said. 'Sorry.' I couldn't remember. Was that normal?

'Not your fault.'

'Sorry' I opened my eyes and moved. Memory. I remembered. 'The kerb' I said.

'Sleep' said Juno. The triangle shrank and closed. You've lost it completely, Juliet said a calm voice. Me. My self. I said that, to my self. So my self's back. And my self says I've lost it completely . . . Well, that's good. If I know I've lost it completely. If I'm here to know I've lost it. Then I can find it in the morning.

Juno's nightdress had ridden up and I rested my forehead on the tender cushion of what we had once learned in biology to call the mons Veneris. The crisp hairs shifted against each other under the weight of my head with a tiny crackling noise that I could hear direct through the bones of my skull, a sound like the world's smallest chips going into the world's smallest deep fat frier. I swallowed, but my mouth still tasted like licked aluminium. Juno's smell was rich and strange, all warm air, spicy, with a tang of vinegar that made me fill and swell with emotion, that made me love her so much, I don't know why. 'Oh Juno' I said. 'Yes?' she said. My heart filled my mouth so I couldn't speak.

'I have to piss' I said.

37

In the bathroom I looked into the mirror.

'Who the fuck is that?' I said. My voice was dry and crackly. My ghost mouthed back at me, and smiled. I smiled back. My ghost's eyes looked huge and exhausted. My eyes swam and lost focus trying to look into hers. I closed one eye, and studied my ghost's huge black pupil and disturbingly complicated iris, and the web of red threads running through the white, like a roadmap drawn with a fine red pen on a boiled egg. My second eyelid slid closed, and I felt muscles relax into rest all over my face. In darkness I slowly touched my forehead to the cold glass. So this is me, I thought.

Later. When I sat on the cold seat, I paused. Closed my eyes again. It was too exquisite. My bladder was so full I was almost afraid to start. It was like a basketball. I had a moment of fear that I was still in bed, opened my eyes, had a moment of fear I was still wearing my clothes, looked down. No, I was naked, it was safe. I relaxed, and the sound of the splashing water and the feeling of utter abandoned bliss, of giving up, the release of tension, was almost mystical. This is what the afterlife must be like, I thought. The sound of running water, and perfect peace.

38

'Really?' I said, and supped deep of black tea as our mother rattled on.

'The Allied Irish Bank they were after, of course, they'd stolen a lorry with one of them platforms on it from the ESB yard on the Dublin Road, obviously a well planned affair, they knew exactly what they were after . . . is that too hot for you love?'

I nodded, added milk, and gulped so much tea half of it ended up on the pillow. I busied myself mopping with Kleenex, face averted. I caught Juno's eye. She buried her face in the other pillow.

'Juno, are you in pain?'

'No no. Go on' said Juno through the pillow.

'Anyway, Guard Toohy says the plan was obviously to cut the wires to the alarm and break in the upstairs windows because they've no bars on them and get in that way. All very clever, fellas down from Dublin he expects, hardened criminals. Or they might have been from Limerick, but Guard Toohy reckons it had all the hallmarks of a Dublin gang.' I tangled my toes delightedly with the toes of Juno's good foot. 'They must have had a getaway car parked nearby, because there wasn't a sign of them by the time the guards arrived.'

Which was probably half an hour after the lights had gone off. I knew Guard Toohy, and Guard O'Meara, and Guard Gill. Anything more dangerous than double parking and they'd hide in the station till they were sure it was safely over.

'They seem to have put up the lift, the platform you know, too early though. Knocked all the Christmas lights, I went down to have a look. It's an awful mess, glass everywhere. A child could get hurt.' Juno twitched beside me. 'The Council sent Sean Hickey down to clear it up with his cart, but sure his back's been out since Halloween, he only got half it cleared before he had to go to casualty to get it set right again. And on Christmas Eve. That man shouldn't touch a brush in his condition, and the size of him the poor eejit with that big awkward cart, it's no wonder.' I could feel it building up. Juno had begun to shudder. 'The shops swept the pavements, most of them, but the gutters are full of bits of light bulbs. The cars are afraid to park. Thank God they didn't get into the bank, the lorry's still sitting outside it, for forensics, but of course every gurrier in town's been swinging out of it since morning, they'll be arresting every child in the park if they go by the forensics on that. Little Timmy Sheehy was sitting in it banging the horn when I went by, and sure they'd stolen all the police tape by lunchtime and fecked two of the bollards up onto the low roof behind Londis.' She frowned at this vision of the darkness in the heart of man. 'Right up onto it. Guard O'Meara had to get a ladder.'

We exploded.

'Well if you're going to laugh . . .' Our mother picked up the tea tray and tea pot and turned to go.

'Sorry . . . sorry' we sobbed helplessly.

'I'm glad you find it so amusing.' She disappeared down the stairs, swinging the door shut loudly behind her with her heel.

'Sorry, Mum!'

'. . . And tape *The Simpsons*!'

Juno's hair covered my face as we rolled around the bed, hugging each other and snorting helplessly into each other's ears. We calmed down. Then Juno gave a little snort and I roared and we laughed ourselves out of bed.

'Ow, fff . . . fff . . . feck, my ankle' said Juno as we lay on the floor wrapped tightly together in duvet.

'Sorry' I said.

'It's OK' said Juno.

'I love you' I said.

'I know . . . I'm sorry' said Juno.

'For what?'

'For not . . . last night, I don't know' she laughed 'I don't know. I thought you wanted me to say sorry for something. You said you loved me like you were angry with me.'

'No' I said. 'Not you. Just . . . angry.' It's . . . at the world, I thought to myself, I'm angry at the world. It was too much, the world was, last night. I wasn't enough, on my own. I was just me without my defences and it wasn't enough, I was crushed . . .

'Juliet . . . what are you thinking?'

'Nothing.'

Juno was shaking her head, making her hair brush against my cheek and nose, it annoyed me, I turned my head away.

'That's not true, Juju. What were you thinking?'

'Nothing.' I was shaking for some reason.

Juno sighed. 'I understand, Juju.'

'No you don't, everything's perfect, you've got your boyfriend and your exams, your notes make sense, you have a highlighter . . .' Juno started laughing. 'You know what I mean!'

'I'll buy you a highlighter.'

'You know what I mean.'

'I'll give you my highlighter.'

'You know what I mean.'

We were tied too tightly together by the duvet for me to be able to hit her properly, but I hit her, and she stared at me.

'You're not joking' she said.

'Of course I'm not joking. You saying you understand me, don't say that, you don't.'

'I do. We're the same, Juju.'

'Well I don't understand you so we're not the same then are we.'

Our faces were up against each other. I could feel her breath, taste it. It tasted of mint. She'd gotten up in the morning and hopped to the bathroom and brushed her teeth.

'It's easy for you' I said. 'It's easy.'

'This is . . . I don't understand what you're saying' said Juno, wriggling to loosen the duvet, to get further away from me, wincing as her ankle twisted in the tight shroud.

I looked into her face and it was nothing like a mirror. Was she mocking me? 'I always thought you were perfect' I said. 'But you're not.'

'Juju, that's crazy, of course I'm not perfect. I never said I was.'

'But I thought you were. Everything you said, and . . . Everything. The soap you bought. The way you could talk to boys.'

'Oh, Juju, no . . .'

'You had opinions about everything, these really quiet,

confident opinions, and I just had chaos and noise in my head.'

'Oh honey, I had too, I have too, I didn't know.'

'And you didn't save me.'

'When?'

'Last night. You didn't understand me at all.'

'Baby Juju, I never did.'

'I thought you did, you just said you did. I thought you understood everything but you just weren't telling me.'

'I don't understand anything. Nobody does. But you don't have to. You get up in the morning and get on with it.'

'You get life, and I don't.'

'That's not it at all . . . maybe I just trust the world a little more, that's all. But that's all. That's all.'

I looked into the complicated mirror of her face and we smiled together.

'Did we just fight?' I said.

'I think we sort of did' said Juno.

'Cool' I said. Life changes. 'Cool.'

39

We went to midnight mass. Not the modern, McMidnight, convenience mass at eight p.m. Christmas Eve, but the real one, starting at the stroke of midnight. When we were very young midnight mass meant being woken up gently and carried to the car, when we still had a car, and driven half-asleep the short distance to the church, and carried inside with our jumpers and coats on over our nightclothes, with Paul trying to make us laugh, fidgeting and giggling and making faces at us as Juno and I held each other's hands and stared solemnly back at him, too in awe of the lateness of the hour and the seriousness of so huge a crowd whispering and shuffling to even smile at our brother. It was so unlike an ordinary mass, more like a great secret meeting of the persecuted early church. The unaccustomed smell of incense shocked and thrilled me. The great crib with its child-God and animals and kings and straw was such a potent mixture of toyshop and Revelation that it could bring me literally to my knees, dragging Juno with me. When the mass had ended I would walk reverently towards it in its side aisle, with its fairy lights illuminating the tiny cardboard houses of Bethlehem in the diorama that stretched out behind the papier mâché cave, itself lit with a huge bulb that, now that I think about it, must have been an appalling fire risk touching the roof of a paper cave floored with straw. I'd kneel in front of it, tugging down Juno, and stare at the baby in the crib till our father got bored and urged us home.

Walking to church in the rain as a sort-of grown-up who didn't even live at home any more wasn't quite the same, but a little awe tingled the back of my neck as I helped Juno up the broad steps and through the great oak doors, flung wide to embrace us all, through the inner doors and into the huge nave with its crammed, murmurous pews under the distant wooden vault, ribbed like a tremendous longship mysteriously tipped and hoist high above us to provide a viking roof on a Catholic church. All us fallen sailors, oblivious to the looming hulk above. Only children ever looked up at the roof, I'd noticed that years ago. And me.

My sense of awe and wonder dissipated somewhat, or at least changed direction and fixed on a new source as we found our seats and I began listening in to the murmured conversations all around me that preceded the priest's appearance.

That the shenanigans of the night before which had made a shambles of O'Connell Street and left the town without electricity till the middle of the morning were the consequences of a botched bank raid by Dublin criminals was by now undisputed truth. It was only the surrounding details that still held the status of rumour, and even these were beginning to settle down nicely. There was general agreement on the matter of masks (check) and guns (check). The issue of getaway vehicles had not yet been resolved, though a strong majority favoured two BMWs ('Stolen in Dublin, of course. I'd never take the car to Dublin these days. The train's as handy and for the Christmas wouldn't you spend the day trying to find a place to park. And isn't it pure gangsters run the car parks, the price of them, and security cameras my arse, begging your pardon, sure it's watching videos they'd be, while some scut of a ten-year-old's fecking your tape machine and maybe going back to break off the aerial if they don't approve of your taste in music. Sure they'd slash your tyres for leaving Daniel O'Donnell on the dashboard, them boys. 'Tis all rap, and the grunge.')

An altarboy emerged from the vestry, swinging the thurible. Clouds of incense mingled with the steam rising from the damp congregation. Outside, rain flogged the saints on the tall, narrow, stained glass windows that gave onto the dark on our side of the church, you could hear it slap hard against the glass in gusts. I could feel the cold as the glass sucked the heat from the aisle beside me.

('They were seen driving through Birr, you know.' '*Really?*' 'Oh yes, no regard for the lights, at a terrible speed.')

I developed quite a cough, and sadly missed some of what the couple behind me were saying.

('. . . burnt out in the Curragh. A rogue IRA unit they say.' 'Really?')

The priest walked to the altar.

'Hrumph . . . ah . . . yes . . . hrmmm' he said, and stilled the secular tongue.

Lulled by the priest's voice and soothed by the richly satisfying blend of candle and electric light softened through incense smoke, I fell asleep against Juno's arm.

40

'Well isn't this fierce Dickensian altogether' said my father, hoisting the knife above the turkey at the head of the table and surveying the family with a sardonic eye. It wasn't exactly a remark you could reply to, so I kept my head down. We'd already had a row about who'd won the contents of the Christmas cracker we'd pulled, and I was pretty sure he was aiming his remarks at me, but I said nothing. A horrible, painful suspicion was growing within me that I'd made a total fool of myself over the cracker incident, and I was too busy avoiding acknowledging that suspicion to myself to risk opening another unwinnable front in our long war. The tiny, malformed purple plastic ape that I had screamed to get sat on my sideplate in mute, one-armed reproach. I felt like pulling my pink paper hat down over my eyes and sliding under the table.

'Oh do they know it's Christmas time at all' sang my father as he carved.

Another dig at me that I couldn't respond to without being put in the wrong. He'd give me a hurt look and nudge my mother as if to say 'Look what I have to put up with' and I'd be left storming at nothing. My blood fizzed with fury and I felt my face go hot. *Bloody* plastic *bloody* gorilla. I'd started fighting for it before I'd even seen what it was and then I couldn't go back. Oh God. He'd picked it up from behind his chair and he must have been so *delighted* to see what a piece of crap it was. I'd felt my heart shrink as I saw it, as he dangled it between finger and thumb by its solitary arm. 'Oh, I like monkeys' he'd said, which wasn't even *true*.

I was in danger of flaring again and I couldn't afford to so I closed my eyes and ground my teeth as he hummed 'Spread a little happiness . . .' Oh, *Jesus*.

But *I'd* got the big end of the cracker. It wasn't *about* what was in it, it was the principle of the thing, it wasn't *fair*. Just because it jumped out and bounced off his side of the table . . . My blood bubbled and boiled like lemonade in a wok.

'Do you want some more potatoes, love?' said my mother.

'*No*' I snapped. Oh shit, that wasn't clever. I tried to retreat but I couldn't make the words come out. And here we go.

'Don't speak to your mother in that tone of voice young lady.'

Oh I couldn't *believe* it. Young fucking *lady*. Who'd he borrow *that* from?

'Well? Are you going to apologise to your mother?'

Oh shit oh shit oh shit totally outmanoeuvred, apologise to my *mother*, as though *that* was what it was all about, oh how did he do this?

'What's it to do with you?' Oh fuck what a stupid thing to say, it wasn't even witty, why did I say that, and here he comes –

'I am your *father*, girl, whether you like it or not, and you will not talk to your mother or me in that tone of voice while you are under my roof' as though he'd built the fucking roof himself 'so I want you to apologise to your mother *now*.'

I opened my mouth and I said the first thing that came into my head. And the second. And the third. The first thing that came into my head was an astonishingly awful thing to say to my father. But it wasn't as bad as the second. The third was unforgivable. In fact I managed to go well past unforgivable before I stopped, and what kept me from stopping was knowing that somehow he'd started all this, he'd goaded and provoked all this, but it didn't make me feel any less sick at myself after I'd stopped.

I ran to my room and locked myself in. Cried.

After a while I looked up at Christ on the cross.

'Happy *fucking* birthday.'

Part Three

GALWAY

41

Three days later, Juno wanted to get back to Galway to meet Michael and I went with her.

The country was white with frost right to the edge of the bay. We'd forgotten that there was hardly any fuel for the stove, so we used up everything the first day back and then Juno basically retreated to bed with Michael for a couple of days, leaving me to fend for myself. For some reason (for the masochistic romance of it, because it made me feel like a brave doomed babushka scrabbling to survive in a besieged Stalingrad) I didn't buy coal and briquettes and have them delivered. Instead I wandered the streets aimlessly at all hours with a big grubby coalsack and filled it with scraps of wood from the skips, piles of discarded newspapers, and offcuts from the lumberyard further along the docks, and dragged all this back home and up the stairs to create weird, messy fires, with bits of planks I hadn't been able to snap short enough sticking out of the open door of the stove, bringing flames out into the room. I'd stare into the stove for hours, my face roasting, and I'd feed it scraps as though it were a sick animal I was coaxing to health. I never tired of the fire. I sat by it for company, not heat. Copper staples in bits of broken packing case stained the flames green and blue. I'd put on music so I couldn't hear Juno and Michael, but the albums would end and I wouldn't always bother turning the tape over. A lot of the time they just seemed to be talking quietly, with lots of silences. Friendly silences.

I fed the fire. When I got too hot I would sometimes get up and walk to the window where my face would cool as I watched the winter harbour and my clothes would leak their heat away till they were comfortable again against my skin.

We didn't do anything special for the New Year. Well, that's a little disingenuous. I didn't do anything special for the New Year but I'm pretty sure Juno and Michael did because I could hear them.

42

A couple of days into the New Year Conrad and Dominic clattered up the stairs and burst in, both full of Christmas spirit, each waving a bottle sloshing with more Christmas spirit.

'Oh, hi' said Juno.

'What's that?' I said.

'Jameson' said Conrad, kissing Juno on the cheek.

'Black Bush' said Dominic, leering at my crotch.

'Sit down and I'll make you coffee' said Juno.

'No!' said Conrad in horror. 'Never mix your drinks.'

'Have you glasses' asked Dominic 'and we'll celebrate.'

'Celebrate what?' I said.

Conrad counted on his fingers 'Losing the insurance, losing the Aula, half the cast leaving, so we're cancelling the Coward play . . .'

'That *fucking stupid* Coward play' Dominic corrected Conrad. They were both quite astonishingly drunk.

'Oh, no' said Juno.

'We're doing *Endgame* instead' said Dominic. 'And I want you to play Clov.'

Juno didn't know what to say, so I said something. 'What's *Endgame*?' I said, and bit my tongue, for my inanity, for showing my ignorance, for everything. Dominic took it in his stride that I hadn't even heard of it, not a flicker. I was relieved and insulted.

'Play by Beckett. Only four people, which is good, and two of them in dustbins.'

'A tragedy exploring the meaningless horror of existence' said Conrad.

'Comic classic. Funny as fuck' said Dominic.

'Ah, you'd laugh at Dostoevsky' said Conrad, disgusted.

'The Russian Spike Milligan' said Dominic.

Juno had been thinking. 'I can't do it, Dominic.'

It took them nearly half an hour to talk her into it, but they finally did. Relief, delight, celebration. We drank to Juno's health. We drank to the repose of Beckett's soul. We drank to the success of *Endgame*. The conversation drifted on a mellow tide of whiskey till I asked a somewhat insensitive question.

'So what are *your* plays about, Conrad? I've never seen them.'

Dominic and Conrad both looked at me like I'd farted 'God Save the Queen' at an IRA funeral.

'Love' said Conrad eventually.

'Ah, bollocks' said Dominic.

'Love' said Conrad.

'Sexual repression. In a kitchen' said Dominic.

'Your first play's very good, I've read it' said Juno.

'Really?' said Conrad, with a relief and gratitude that was almost painful to watch. His face opened out and his shoulders rose, like sped-up footage of a desert plant blooming in a sudden shower of rain. 'No one reads them . . . no one performs them. I'm a dead man.'

'There's copies in the library.'

'Copies in the library . . . yes. But no one takes them out. I've checked.'

'I read all of them, in the library. *The Living* is really good.'

'You think so? You think so?'

I couldn't bear to look at him, it was too sad. Does everyone feel broken? I looked at Juno, smiling and talking, her voice so kind. Just like a human being. Just like a human being.

So unlike me. I could see what they saw.

'Pity' said Dominic, conversationally, 'that all your other stuff is shite.'

Conrad suddenly seemed on the verge of tears, or anger, his throat working. Juno reached out to touch his hand.

Conrad pushed back his chair and stood up.

'Bathroom' he said thickly, and walked straight into Juno's room, slamming the door behind him. The doorhandle fell off.

Juno glared at Dominic and went to the shut door. 'Conrad, you idiot' she said to the door. There were confused noises inside, then silence. Juno tried to open the door, but the spindle was attached to the far handle, which had come away on the inside in Conrad's hand. 'Conrad!' No reply. A muffled banging noise, then silence again.

Dominic came over to help. 'Connie' he said. Silence. Dominic half leaned over, said 'Woah, there' and stood back up. 'Perhaps you could have a look, Juno' he said.

Juno dropped to her knees and looked. 'Handle's gone' she said. 'Can't see anything . . . No.'

Dominic gave the door another push.

'We could pop the lock' I said. Juno turned and gave me a startled look. Dominic did the same. I laughed. He raised an eyebrow, and I laughed again. The tableau looked so absurd, Juno on her knees in front of Dominic, the two with their mouths open.

'Like in the movies' I explained. 'With a credit card.'

'We don't have a credit card' said Juno.

'Or a callcard' I said.

'I've a credit card' said Dominic. 'Well, a half one . . .' He tried to find it, farted suddenly, looked thoughtful and subsided. There was an expired callcard with a Santa Claus on it, on the living room table. I got it. Dominic, looking even more thoughtful, walked with tense buttocks to the bathroom. I got to work with the card. It was easy. The tilting, ancient house had gaps between doors and frames nearly big enough to stick a finger in. The callcard slid the curved metal latch back into the door, and I swung the door in. Juno and I stepped inside. Conrad wasn't there.

The window was open. Juno walked over to it, looked out, looked down. I joined her, did likewise. There he was, lying face down on the edge of the flat-roofed extension that jutted out the back of the next building. The roof ridge of the next building, facing the harbour, threw its shadow over him. His back gave a convulsive shudder and something fell from his mouth in a silver line down into the dark yard of our neighbour.

'Oh Jesus' I said.

'It's OK' said Juno, and stepped up onto the windowsill. She turned and climbed down the fire escape ladder to the flat roof. I followed her down.

Conrad turned away from the edge to face us as we arrived. 'I didn't want to do this in your room' he said to Juno.

'Why didn't you just get sick out the window?' said Juno.

'I didn't want you to hear me. To hear it. I'm sorry.' He turned back to the edge. She shushed him, and laid a hand on his back. He spoke away from her. 'I'd write for you if I could, Juno. I would. This isn't me.' He mopped his chin on his jacket sleeve as Juno made soothing noises and circled her palm on his broad back. It shuddered under her hand. 'How did I get old?' mumbled Conrad to himself, half crying. 'How did I get old?'

43

When Conrad had recovered a little, Dominic joined us on the roof, brought the glasses down full and his bottle of Black Bush open in his pocket, with the careless grace of the happily drunk. Juno and I, unused to spirits in instantly refilled triple measures, grew a trifle tipsy.

The cold, clean air gave us the illusion of sobriety. I found myself lying with my head in Dominic's lap. How did that happen? I adjusted my buttocks and wriggled up a little to avoid an uncomfortable seam in the tarpaper roof. As I rested my head back, I felt Dominic's lap change shape. Wow.

'So where are we going to do it?' said Juno.

'The IMI' said Conrad.

'Better off there' said Dominic. 'The Aula's a stone barn. Desperate sound.'

'It's a great play' said Conrad.

'We're gonna have you, Beckett!' roared Dominic at the sky. 'Hey, Beckett! We're gonna fucking have you!'

Eventually the bottle was empty. 'I'm cold' said Juno.

'Mmm' I said, half-asleep, warm against Dominic.

'Wear my jacket' said Conrad.

'No, I think I'll go in. I'm meeting Michael later, I want to get ready.' She stood and swayed, on the edge of the roof, by the long drop to the concrete yard.

'Let me help you' said Conrad, rising, holding her sleeve to get up, swaying himself. Lonely, lonely, lonely man I thought. God's Lonely Man. I hate that film. Scorsese loves violent men so much. He should marry one.

Conrad helped Juno up the iron ladder. She, then he, vanished into the bright block of light at the top of the ladder. I closed my eyes. Lonely man. Very sad. Marry him, Juno, I thought. Romantic man. Burn his jackets . . . marry him. 'Poor Conrad' I thought. No, I'd murmured it.

'Ah, fuck Conrad' said Dominic.

'Lonely man . . .' I said.

Dominic snorted violently and his lap began slowly to change shape again. 'He's free and he's single and he's fairly well off for the first time in his life and he fucking hates it. Fuck him. I'd swap anyday. All the drink he can drink, women throwing themselves at him, and is he happy? Is he fuck. Oh get behind me Satan.'

I awoke a while later with a start. My heels drummed on the tarpaper and I blinked the tears of sleep out of my eyes, trying to see too fast. My leg. Something on my leg.

Dominic's hand. High on my thigh, my right thigh, inside, stroking and caressing. My legs wide apart. It's lovely. I don't want this. Should've asked.

'No' I said, my voice slurred with sleep and Black Bush, and I rolled my head out of his hard lap and stood shakily.

'Juliet' he said.

'No' I said and walked across the flat roof to the iron ladder. I felt him rise, behind me.

'Listen . . . Jesus' he said, and I turned to see his right knee buckle, and he twisted to try and soak the blow with his shoulder as he hit the tarpaper full length. I almost walked back to him. He groaned. 'Dead leg' he said. I turned back, climbed the ladder into the light, and left him on the dark roof.

Juno's room was like heaven, so bright and unreal. The smell of her and the scatter of her things. I walked through into the living room. Someone had fixed the doorhandle.

The living room was warm and empty. I threw a broken piece of scrapwood into the stove's glowing ashes to see the sparks swirl and vanish up the flue. A quick flame ran along the rough wood and all along it splinters flamed in bright orange, then bent slowly into glowing neon red curls then switched off to black. A real, enduring flame caught it at the bottom, and started to haul itself up. I sat back into a chair and watched it like television.

I heard Dominic cursing as he tried to get his dead leg over the windowsill in Juno's room. My pants felt hot and tight against my skin and between my legs and I couldn't tell if they were hot from the stove or from me.

I turned round in the chair. Dominic was leaning in Juno's doorway.

'Jesus Christ, fucking pins and fucking needles' he said.

'Fuck off home, Dominic' I said, turning back to the fire. I didn't like having my back to him, but I didn't like looking at him either.

'You don't mean that' he said.

'You were groping me in my sleep' I said.

'You're overreacting, I was just . . . you looked lovely and I was just, rubbing, you know, stroking your leg, absent-mindedly. Like you would with a cat.'

I swung round in the chair. 'Between their legs?'

'It wasn't between.'

'I woke up with my legs spread, Dominic, and they weren't like that when I went to sleep.'

'Well, er, Juliet, I mean I hate to say this, but whatever you were dreaming about, it was you that spread your legs, not me.' Dominic walked very, very carefully towards me. 'And to be honest you hadn't seemed too unhappy with me stroking your leg. How was I to know?'

'Ask me! Ask me! Ask me!'

He came around the table and stood in front of me. He gave me a melting, apologetic, puppydog look. Actor, I thought.

'Juliet . . .'

If he touches me . . . I thought.

He put his hand on my shoulder, and dropped into an awkward crouch. His eyes looked into mine. Oh God, I thought.

'Juliet . . .' he said.

'Yes, Dominic?' I said in a voice remarkably like that of a Victorian headmistress, albeit a rather drunken Victorian headmistress. I felt transported in time, not very far admittedly, back to the school discos of transition year with their ghastly fumbles and stilted conversations. If I squinted he could almost be Harry Brannagan, who had actually got his hand under my T-shirt once in the dark behind the gymnasium, and been so stunned by his success that he had just left it there, entirely unmoving, for ten minutes while we kissed with the Hollywood-influenced hoover-action of the very young and very drunk.

I realised I was squinting, and stopped. He turned back into Dominic. Oh balls.

His face drifted closer to mine and I was distracted by the oddest feeling I'd done all this before. Then his lips touched mine and his rather pointed chin crushed its stubble into my chin and I could smell his whiskey, cigaretty breath.

'No' I said into his mouth, and turned my head sideways. He leaned his face against my cheek and stuck his tongue in my ear. He's bloody read that somewhere, I said to myself furiously, he's bloody read that it's erotic and seductive to stick your bloody tongue in her ear and he's trying it on like a key in a fucking lock.

I stood up, and my shoulder caught him under the chin and snapped his jaw shut.

'Om, f'hk, oh Jeshush' he said, clutching his mouth and rolling back onto his behind.

'Oh no, oh God, are you alright?' I said, horrified to see blood on the fingers he held to his mouth.

'I bit my fucking tongue' he mumbled, none too clearly, through his fingers. 'Oh fuck, I'm bleeding.'

I began to laugh. 'Oh dear, I'm terribly sorry' I said. 'Oh gosh . . .'

Gosh? His swearing had made me all prim, a nice way of isolating him further as he swore, bled and winced in pain, sat on his slender rear on the orange rug. I bent towards him, but thought better of it.

'I'll get you something . . . for the bleeding' I said with drunken, owlish dignity and made my way with self-consciously ladylike steps to the bathroom, where I closed the door, sat on the toilet seat and cried with laughter for a while.

Eventually I summoned up the courage to return to the scene of the crime. Some spirit of mischief possessed me to pick up a couple of Tampax on my way to the bathroom door and I emerged holding these, for reasons unknown, aloft like the torch of the Statue of Liberty. I tracked Dominic down, with his head in the kitchen sink, spitting pinkened tapwater straight down the plughole with the accuracy of one who had been doing this for some minutes and was now rather good at it. He looked up, and seemed startled to have a couple of tampons thrust in his face.

'For the bleeeeeding' I explained solemnly. He didn't know how to react and I wasn't in the mood to help him. I stared at him unblinkingly till he with grave reluctance took them from my outstretched hand.

'Ah . . . thanks . . . but I'm, ah, it's better now. Almost stopped.'

'You'd better take them, just in case.'

'Oh, alright so. Yes. Thanks.' He held them helplessly.

'Are you sure you'll be alright, now, walking home in your condition?' I said solicitously and he gave a reflexive 'Oh, yes, no problem.'

Bang! Gotcha! I thought, and he began to look rather thoughtful himself.

'Look, ah . . . actually . . .' but I was already bringing him his coat.

I left him to make his own way downstairs, still clutching his tampons as I closed the door to our flat on his mournful goodbye.

I went to bed in high good spirits, with a hot-water bottle, and a pint glass of water by the bedside for the morning. After switching the light out I hugged my pillow with glee and wriggled about in the bed like a salmon in a net. When I surfaced for air, I had that giddy pleasurable moment of not knowing which way I was facing, of feeling as though the room had been spun for my entertainment. I blinked and the dim outline of the curtained window emerged like the picture on a polaroid, on the opposite side of my vision to the one half-expected, and the room whizzed into place around it, boom. With my head sticking out over the side of my bed, I laughed till I got hiccups.

In my own bed, in my own room. A low-key revelation this time, spreading like the warmth of the Black Bush through me. Galway had become home.

44

A few days later, down by the dockside, dragging my coalsack of debris and offcuts home, I saw David Hennessey. He was stepping off a boat onto the narrow, slippery steps that lead up from the water to road level. He hadn't seen me, and I rushed to make it to the top of the steps before he re-emerged up into view.

When his head did appear, he was still looking down at his feet, fairly vital work when negotiating the quayside steps, so he didn't see me till he was safely at the top, and looked up.

I seemed to startle, almost shock him. For a moment I thought he was going to undo all his good work and take an involuntary step backward, off the edge of the quay.

'Juliet' he said. 'Good God.' Half-step back. I nearly grabbed him.

'Hello Mr Hennessey.'

He gave his 'Mister Hennessey?' grimace. 'Mister, schmister. What on earth are you doing here?'

'I live here.' I pointed. 'The tall building. Top floor.'

'You live in the *docks*?' He shook his head. 'You Capulets. A fine view, though, I'd imagine?'

'Oh yes.'

'So were your agents tracking me across the bay with binoculars or did you just, ah, happen to be standing at the head of these steps this morning?'

'I saw you stepping out of your boat and I, I sort of decided to, to ambush you. I didn't think you'd mind.'

'Oh I don't, far from it. I was just a bit . . . startled. Sorry if I was abrupt with you. What's in the bag?'

I blushed and explained. I even mentioned my babushka-in-Stalingrad fantasy, to my own horror as I heard myself, but he seemed heartily amused by it and laughed.

'Were you out fishing?' I asked, to change the subject.

'No, not fishing.' He looked back down at the boat, a sturdy little launch with a half-cabin and a big bulge of what I assumed to be engine at the back. Not quite a proper working boat, not quite a pottering-about toy. 'No, I just came in to do the shopping actually. Horribly mundane explanation. My father's house is a few miles up the coast, right on the water, and you know the Connemara roads. On any kind of decent day like today it's easier to pop in by boat than take the car.' He gave a sort of apologetic smile-and-shrug. 'And much more enjoyable, of course.'

I was absolutely delighted to learn that he commuted by boat, it appealed to the romantic idiot in me. I couldn't have been more pleased if I'd discovered he came to work in full armour, on horseback, but he seemed terrifically embarrassed by my delight, as though I'd caught him showing off somehow.

'It's very practical' he said helplessly.

'What are you shopping for?' I said, to put him out of his misery.

He cheered up. 'Food and . . . um . . . stuff' he said.

I sighed. It was such a hopelessly boyish answer that I felt older than him for a moment. 'Do you have a list?' I said.

'Er, no. I sort of wander around . . . I mean, I know we need light bulbs . . .'

I must have given him my mother's Disapproving Look, because he grinned and said 'God, is this what it's like when I'm grilling you all on a book you haven't read? I swear I'll have a list for next week, Miss Taylor.'

I grinned back at him. This was just like a Real Conversation. 'Would you like a hand? Shopping? I'm quite good at it.'

'Oh, would you do me the honour, Miss Taylor?' he said and fell on one knee and kissed the back of my hand mock-reverently.

'Why Mr Hennessey, the pleasure is entirely mine. And get up, you'll ruin your trousers.'

He got up. 'What about the, uh, ruins of Stalingrad?' he said, pointing at my coalsack.

'Oh, they're fine here. I'll pick them up later. They're out of the road, and who'd steal them?'

So we left Stalingrad behind us at the head of the quayside steps, and went shopping.

45

'But it's on special offer' said David.

'Great, 650 grams for the price of the usual 500. It's *still* dearer per gram than Super-Valu's own brand, which is frankly just as good. You're paying for the name.'

'Oh God, this isn't shopping, this is mathematics. I just can't do all those calculations in my head.'

'Shopping *is* mathematics' I said, in a fair parody of him at his most serious. 'And put those down.'

'What? But these are the cheapest.'

'You're buying air. They wind the rolls loose and puff the pack-wrapper full of air to keep it firm. You'll never save money buying the cheapest toilet rolls. They last no time, and it's not worth it for the annoyance of having them run out constantly.'

'So what do you recommend?'

'Steal the industrial-sized ones from the lecturers' toilets like I do.'

'Jesus, do you?'

'Well, they don't padlock the toilet roll holders in the lecturers' toilets' I explained, breaking character. 'The toilet roll in the student toilets comes out of a thing like a small fallout shelter bolted to the wall, I think they have to cut it open with a welding torch when they want to put in a new roll. Maybe it's different in the boys' toilets.'

He shook his head. 'No, I know the dispensers you mean.'

'Well, I raid the Arts tower. History usually, it's the easiest. They just leave these *enormous* rolls on the cistern . . . You don't mind, do you?' I said, suddenly anxious.

'Christ no, fascinated.'

'I *never* take the last roll.'

'Very Christian of you.'

'It's just that we don't have any money, really, or not enough. I can't ask our parents for more.'

'We?'

'My sister Juno and I.' I'd have said Me and Juno if it had been anyone else. Now that the conversation was about something real, albeit stupid, I was anxious again. I didn't want him to disapprove of me, but I didn't want to fib either. 'My twin.'

I was surprised to realise I must never have mentioned her to him before, that to him I was unique. How strange, that he only knew me. How . . . incomplete? No. Misleading. Or was it? My being Juno's twin was such a constant that I couldn't get a clear picture of its importance.

'Cheese' he said. I pretended to take a photograph. 'No, I've remembered we need cheese.'

'We?' I said in my turn, pleased he hadn't asked about Juno, hadn't said 'And is she just like you?'

'My father and I' he said.

I blushed as though reprimanded.

'Oh, of course' I said.

46

'Don't put the sugar on the firelighters' I said. 'The sugar will taste of firelighter.'

'Good thinking, Batman' said David, and moved the bag of sugar to the other end of the trolley. 'That really *is* it. I think.'

We'd covered every aisle at least twice as he remembered items we'd already passed. By the end I began to suspect he was doing it deliberately, that he didn't want the game to end.

'Ostrich eggs!' he exclaimed, slapping his forehead. 'Nearly forgot.' He turned the trolley.

'I don't think Super-Valu do ostrich eggs' I said, turning it back. 'Besides, you're better off getting them down the Saturday market. Fresher, and they'll usually throw one in for luck.'

'You're right' he said. 'We're done, then.'

He wheeled the laden trolley toward the shortest checkout queue. I pointed to the second-shortest queue.

'Aye, aye captain' he said, and joined it. 'Why, Holmes?' he stage-whispered.

I sighed and whispered 'This queue is only one person longer and look at the trolleys. Practically empty. It'll whizz through. That queue has two *gigantic* trolleyfuls and they're bound to pay by credit card as well, they look the type. Much slower than cash. Lots of form-filling, counterfoil signing. Probably want them delivered, that's another form.'

'By Jove, Holmes' he whispered. 'You never cease to amaze.'

After we'd got through the checkout and I'd made him take the firelighters out of the bag with the bread in it and give it a bag of its own and he'd paid for everything, we looked at the huge pile of plastic bags.

'Hmm' he said, 'I could probably sneak a trolley out, and dump it in the harbour when I'm finished.'

The checkout girl gave him a dirty look. I smothered a laugh.

'I'll help you' I said.

'Oh no' he said aghast, 'I couldn't possibly allow you . . .' but I just picked up as many bags as I could carry and headed for the exit, which didn't really leave him with a hell of a lot of options.

47

'Have you drink taken?' I asked him as we put our bags down on the quayside at the head of the steps.

'No, God, sorry, do I seem drunk?' he said, concerned. 'Oh dear.'

'No' I said, 'Not *drunk*, but . . .' I paused for thought. I was sick of stuttering and sounding incoherent whenever I tried to say anything serious, so I took my time, trying to get it right. Gulls made their alien noises and a trawler further down the quay throbbed quietly, about to leave.

What I thought to myself was that all of his gravitas had imperceptibly transmuted into levitas in the last hour or so, but I could hardly put it like that.

And pretty soon I'd thought too much about it and couldn't say anything at all. I shrugged, mute and furious with myself. He made urging gestures, raised eyebrows, mimed pulling it out of me with a rope. Made the charades gestures for film, book, play? First syllable? I smiled despite myself. I pointed at him, pointed at my wristwatch, mimed the hands winding back an hour with an anti-clockwise forefinger, pulled my mouth-corners down. I pointed at him again, pointed at my watch now, lifted my mouth-corners into a smile. Shrugged. Gave him a questioning look.

I thought for a second he was trying to mime a reply. A shudder shook his upper body and his head swayed for a second, but he pulled himself together at once with an effort that tightened the skin across his face and said 'I can't . . . I don't . . . It's a long time since I had any *fun*.' He said the word with a weird anger. 'I'm sorry, Juliet. Because . . . of my home situation . . . because' he looked at me questioningly 'my father is dying.'

I nodded miserably. I hadn't meant to open up whatever I'd just opened up. He was speaking quite calmly now, not angrily, almost as though he was thinking of something else entirely, as though he was giving absent-minded directions to a tourist while thinking separately how best he himself should go home.

'I have not had a particularly enjoyable Christmas or New Year, and this morning was very enjoyable indeed. I was very grateful for your company. I allowed myself to forget about . . . all of that, and if I embarrassed you or behaved foolishly then I really am truly sorry.'

He was so awkward and sad and dignified I wanted to hit him, how could he think that I wanted him to apologise for the last hour of silly, innocent nonsense?

'Don't be *stupid*' I said violently, nearly crying. I'd thought he understood me. 'It was *lovely*, I wouldn't have *gone* shopping with you if I didn't *want* to and I wouldn't have *stayed* if I wasn't enjoying myself, I was *pleased* you got happier, how could you possibly *apologise* to me for it?'

'Oh no, oh no . . .' he seemed appalled at my distress.

'I had a *lousy* Christmas' I interrupted. 'And today has been *great* and for *Christ's* sake don't apologise again.'

He seemed lost in thought for a moment, then fumbled in the pocket of his jacket and brought out a battered packet of fruit pastilles.

'Fruit pastille?' he said. 'You can have one of the black ones, they're the nicest. Blow off any fluff, they've been in the pocket for weeks.'

Miserably I took the first one, orange, and chewed it.

Five minutes later we were both sitting on the ridiculously cold stone of the quay's edge, our legs dangling above the harbour water, happily miserable together. We exchanged the horror stories of our Christmases, just the outlines, nothing too grim, made them sound funny. We talked about films, and the weather, and Christmas television. Eventually a very light drizzle began to fall.

'Why don't you come in, for coffee?' I said, nodding back towards the house.

'Oh no, I couldn't. I really should be getting back, I mean he won't worry about me or anything like that, but I said I'd be straight back, and we're cooking dinner . . . Look' he said, and seemed to startle himself with the suggestion, 'why don't you come to dinner?'

He didn't startle himself half as much as he startled me.

'Yes, do' he said, pleased, as though seconding someone else's suggestion. I hovered on the brink of saying no for what seemed like a month or a year or some ridiculous length of time entirely unsuited to a conversation, until I realised that absolutely every atom of me was roaring yes.

'Yes' I said, without thinking about it at all, like I was reading the word off a blackboard.

48

I sat in the half-shelter of the half-cabin on a plastic beer crate, feeling grotesquely busty in an oversized bright orange life jacket, attached as tightly as the straps would allow over my grey wool coat.

'If we go fast enough, the drizzle won't get us' said David, gunning the engine as we emerged into open water and headed up the coast into the wind. Sure enough the drizzle fizzed against the window at the front of the cabin but nothing came in the open rear. I peered out the window. Windscreen? I wasn't sure what to call bits of boats. The engine was incredibly loud, but the boat smacked through the choppy water surprisingly smoothly. I'd been on buses that bounced more. The view through the windscreen was tremendous, an endless expanse of grey water, ridged with low white wavecrests, pouring towards and under us endlessly, with the mist and drizzle hiding Clare from us on our left so that it felt like the ocean, not the bay.

'This is *brilliant*' I yelled. The coast of Galway drifted by, far to our right. I recognised a building, a hotel, then it was gone behind a sheet of rain and the windscreen spattered hard as the rain hit us, but the cabin stayed dry.

'Glad you like it' yelled David. 'Want a go?' He nodded at the wheel.

'Oh *yes*' I said, pleased and scared.

He stood up from his little seat, still holding the wheel, and stooped under the low roof, legs braced wide for balance, while I left my beer crate to slip by him into his seat.

'Grab the wheel.'

I grabbed it. He let go. I could feel every wave through the palms of my hands.

'Throttle' he said and took my right hand from the wheel and put it on the throttle. 'Turn it.'

I turned it. The engine roared still louder and the boat surged under my hands. 'You can swing her around a little if you like. Never hold her sideways to the waves. She's much more comfortable taking them head on. Anything makes you nervous, other boats, buoys, rocks, slow right down but leave the engine running. Don't point her at the shore. Got that?'

I nodded.

'Comfortable?'

I nodded.

'Good.' He stepped back, out of the half-cabin, and stood up into the rain and wind. I heard the palms of his hands slap the roof above me to brace him as the wind and water ripped into him. I turned the throttle more and the engine roared louder than love. Where did I get that from? It was an album Michael played sometimes. Louder than love. The wind was enough to keep the angled windscreen clear now, water pushed to the edges by the pressure of our speed through the water and the air. Everything louder than everything else.

I swung the wheel, just a little, and the horizon wheeled, and I swung it back, and I shouted silently for joy in the middle of the great noise. Above me I could hear David singing, it was something I knew, words torn ragged by the wind. 'Rainy Night In Soho', the Pogues. I joined in but I'm sure he couldn't hear me there, outside the cabin, his face in the storm.

Roaring across the grey plane of the water, the wheel and the seat beneath me transmitted the details of the neverending, complex kiss of the boat and the water, up through my bones.

When eventually he stooped to come back into the tiny cabin, soaking, shaking rain from his hair, and put a hand on the wheel by mine, I was as startled as if I'd been caught kissing by my father.

'We're almost there' he said. 'Shall I bring her in?'

I nodded and reluctantly handed over control. Back on my beer crate I felt as though I was about to start trembling, and put a hand to my face to check if it was hot, it seemed roasting to me but it was cool under my hand.

He was lost in concentration, bringing her toward the shore and around a great dark bulk under the water, rocks, and then there was a gap in the low grey stone of the shoreline, an inlet with high sides of a darker rock, and the high sides fell away and we were in calm water idling toward a wooden dock, under a low grey sky.

I realised with a shock that it was an ordinary day, quiet, calm and raining, and that the storm had been private to us, just a creation of our speed, and that for everybody else around the bay it was just raining.

My storm. Juno had missed it. I felt absurdly cheerful about this.

49

'It's got a *tower!*' I said to David as he tied the nose of the boat to a rusting iron ring set into the end of the wooden dock.

He looked over his shoulder towards the house. 'Mmm, yes.'

I passed up the last of the shopping bags and hopped out of the boat onto the dock. '*Wow*. It's *brilliant.*'

David was embarrassed again. 'Mmm.' He finished securing the boat and stood up straight. 'Just chuck your life jacket in the cabin, it'll be fine.'

I got in a tangle with the straps and he made as though to help, then checked himself. I grinned at him. 'Hah. I just missed out on a big payday there, didn't I? Report you to the ethics committee and sell my story to the *Sun*. "He Took Off My Life Jacket" Sobbed Student. Damn, it's stuck . . .'

He smiled back. 'With your permission, Ms Taylor?'

'Granted, Mr Hennessey.'

He dealt with the knot I'd made of the straps at the small of my back, and I slipped the life jacket off over my head and threw it down into the cabin.

He'd picked up the shopping bags before I could get to them.

'Spoilt Victorian Child' I began singing softly to myself as we started up the path towards the house with the tower.

David laughed. 'Your subconscious is showing' he said.

'What?' I said

'Do you think I'm . . . dreadfully old-fashioned?' He was smiling.

'Oh no' I said. 'Or if you are, it's lovely. I mean, I like it about you. You're old-fashioned in a good way.'

'Mmm.'

'Every time I say anything nice you clam up and go mmm. I'm going to have to start being horrible to you to keep the conversation going.'

He'd said 'Mmm' again in the middle of that, and now laughed. 'Yes, sorry. But aren't we living in rather a neo-Victorian age, Ms Taylor? One very concerned with correct appearances and with, ah, genteel speech. Always making sure we discuss the unspeakable without offending anybody's delicate sensibilities. An age where . . . we are careful not to touch each other, because altogether elsewhere others rape and murder and that starts, does it not, with a touch? An age where the privileged try to cure the world by talking.' He laughed at himself, made a helpless moue. 'If I am old-fashioned . . . am I not a model modern citizen of a most old-fashioned age?'

I smiled at him. I liked him like this, a little embarrassed at his own fire, but still meaning it, not backing down.

We'd got to the house, but he didn't reach for a key immediately. That suited me, I didn't feel quite ready to meet his father, on a drip or in a wheelchair or slack-jawed and dribbling. I took a couple of steps away from the house, toward the sea. The view was bleak, grey, vast, thrilling.

David put down the bags against the big, yellow-painted front door, and moved to stand beside me.

'You're lecturing again' I said.

'I'm more comfortable lecturing' he said.

We looked out across the tremendous sweep of the bay where the rain, falling lightly on us still, thickened and blackened as it grew closer to the Clare shore, the small Clare hills buried under black clouds vast as flattened, molten Alps. I put up the collar of my coat and shivered, half from the cold and half from the glory. The power and scale of it. Its indifference to my existence thrilled me, I loved the world when it forgot about me.

As we watched, a bright rod of gold joined the dark sea to the dark sky, far out in the bay.

'That's a bit over the top' I said.

'Gaudy' he said.

'Cliched.'

'Sentimental.'

'Victorian.'

The gap in the clouds widened and the gold spread like butter, lush, thick smears of light that almost hurt to look at, as countless raindrops fell across the path of the light and spun it through their accidental lenses to our eyes.

It became too beautiful to be flippant about and we shut up and just looked at it.

After a while David stirred. 'My father would like this very much. I think I'll . . .' and he turned abruptly back toward the house. I stayed looking. Great spears of gold, embedded in the sea, shafts rippling with the pressure of holding up the sky.

Footsteps on gravel, then grass. He stood beside me. It was hardly raining over Galway at all now, the last of the low, heavy clouds were moving out across the bay to Clare. The crack in the clouds tightened, the waterfall of light brightened, twisted, flared as a heavy squall of rain blew through it, then dimmed and narrowed to a thin scratch of silver, flickered, flared, vanished. Black clouds over grey water. No light.

'My God.'

I breathed out and turned my head. Not David. David's father. He turned too. We smiled at each other.

'Gerry Hennessey. David's father.' He held out a hand. I was shocked at his accent, far more Irish than David's. Broad West Galway with only some of the edges smoothed off.

'Juliet Taylor' I said, very formal, and shook his hand. God, I practically curtsied.

'Delighted, delighted. David's talked a lot about you.' He laughed at the look on my face. 'Only good things, don't worry. He showed me an essay you did, on Jane Austen was it? Didn't mean a thing to me, but he seemed very impressed. Oh indeed, I nodded wisely and pretended I'd understood it, ach, a bad mistake. I hadn't read more than a page of it and he caught me rotten with a couple of questions about God alone knows what. Wasn't that a magnificent display?' he said, sweeping a hand at the horizon.

I nodded.

'Are you hungry?' he said.

I nodded. He looked a little like David but fabulously old and leathery. I looked again. No, not old.

'Good, good. David's preparing dinner. You're not a vegetarian are you?'

I hesitated. I didn't buy meat, or I tried not to, but I wasn't really a vegetarian because I ate it if I was given it although I sort of *thought* of myself as a vegetarian sometimes, even though I'd buy the lasagne in UCG canteen when I was really hungry because their vegetarian food came in tiny portions and always contained carrots for some reason . . .

'No' I said. We walked back to the house. David's father pushed open the front door. I looked up at the tower for a moment before realising that he was holding the door open for me. 'Oh, thank you' I said, and walked into the house.

50

Let me rephrase that.

'Oh, thank you' I said, and walked into a temple of transformations.

Look, now.

Down the corridor, paintings blasting colour at me like heat as I pass them, fat with chrome yellow and petrol bomb orange, bulging out of their frames like the freaked-out spine-damage erections of accident victims.

Maybe I shouldn't have stared at the sea and the sky for so long in such silence, but now as I return to the world of furniture, conversation and dinner my nerves seem to be sticking out of my skin like tiny sea anemones flowering from the open pores. I'm super-sensitised, the damp cotton of my skirt crashes across my thighs as I walk toward the open door at the end of the corridor, my breasts kiss hard against the cups of my bra, kiss, in the dark of my dress, kiss, with every step, kiss, and I'm anointed in adrenaline, I'm fizzing like an aspirin, the folds of my skin are spicy with arousal and social terror. If you licked me, you'd trip.

High on shyness. I'm buzzing.

I take the two steps down into the kitchen.

Kiss, kiss.

He's beautiful. His hair's still wet with rain. Some of it tumbles forward as he leans over the range. He runs his left hand up through it, and his fingers ripple it back into order in one stroke and little droplets of rain are spun out and away by the whip of the hair as the hand passes through it, like the great teeth of a plough through pastureland.

Everything's hyper-enhanced. I'm standing in a Connemara kitchen, thinking in symbol and metaphor. As our cousin Gareth's mother would put it, I'm tired, I'm excited, and I'm beginning to show off. And I'm staring at David, which I only notice when he notices me.

'Hi, Juliet', oh God his eyes. Cue more damp cotton.

51

'Ah, what's for dinner?' I said, and immediately boiled with self-loathing at the inanity of my words.

'I've no idea' said David. 'This thing, whatever it is.' He pointed at an extraordinarily large, recently deceased oceanic beast that completely hid a merely very large frying pan beneath its bulk of fins and eyes. 'Fried sea monster. Dad catches them and expects me to know how to cook them. Creatures previously unknown to science, and he expects me to know if they go well with a butter sauce.'

I stood beside him and we stared at it. It stared back.

'Jesus' I said. Partly an expression of my shock at the odd fish in front of me, partly an expression of my shock at the odd fish beside me, both of whom I felt I was seeing as if for the first time.

I know. I'm a pretty dim bulb. You probably knew I was in love with him halfway through the acknowledgements.

But I was a simple, fucked-up, country girl. I endured great emotions the way Belgium has traditionally endured great European battles. I mean, they were *painful*, and I was often quite profoundly affected by them, but I didn't really think of them as having much to do with me. I was just where they happened to be taking place. Happy geographical accident. From Waterloo to Ypres. There go those guns again. I wonder what it's all about this time?

So, as wave after wave of nameless emotion swept over me, emitting battle cries of 'Name me! Name me!', I rocked from foot to foot, shellshocked. Here we go again.

I swayed and stared at the sea monster and felt turned on, turned inside out, and on the verge of tears.

Jesus.

He really was ferociously sexy that day, by the way. At the time I was too busy not-noticing-anything to notice that I'd noticed, but looking through the folders of memory now, oh yes. Oh Jesus, he was sexy. It wasn't the clothes, though they were grand, and it certainly wasn't the haircut, which was the subtle, natural look of a man who's been out of prison six months and hasn't gotten round to visiting his stylist yet, but by God he was sexy. And there I was with my hip brushing his as I swayed, and me wondering what on earth was wrong with me.

Believe me, my wilful ignorance of the geography of my own heart throughout all this is at least as annoying and frustrating to me as it must be to you. Bear with my youthful self.

His father came in behind us and put a hand on each of our shoulders. It's a wonder he wasn't electrocuted.

'Well, can you cook it, son?'

'I found its guts where its brain should be and it took me two goes to find its spine, I think it had only just evolved one and wasn't sure where to put it, but yes it probably won't kill us.'

'And how'll the maestro be serving it?'

'With lashings of garlic and a prayer to Saint Anthony.'

'There's the boy. And a wine to go with it?'

'I was thinking a Newcastle Brown Ale of recent vintage.'

'Ah, you and your beer. I have a cellar to get through and it's seldom we have guests as radiant as young Juliet here.' He patted our shoulders and made for the door. 'Makes a change from your bloody fish farmers. I know the very thing.' He disappeared up the two steps and out of the kitchen.

'He's a bit unreconstructed' said David apologetically as I blushed all over the place.

'Oh no, he's lovely' I said, and meant it. 'Who are your fish farmers?'

'Ah, Cian and Eamonn. They work in the bay, friends of mine. And his, at this stage, but it's a running joke that the three of us can't tell a glass of Château Zut Alors '61 from Pepsi in a shoe. I'm not very interested in wine, and my sister doesn't drink, so he's drinking his cellar before he goes.'

I was almost thick enough to ask 'Goes where?' but remembered in time.

'He looks great' I said.

'Hmm. Yeah, yeah he does' said David, and his father's footsteps came down the corridor and he was back, bearing aloft a dusty bottle.

'The very one!' he said. 'Even the shagging dust is probably worth money by now' and he turned to me 'Have you e'er an interest in wine at all, Juliet?'

I shook my head, no.

'Well, it's a monstrous world of charlatans, snobbery and bullshit, but at the heart of it all is some lovely booze. I've three bottles of this fella left, and if my bank manager could see me swinging it about like this he'd have a shagging heart attack. I *invested* in wine, can you imagine, in the early eighties, sold most of it on again before everything crashed in the late eighties, made a fortune. No way to treat wine, though. I'm making amends for my sins now by drinking the few crates I have left.'

'Was that . . . what you do for a living, selling wine? Trading it.' Blush blush, kick self.

'Ah no. Sit down there, sit down. No, the fortune I made out of wine was a fairly small fortune, I'd already made my few bob in the oil industry. Working in Scotland a lot of the time, and travelling a bit. Saudi, the Emirates, Malaysia, all the usual suspects. Plying my trade. A wandering Irishman with a family to feed, like many another.'

'He also invented a deep-water pumping system that's opened up new oilfields all over the Indian Ocean and the North Sea' interrupted David from the range. 'Which he's too shy to mention. He'll have you thinking he was sweeping the canteen floor of a rig for twenty years if you're not careful.'

'Arra it was a few valves and a cutting-head, David. "Deep-water pumping system", Jaysus. You make me sound like a fecking engineer.' His accent was getting more Galway by the moment.

David continued to address me, as his father writhed in embarrassment in his chair. 'Dad not only invented "a few valves and a cutting-head", but he patented them and got some of the most tight-arsed companies on earth to pay him a handsome royalty to use them, including BP, who employed him. What's really funny is that if they'd given him a decent job in research and development to begin with, he'd have had to sign a waiver as a condition of employment and they'd have owned his ideas. But of course, as he constantly points out, he's an uneducated Galwayman not a feckin' engineer, so they employed him as a Paddy with muscles, he got his diving cert in his own time, and he figured out better ways of drilling and pumping as a hobby to pass the hours while he was decompressing.'

'Oh would you stop, I'm sure Juliet has no interest in all this.' The leather of his face was managing to blush somehow. 'And besides, it was Pat Shanahan did the real work, or I'd have never made a shilling out of it.' His accent had retreated in his embarrassment to the very borderlands of comprehensibility. I'd thought for a second he was speaking Irish.

'And did David and . . . David's mother, and sister, did they travel with you to all these places?' I said quickly, letting him off the hook, and putting him on another one.

'Ah no, no. Their mother, my wife, she died young.' Christ, I thought, I will never open my stupid mouth again. He waved away my attempted apology. 'We were living in London, for the job. Their mother was English, well French-English, a Hampstead Huguenot, great woman altogether, anyway. I thought I could either look after them or make enough money for them to look after themselves. I probably made the wrong decision, but this was back a long way. Back then a father went out and earned. That's how you were a father. So I left them with the relatives a fair bit, their mother's sister, and their gran, my mother, while she was alive. And when I'd enough money put away, I retired. Missed a lot, though. Missed a lot.'

'You missed shag all' said David, adding some sort of sauce with a sizzle to the sea monster. 'A lot of puking and crawling. Learning to say "fuck" from the estate kids. Sarah's Bay City Rollers obsession.'

'Oh Jesus' said David's father, settling back in his chair with a satisfied sigh like a proper father. 'I remember. Back from Brunei with a ruptured eardrum from a bad pressure drop, and Sarah in tartan from bloomers to nightie, screaming along to "Shang-A-Frigging-Lang", day in, day out, morning till night. I thought I'd go mad. I thought I'd *gone* mad. Surely life isn't meant to be like this, Lord? I'd say to myself. Have I committed a grievous sin unbeknownst to meself? Am I being punished? And sweet Jesus, do you remember Mud? Where did a child that young get the lungs?'

He uncorked the bottle, David served up a melon and a knife and told us to get on with it, and dinner lazily began in a haze of nostalgic stories about David and his older sister, Sarah. David and I took turns to prompt. By the time the first bottle of wine had been polished off I was contributing amusing childhood stories from Juno and Paul's lives, and by the time a second had been dusted, uncorked and demolished, I was digging up some of the most embarrassing incidents from my own. So was David. So was his dad. We were roaring with laughter at a story of mine which I assure you requires a lot of very good wine indeed to be funny, when David's dad fell off his chair. I nearly sobered up, I was so scared he'd died. Then David fell off his chair, quite deliberately, and I realised they were both still laughing, and I was so flushed with relief I deliberately fell off mine too and we all lay on the kitchen floor like complete idiots, laughing hysterically.

It was David's dad's idea we all go for a walk, and a jolly good idea it was too. In fact, at the time, it seemed like probably the best idea anybody had ever had, ever. I think I said as much. Loudly. I may have sung it.

David's dad disappeared through a small door into a space slightly larger than a closet and slightly smaller than a room, tucked away to the left of the range, and began hurling wellingtons and oilskins back over his shoulder into the kitchen.

'Hi-ho, hi-ho' he sang, 'It's off to work we go' and we all joined in, ba-rum bum bum, baba rum bum bum, hi-ho, hi-ho, and I sat in the middle of the floor and slipped off my shoes and slipped on a wellington and, after a couple of brave attempts, another wellington. I frowned at them quizzically. One of them was on the wrong foot. How could only one of them be on the wrong foot? Ah. The green one was on the wrong foot. The black one was fine.

David's head emerged from a bright yellow oilskin. Straight out the neck hole, first time. I admired his *savoir-faire*.

'Your sea monster' I said carefully, catching his eye, 'was <u>divine</u>' and I started giggling. 'And may I also say how much I admire your *savoir-faire*. And your *sang-froid*. And your ... Savoy 'otel.'

'Miss Taylor' said David, taking my heart in his hand, no, my hand in his, 'May *I* say how much I admire your certain ... *je ne sais quoi* ... your certain ... *joie de vivre* ... your certain age ... your uncertain smile ...'

'Your grace under pressure'
'Your face under water'
'Your place or mine?'
'Your . . . fruit of the vine'
'Your hand on your heart'

'My hand on my heart.' He put his free hand on his heart. He grinned down at me, I grinned up at him, and he pulled me to my feet by the hand he'd continued to hold as we babbled nonsense at each other. I thought I'd explode. I felt as though I was still rising and rising, even though I was now just standing in the kitchen holding his hand. I swayed, and opened my mouth to say something and he let go my hand.

His father came out of the boot room backwards, zipping up a bright orange ensemble that looked likely to get him through an outbreak of chemical warfare unscathed, let alone a patch of Connemara drizzle.

'Still deciding on an outfit, are we?' he said, looking at my boots.

I blushed.

'Black suits you' he said, and handed me the other of the pair. I leaned over and sorted out my footwear, wishing I had Juno's hair to hide behind. The enormous green left boot came off my right foot with ease. What on earth had I been thinking of? I must be the teeniest bit drunk.

52

We must have been pissed out of our heads. It was *flogging* rain. The inlet with the little wooden dock lay on the sheltered side of the headland, so of course we marched down the other side, onto the beach, into the teeth of the wind. I tried to work out if the wind had changed direction since I'd entered the house, but somehow it seemed to have gotten dark in that time, and I hadn't a clue which way Clare was any more. I was having enough trouble remembering which way up was. We sang a medley of our favourite Irish Eurovision entries as we stumbled arm-in-arm-in-arm down to the sea.

God, we were drunk. A certain amount of Newcastle Brown Ale had managed to sneak in between the bottles of white, not really adding to the sobriety of the evening. Night. Whatever. We reached the high tide mark, and the kelp and the carragheen squelched beneath my wellingtons. My eyes adjusted to the fractured moonlight coming through the broken clouds that tumbled in perpetual avalanche above us.

A black and white landscape with hardly any land in it. Seascape. That's the one. A black ocean. The black sea. Just enough light to frighten you with the colossal amount of darkness it revealed, but only if you were a scaredy-cat. I wasn't frightened. I let go of everybody and ran the last few yards to the sea. The men stopped singing.

'Juliet' said David.

I picked up a rock and threw it out into the dark sea. It made a good splash in the bad moonlight. I picked up another rock. The rain hissed on the sea, and the sea went 'SHUSSSSH . . .' as it rattled some pebbles in its crawl up the beach to my feet.

Why should I be frightened?

The moon broke free of the clouds and a silver world froze. I had lifted my arm to throw the second rock but now I studied the curve of my arm as though it were that of a statue. I was a statue in the moonlight. Diana, the hunter. I laughed. Diana, in oilskins and wellingtons, with a rock instead of a bow. A wave made it as far as my wellingtons, tried to sneak past me, 'SHUSSSSSH . . .'

I wasn't frightened. I dropped the rock on it. I made a little bomb noise, 'Boosh', as it splashed.

David came up behind me. His father stood higher up the beach, looking back at the steady black of the house against the changing greys of the sky. My eyes were getting better and better. Diana the Hunter. I could even see a tiny moon in each of David's eyes. The rain wasn't as strong now. Everything was so changeable, here. I swung my arm across my breasts, to press my heart back in.

'Juliet' he said again. I didn't want to hear it, whatever it was. The sea said 'SHUSSSH . . .' again. I bent and picked up a rock from the rocky beach. I handed it to him and put a finger on his lips.

'Shush' I said. 'Present. Stay' and I turned and walked away from him along the shoreline, my wellingtons kicking fans of water ahead of me. I could feel him looking after me.

Looking after me. I wasn't frightened.

53

My father was frightened of everything, on my behalf. I'd never needed to be frightened. He'd always done it for me.

'Jesus, you could've been killed.'

Walking home alone at three a.m., drinking a bottle of vodka and passing out, getting a lift to Limerick on the back of Jimmy Gleeson's Suzuki with the stupid heavy metal painting of a girl chained to a rock on the petrol tank (Me: 'Jimmy, that's sexist.' Jimmy: 'Yeah, it is, isn't it', patting the painting approvingly).

Men and alcohol, mainly, he was frightened of on my behalf. The combination left him stuttering. A pissed Jimmy Gleeson bringing me, also pissed, home at three a.m. on the Suzuki. My father's reaction was a treat worth repeating, so of course I did. Patting Jimmy on the head, 'Goodnight', and his shiver of pleasure, as he made the bike roar goodbye and was off. Me ringing the doorbell because my father had taken my key off me. (That didn't last long. I cut a copy of my mother's, and nothing was said.)

I think one of the things that I most held against him was his assumption that I was sleeping with the Gleeson twins. He didn't understand (how could he? I never even tried to explain to him) that the Gleeson twins were natural knights. Not in every aspect of their lives, true. Gawain and Galahad didn't deal in drugs and stolen electrical equipment. But to me and Juno, they were chivalrous, worshipful, chaste. They sought our favour, and they beat people up on our behalf, whether we liked it or not, until we eventually managed to persuade them to stop. They beat up Jem Toohy for saying something crude about Juno (they never told us what, they just blushed and said 'it was fuckin' disgustin'. Cunt deserved it.')

Toohy called round the next day with a black eye, a wrist in a sling, and a small box of Cadbury's Milk Tray.

'For fuck's sake tell them I apologised' said Jem to a bewildered Juno, before he shoved the chocolates at her left-handed and hobbled home.

Next day we found out that they'd told him they'd drop him off the railway bridge if his apology wasn't up to scratch. They'd told him this while holding his ankles, as he swayed in the light breeze twenty feet above the road, so he had little reason to doubt them.

The Gleeson twins liked the railway bridge. It had dinky little fences at its edges instead of the stout walls of stone or concrete the other couple of bridges around the town had, so they didn't have to bring boxes to stand on when they wanted to dangle a miscreant above the abyss. They'd had an accident early on in their career when a beer crate collapsed and they'd dropped Sheamus Hickey off the bypass flyover onto a brand new Mazda parked in Huchinson's forecourt. The insurance battle went on for years. They'd only wanted him to help them with their maths.

Suddenly my feet were very, very wet and cold. I snapped out of my reminiscence and was bemused and pleased to see where I was. A bloody long way from Tipperary. Standing in the sea, which had just swept up to my knees and flooded my wellingtons. God I was drunk. Drunkety drunk. Drinkety drankety drunk. Drunk as a monk's flunkey, in a bunk with a funky monkey, on skunk . . . blink.

A lighthouse blinked at me from far across the black and silver bay. I waved at it, hallo Clare, and slipped, and fell backwards, and didn't hit the water. Hands held me up, under my arms, and only my bottom got wet. Then the hands shifted and I was lifted right out of the water, with one arm supporting my back and one arm in the curve of my knees.

'David' I said, dreamily thinking to myself My God, this is the most romantic thing that has ever happened, I could happily die now, 'You saved me.'

'Christ you're heavy' he said.

He carried me up the slope of the beach, out of the sea. I looked up at his face in the moonlight and, dizzy with Château something Seventy something, lifted my head enough to brush against his cheek. A tiny rasp of stubble on my lips and cheek, and a noise like a sigh, or a kiss. I couldn't tell which it was, or which of us had made it. I was halfway between deliriously happy and delirious.

The lighthouse winked at me over David's shoulder. Moonlight on the wavecrests. Great grey, butchered tentacles of cloud boiled above me in the dark, cooking in their own black ink.

He put me down on a rock and collapsed beside me, exhaling hard as he did so, like a mortally wounded zeppelin crumpling to earth. Like Icarus falling.

My mind was away with the fairies, describing metaphorical arabesques. Wheee! I thought to myself, and leaned sideways, into David, my head bumping his shoulder and sliding down the Eiger of his oilskins till I lay comfortably on my back with my head in his lap looking up at him looking down at me. Rain fell in my eyes. I blinked it away.

'What's a nice girl like you doing on a beach like this?' said David. It sounded funny but he looked very sad.

I shut my eyes and the wind went wheee . . . 'Tell me a story' I said.

'I can't tell stories' he said. 'I've tried, and I can't. I can only tell you about stories. That's my job. You tell me a story, and I'll tell you about it.'

'Shall I tell you a story?'

'Yes.'

'And you'll tell me about it?'

'Yes.'

I kept my eyes shut and thought for a while. 'There was a girl' I said.

54

And stopped. No. That was the wrong story.

'There was a boy' I said. 'A handsome . . . knight. And he was very, very serious. And he was very, very sad.'

I opened my eyes to see that he had closed his eyes. The rain fell down his face. I closed my eyes.

'The boy lived in the king's castle, by the sea. Every day he would protect the old king . . . from sea monsters . . .'

Suddenly I was very tired. I settled my head more comfortably in his lap. He started to say something and stopped.

'Mmm?' I said.

'Nothing. Go on.'

I yawned, and with my mind quite blank I said 'And one day a girl came to the castle . . .'

'A beautiful princess.'

'No, just a girl' I said. 'The girl comes to the castle . . . on a quest . . . to rescue the knight.'

'The *princess* can't rescue the *knight*' said David. 'It's against the rules of the genre.'

'She can try' I said.

'And what's she rescuing him from?'

'Being sad.'

After a while I opened my eyes. His eyes were still closed.

'That's the story' I said. 'Tell me how it ends.'

He opened his eyes and looked down at me and then looked away at the sea. After another while he said 'She doesn't rescue him.'

I felt sick. 'Why not?'

'Because she's too young.'

I felt sicker. 'That's not true' I said. 'That's so not true.'

'I know these stories' he said. 'I know them backwards. And she's too young. Another thing I know, she isn't just a girl. She's a beautiful, intelligent princess . . . under a terrible spell . . . that makes her think she's just a girl. But she could rescue anyone in the world. She doesn't want a sad knight. Maybe she feels sorry for him, because he's sad, and that's . . . very lovely of her, but they've both drunk too much Château Magic Potion' I hate him 'and a bucket of Newcastle Brown Elixir and when the magic wears off . . . Juliet, are you alright?'

I'd listened to most of this with my eyes closed and now I'd opened my eyes and the rain fell down into my eyes and they looked like my tears falling up into the sky, and I was unsure again which way was up. I felt dislodged from the world. I felt about as bad as I ever had. I had drunk enough to have the courage to so nearly say how I felt, and I'd been so misunderstood. He thought I was some silly girl. Too young. Silly. Drunk. I felt older than the moon, and as cold, and as ruined. 'It's nothing' I said.

'You seem . . .' he said. 'Are you sure you . . . Are you feeling OK?'

I felt like I'd been exploring a magnificent palace all day, one famed for the view from the turret of its highest tower, and that I had discovered ever more wonderful things as I moved ever upwards until now I'd just stepped through the final door to discover not the rooftop's panorama but a liftshaft. Wheee. 'I'm fine' I said. 'Really.'

Crying in the rain is brilliant. You can just get on with it. No stupid questions. Just keep your face from crinkling, and don't make any noise. I wondered if he was dim enough to really think I just felt sorry for him, or was he trying to give me an out, a way of not feeling rejected. I wondered why he'd rejected me really. My age just wasn't a good enough excuse, certainly not from where I came from. If you made it into your teens in Tipperary without being impregnated by your grandfather, the county council gave you a medal.

I suppose I could have *asked* him.

That didn't really occur to me at the time.

Boy, was I young.

55

He walked me back to the house and called a taxi. I refused the offer of dry clothes, said I was fine, that I'd just have a shower and go to bed when I got home, everything was fine. His father, who had quit the rain before us, made me coffee before shaking my hand with both hands and saying how delighted he was to have met me, delighted, really, it'd been a great auld evening, but he was too pissed to stand so he thought he'd better go to bed. And he disappeared off into the house, toward a bed from which he said he could see the sea.

David and me, alone in the kitchen. The taxi was late. Rain banging on the windows. A lot of demand for taxis on nights like these.

Tick, tock. Silence, et cetera. David laughed. 'I've really fucked up the evening, haven't I?'

'No, no' I said, agreeing with him completely.

'Yes, yes' he mocked. 'I suppose I should have just gotten you pregnant and called the kid Lancelot. Too late now, though.'

My insides disagreed, and it showed through on the outside. He lifted a warning eyebrow. 'Hoy. Less of it. You don't think I find you madly attractive? Of course I find you madly attractive. Not the way you look, well not just the way you look, but the way you are.' He searched for words, raised his eyebrows, made a face. He squirmed, found a word. 'Special.'

I squirmed.

'You *are*, you idiot. But I'm riddled by scruples, by angst, by all manner of things, I'm brittle as a wafer at present, you don't want to be *near* me, you hear? I'm warning you off. Not because I don't like you, but because I like you too much. If I let myself fall for you, the way I'm feeling now, I'd never stop falling. And that wouldn't do you any good at all. As it is, I absolutely refuse to fall for you. I refuse. I don't want to get hurt, I don't want you to get hurt, I don't want anybody to get hurt. And somebody would be bound to get horribly hurt. And I just couldn't bear it. I'm up to my fucking ears in hurt, and I just couldn't bear any more anywhere near me. I was mad to invite you here, but I'm drunk enough now to see sense. I thought we could . . . talk, and eat, and orbit each other at a safe distance, and go home and it would be very *nice*. But we can't, Juliet.'

And he got up from his chair and walked to my side, and sank to one knee, took my hand, as though it was natural, as though people behaved like that, as though it meant nothing, as though we were having a conversation, 'I thought we could keep it light, and pleasant, and fun, and today has been so much fun, but there is too much gravity in the situation, you generate, we generate too much *gravity*, and I don't want to fall Juliet, not now, I can't, I'm needed, it's already so hard to hold everything together, you don't know what it's like, do you understand?' Yes. Yes. 'So will you please not think less of me for being such a . . . coward, and sending you off home when I wish I could . . . wish that I could . . .' He lifted my hand, kissed it 'Wish it was all different. But it isn't and I can't. And I'm really, really sorry for fucking up tonight.'

I placed an imaginary sword on his left shoulder, on his right. 'It's alright' I said. 'It's fine.' It wasn't, but it wasn't as bad as it had been. 'You can arise now.'

He arose.

'So you would if you could?'

He nodded.

'But . . . you can't.'

He nodded.

I sighed. 'I don't really understand. But . . . you still like me? You'll still talk to me? You won't start acting like we've broken up or something?'

He nodded till his head blurred.

'Fair enough then.' Tiredness hit me like a sack of cement. 'Life is awfully difficult, isn't it?' I said.

He shrugged. 'Yes. But it's the price we pay for its great rewards. It's worth it.'

'I don't think I've got to the rewards yet' I said.

He laughed.

When the doorbell rang we were talking about something as though nothing had happened. And, of course, nothing had.

He poured me into the taxi and paid the driver through my protests.

'Look, I invited you to dinner, I'd be driving you home if I wasn't so pissed, so just shush. There's no question. Here, if there's any change give it to her. Thanks. Just give me the change when you see me. Safe home, sleep well, look after yourself.'

The taxi swept away from the house and tower, along the coast road. I turned awkwardly to wave, even though he wouldn't be able to see it. I caught a glimpse of him in the light of the doorway. Waving.

56

When I got home the light was on in the living room and the stove was still warm but there was no other sign of life. I threw some offcuts into the stove and got some change from my room for the shower. Superstitiously, I wouldn't use the taxi change. I left that on my windowsill. For me, coins had histories. They weren't interchangeable.

The shower was just gorgeous. I stayed there forever.

When I came out, wrapped in my big towel, I was surprised to find Michael alone by the stove.

'Hello Michael. Where's Juno?'

'Juliet! Jeesus! Juno's gone out, to the Warwick, with the rest of the ack-tors. I haven't. Didn't.' Michael wasn't looking his best. 'I'm ossified' he explained. 'Langers. We were going to have a row, but I decided to get rat-arsed instead. Good decision. Fine decision. We decided that Juno would go out and I would get pissed. Division of labour. Much better than a row. Have a Carlsberg.'

He handed me a can. I sat on the chair beside him.

'Tell me about your day. We haven't had a good talk in . . . since last year. Maybe we never had a good talk. Who knows?'

I rolled the can against my cheek. Lovely and cold. I opened it, and told Michael at length about my day.

'Jesus' he said. 'And the fucker wouldn't even sleep with you. The fucker. The sad fucker.'

And Michael leaned over and kissed me and without thinking about it particularly I kissed him back. Warm lips, dry, a little chapped. The pleasantly rough surface of his lips moving very gently on mine. And after a few seconds and a very long day it became less about surfaces and I melted back into my chair and a little bit of me put my can down, on the stove-top, and another little bit of me very deliberately switched off all the little bits of me that were trying to grab my attention, going wait . . .

Click.

And I was melting.

Click.

And for the first time in a long time I wasn't thinking too much.

Click.

And it was very nice.

Reasons aren't really things that make you do other things. Reasons are things that you make up, much later, to reassure everyone that we are all logical and that the world makes sense. We do unreasonable things, because we want to, at the time. No reason. Much later we sit in the wreckage, building reasons out of little bits of wreckage, so we'll have something to show the crash investigators. Look, this is what caused it. So the whole mess at least appears reasonable. So we can convince ourselves that at least there was a reason for the disaster, something we can prevent or avoid, so it'll never happen again. But a lot of the time there's no reason. We just flew it into the ground. Because we felt like it. And we're still dangerous. And it could happen again any time.

It's easier to live with each other afterwards if we give each other reasons.

Much later a tang of burning paint brought me slowly back to proper thinking. Conscious thought. My mind reluctantly switched back on.

I was lying on my big white towel in front of the stove. Michael's dark head between my parted thighs. He appeared to have fallen asleep. I was unsurprised. No wonder his lips are chapped I thought, if he does all that every night. I looked up at the stove. The last of my Carlsberg had evaporated and now the paint was beginning to blister and blacken low on the can. The air was jungly with beer-steam. Me, I felt like I was made out of marshmallow. I felt absolutely delicious. I didn't want to move.

The metallic, harsh smell of the hot paint and the can was getting quite strong, though.

Michael said something that sounded very like 'Juno . . .' though it was rather muffled between my legs, and woke up with a start. He looked up along my belly at me.

'Oh shit' he said. 'Oh fuck.'

'I think I'd better go to bed now' I said, pronouncing each word carefully.

'Oh God' said Michael. 'Yes . . . wait! What am I . . . huh. We should talk, about . . . this.'

I extracted my legs from under his arms and stood, as he lay there trying to climb up the ladder of a sentence from out of the swamp of sleep.

I picked up my towel, wrapped it back around me, and laughed at myself. Bit late now. My nipples were tender from his teeth and tongue. Absently I brought my left arm across my body so that my forearm lay lightly against my breasts. A mild pain. Not a pain at all. Pleasure, really. And under it some different kind of pain. It's odd how the things felt by our bodies and the things felt by our minds get so mixed up sometimes.

'Goodnight' I said.

'Oh Christ Juliet, don't be silly. You can't just *go to bed.*'

'Yes I can' I said very politely, looking down at him.

'We have to talk, you know we do.'

'No we don't' I said. 'I'm tired.' And I was, I was, I was going to cry if the conversation lasted another minute. 'Night, Michael. Don't burn your fingers taking the can off the stove.'

And I went to my bedroom, hunted through my underwear drawer for the key I never used, and locked my room.

And of course I cried, but that didn't mean very much. My tears weren't hard currency in those days. Devalued by overproduction. I wouldn't give too much weight to my tears.

Still . . . But . . .

Still, I'd known Michael loved Juno, even as I was kissing him I'd known it, and I'd always known Juno was different from me in a great bundle of important ways, but I wished Michael hadn't looked at me like that, in the moment after he woke, as he realised I wasn't Juno. I wished I hadn't seen him wake. I wished I hadn't seen him see me, and heard him speak when he was just letting his emotions fall out of his mouth because his consciousness hadn't yet arrived to filter his words. There probably wasn't enough of Michael there at the time to even hear himself say what he said.

As I cried myself to sleep they felt like a careful description.

Shit.

Fuck.

Slowly they turned from words I heard into things I observed, as I spiralled down the gravity-well into sleep. They gained mass, became bat-like, bulky, enemies, part of me. Just before we arrive at the event horizon of sleep and we impact with it at the oblique angle required to smoothly enter dreams, in the moment outside time just before we disappear, the world sometimes suddenly reappears around us, very sharp, very clear, quite transformed. Doesn't it? Sometimes? More real than life. More real than dreams. Just before we disappear. And we can't move, and we can't wake, and we can't dream. We're just there, super-sharp, super-clear.

I was there, super-sharp, super-clear. I was transformed. Lying on my back, in my bed, in one of those states so hard to describe because everything has changed its shape and significance and name.

(Beneath my right hand, my belly was still a little sticky, though I'd wiped most of it off.)

(The tracks of the tears that I'd cried earlier, standing up, were cooling and tightening on my cheek as the water evaporated and left faint trails of salt.)

(A new tear was taking the shortcut down to my ear.)

(Never cry on your back. Your ears fill with tears.)

My eyes were closed but they felt open. It was dark but I could see. I could see me, I was the world looking at me instead of the other way round.

And Michael was right.

I was Shit.

I was Fuck.

And then, at last, after a while, I disappeared.

It's so easy to say you cried yourself to sleep. It's so hard to do.

57

It was morning.
   'Ouch' I said, and my eyes flicked open.
   'Jesus' I said.

58

I walked into the living room. Juno was looking out the window. I walked across the room and stood beside her. The harbour and the bay. Crisp, bright morning. Sky-blue sky. Sea-green sea. Calm harbour below us. Boats as still as sculptures of themselves. All that moved the spark of sun on tiny waves far out to sea. No clouds.

She exhaled a long breath. The window misted, and cleared. Her shoulder touched mine and I leaned back into it. We watched a sailor walk the length of the deck of the *Aoife*. About a quarter of our navy, she must have come in that morning at high tide when the harbour gate was open. Back from boarding Spanish trawlers far out of sight of land, to check their nets and papers and share jokes in mangled English about the English. There were rumours of a ceasefire in the war over our fish, too. Rumours of peace everywhere, even out of sight of land. Strange days, with the nets being cut and the boy-soldiers shot, and everywhere rumours of peace.

He reached the back of the ship and looked around. In the shelter of a tarpaulined gun and high above the quay, with just a lumberyard to one side and the harbour to the other, he must have thought himself quite unobserved. He lit up a cigarette.

'That's naughty' said Juno. 'I bet his mummy doesn't know.'

Old joke. When we were tiny we used to say it seriously. At thirteen we revived it, ironically. Later again, at sixteen and mourning our loss of innocence, we'd used it all summer, nostalgically. And now we didn't use it at all. I hadn't heard it in a year. What comes after nostalgia, when you're eighteen?

He leaned forward till his stomach rested against the guardrail at the back of the *Aoife*. Lazily he moved a hand to his flies and, after brief manoeuvring, began to urinate in a high, astonishing arc, out and down into the harbour waters.

'That's very, very naughty' I said. 'I bet his mummy *and* his daddy don't know.'

'I bet his granny doesn't know.'

'I bet Father King doesn't know.'

'I bet Father King watches.'

We giggled and held each other. He was still doing it. He made the glittering arc go even higher.

'He must have a bladder the size of a beachball.'

Pause.

'He must have hollow legs.'

Fascinated pause.

'He must . . . I think I can see it!'

He waggled his hand as I spoke and the pale stream waggled too, like a clothesline when you shake a wave along it. We howled with laughter and Juno put her lips against my neck and spluttered great rasps of sound off it till it tickled and I ducked.

The flow had begun to slacken by the time we stopped laughing, but it was still pretty impressive, going out horizontally now before falling.

'What a man!'

'He's cheating, he's got a hose in there.'

'You looooove him' I said, another very old joke, one we'd often used in childhood to get us through a night of bad Irish television, all cheap English imports and old films and RTE sitcoms so terrible they were hypnotic, like the sort of video installation that would later win awards, 'Sitcom Without Jokes Or Acting', brutally deconstructed critiques of the genre.

'You loooooooove him.'

Bob Monkhouse. Nicholas Parsons. Mike Read, God help us, on *Top Of The Pops*. The man who read the cattle prices on *Mart & Market*. The singer with Norway's inexplicable and doomed heavy metal entry in the Eurovision Song Contest. Everyone in *Leave It To Mrs O'Brien*. Clint Eastwood, lapels and hair billowing, in *Every Which Way But Loose*. The orang-utan in *Every Which Way But Loose*.

'You looooove him', giggling on the spavined couch with our father scowling at our mother and our mother going 'Shush.'

Juno giggled. 'I do not.'

'You looooove him and you're going to maarrrry him!'

'I am not!'

He was still, incredibly, pissing.

If I laughed any more I'd be joining in.

'Maybe he's your pervert' I gurgled. '*Imagine* . . . if he can piss like that . . .'

'Oh Juliet . . . that's not funnnny . . .'

We were holding each other up, crippled with laughter.

'*Ju*-no's *per*-vert! *Ju*-no's *per*-vert!'

His super-powers eventually waned.

The arch buckled, and broke.

A last jet, a sprinkle. He tucked it away one-handed. I was vaguely surprised to see that the cigarette he'd started with, on which he'd puffed throughout, was still going. Perhaps he'd lit another while I was blind with tears. Perhaps he'd smoked a pack.

Eventually we stopped laughing. 'I'm sorry about last night' I said.

She shrugged, almost a real shrug. 'These things happen' she said.

'It was my fault, I was drunk' I said.

She laughed, a real laugh. 'He said it was his fault, he was drunk.'

'Have I fucked everything up?'

'Mmm. Yes. I'd just decided I wouldn't break up with him, after talking it over for hours with Gemma in the Warwick, and then I come home and he tells me he doesn't know how to tell me this but he's fucked my sister, I mean, Juliet, Jesus . . .'

'But he didn't!'

'Well *he* came, and he couldn't resist telling me *you* came, so you're trying to get off on a bit of a technicality here.'

'But he didn't' I said sulkily. 'I mean, he . . .' I thought better of it.

Juno sighed. 'Jesus, Juliet, you're getting more upset about me getting the *position* wrong than I am about you fucking him . . . NOT fucking him, whatever. About the two of you coming in the same room as each other . . . you did come?'

'Mmm.'

'Well, there's a good girl. At least one of us got something out of it. He's surprisingly . . . nice . . . isn't he?'

'Mmm.'

'I was surprised . . . I nearly . . . I'll miss him.'

I held onto her a little tighter and she squeezed me back. 'Oh, you are a fool, Juliet.'

'I'm sorry.'

She kissed me on the side of the nose because that was where our faces had ended up.

'I'm sorry, I'm sorry.'

You will be unsurprised to hear I cried.

When I could see again the sailor had gone. Oh God. Poor Michael.

'He loves you' I said miserably. She nodded. 'I'm sorry' I said again.

She nodded, and held onto me.

59

I hid in my room for a couple of days and read a lot of Beckett. Time passed very slowly, and then changed its mind and passed very fast. Michael's visits to the flat were soon again so frequent that I couldn't really avoid him without becoming homeless. The awkwardness faded slowly, like curtains over a good summer. The resumption of college was in many ways a blessed relief. The whole situation seemed in some obscure way to amuse Juno, whose forgiveness ate away at me more than her blame would have done.

Juno and I were sitting snug by the stove one afternoon when Michael stuck his head in.

'I need to buy a book in Boo's, will you run cover for me?'

'Oh no' I said.

'Ah yeah' said Juno. 'Let's.'

So we did. The walk there was nice. You could take us, from a distance, for friends. We walked, we talked, we laughed. I watched Juno with Michael, and Michael with Juno, on the sly, out of the corner of my eyes. Watched the air between them, and the way they used the air between them. The way it filled and emptied. What happened when their hands touched. They were again a mystery to me. I brooded.

Apart from the fact that Michael didn't stay the night any more, hardly anything appeared on the surface to have changed between him and Juno. There were hints and signs that a massive renegotiation of the entire relationship was taking place beneath that surface, but I couldn't tell in what direction, or by whose command. It had seemed obvious to me at first that the balance of power in their relationship must have shifted firmly in favour of Juno, self-evidently, for Michael had put himself so blatantly in the wrong. When Juno said she'd miss him, I had assumed that she had ended everything, regretfully but firmly. As the days and the long nights passed I began to suspect I'd got the whole thing wrong. Sometimes it seemed that Michael, in sleeping with me, had . . . (let's flowery-up the language here, because this is how I secretly thought back then) . . . had shaken off the chains of his love for Juno, and was free.

(And often I still think like that, in great romantic metaphors, unironically. Because sometimes I believe they are more accurate and true than sentences with the words 'relationship' and 'power' in them. Though I use them too. They can also be accurate, and true.)

. . . That because he had broken the terms of their delicate, failing treaty the initiative was now his, and with it the power to renegotiate their relationship. In yet another tribute to my award-winning naivety, I was shocked at this possibility of vice rewarded.

But, Juno didn't talk to me directly about it and I couldn't ask, I was too guilty and implicated.

Besides, I was too busy worrying about my own Relationships, and their mysterious balances of power.

With David Hennessey. For instance.

Anyway. We were walking to Boo's.

Boo's was A Bookshop Of One's Own on Middle Street. Someone had nicked the letter 'K' the week it opened, so A Boo shop Of One's Own it remained for a month, in stern brass letters with its many and wonderfully vulval 'o's. Even after they'd fixed it everybody called it Boo's. When we were almost there, Michael and Juno bumped into one of Michael's theatre friends.

The friend (I missed it, Aaron? Arnold?) talked straight at Michael while staring straight at Juno's tits. When he decided to give his gaze a rest from Juno's chest by switching it to mine, I drifted a few yards ahead of them. I took a deep breath in Boo's doorway, and teetered. I never felt quite ideologically sound enough, quite female enough, quite brilliant enough to meet with the management's high standards. Boo's practically had a dresscode and door policy.

Michael saw me teetering and gave me a little push. 'Get in there, woman' he said. It was a joke, but my toe caught on the lintel, failed to clear it, and I stumbled into the shop, falling to one knee. A startled assistant looked up to see an unshaven man in a leather jacket pushing a girl to the ground. I looked at the assistant. I looked up at Michael. I hadn't wanted to come anyway.

'Please, I won't do it again' I said.

Michael looked down at me, mortified. 'Sorry' he said, and put down a hand to help me up.

'That's what you said last time' I said and got up without taking his hand. He looked at me. I looked at him. The assistant looked at both of us, all her suspicions about men entirely confirmed. I turned slightly so she couldn't see my face and smiled sweetly at Michael. He gave me a wryly admiring grin.

'You know you love it, you bitch' he said.

Behind me, the assistant dropped her roll of sellotape. Over Michael's shoulder, through the doorway, I could see Juno pissing herself with laughter.

Inside the shop, Juno joined in the game. We probably laid it on a bit thick. Michael made me put back the Anne Tyler I'd picked up, gave Juno a Norman Mailer to read, and then made her climb the ladder to get the psychology text he wanted from the top shelf at the back. 'But Michael I'm afraid of heights.' 'Get up there, it'll make a man of ya.' We gurlied it up and said 'Yes, Michael' submissively every time he loudly recommended another classic of misogyny they didn't stock. I was a bit worried at one point that the manager was going to call the guards. Her disgust at our servility overcame her pity at our plight, however, and she did nothing.

With the book bought, we fled giggling. The three of us had a coffee in Neachtain's. Something was fixed. That night, Michael stayed over. Juno was pleased. Repeatedly. I eventually managed to fall asleep around four.

60

The rocket of my rage accelerated me along the corridor and straight into the lift for Tower 2, which cut in (second stage booster) to send me soaring up to the English Department. With smoke coming out of my ears I rounded two corners, more than half an internal orbit of the tower, and crashed to a halt outside David's door, palm first.

'Come in.'

I came in. 'She doesn't even *bloody* know how to punctuate *Finnegans Wake*' I said.

'Calm yourself, child' said David, pretending great age. 'Sit in the seat, gather the thoughts and tell the tale. It concerns Pamela, no? or I know nothing of first-year timetables and the human heart.'

'Pamela Henderson is a moron' I said, loudly. David winced, put down his pen and walked to the door.

'Careless talk costs lives' he said, shutting it. 'And she isn't, really. But continue. Elaborate. Unburden yourself.'

'She put an apostrophe in *Finnegans Wake*! She corrected my punctuation! She doesn't even know the title of Joyce's *bloody Finnegans Wake*!'

I waved the essay about my head in an excess of fury almost beyond words. 'She gave me a C!'

David looked crestfallen. 'Oh, that's hardly a crime. I'd hoped you'd caught her dealing drugs after lectures. Or during. Shooting up at the lectern.'

I was so incensed at his not sharing my fury that I actually stuttered an authentic 'But . . . but . . . but . . .', as frequently seen in film and fiction, but not too often in Galway. '*Finnegan's*?!'

'It's an apostrophe, Juliet' he said, amused.

'It's *Finnegans Wake*!' I said, not amused.

'Well, yes, that's pretty bad' he admitted. 'But she probably wasn't thinking. After a couple of hours correcting the illiterate ramblings, begging your pardon, of a shower of first-years, your head is dead. Your brain can't handle the insult. You start to correct e.e. cummings into upper case. I stuck an apostrophe into the middle of Keats once, after four hours of correcting almost identical answers to an already dull question on the Romantics. I was practically hallucinating with boredom. My mind started playing sub-Joycean word-games to stay awake. I started reading Shelley as an adjective redolent of the seaside. Their footsteps crunched across the shelley beach . . . Have you calmed down yet?'

'No.'

He sighed. 'Give us a look.'

I handed him the essay. He read it slowly while I wandered the office, weaving my way around the tall, coral-like growths of stacked hardbacks and paperbacks that rose from the floor, often to a height of several feet. I examined the deep, stuffed bookshelves that lined the walls of the room, soundproofing it, practically bombproofing it, and I committed the sin of envy.

'Very good' he said when he'd finished. 'B plus, at least. Probably a low A. She does seem to have rather missed the point you were making. But that's partly your own fault, there's leaps in the logic which you haven't really bothered bridging with any planks of evidence, to help your reader follow you. I can, because we've talked about Yeats enough so I know what you're getting at. But you can hardly expect poor Pamela to give you the benefit of her sturdy Non-Conformist Londonderry doubt when you make it so hard for her. You're attacking her all the way through it, I mean it's obvious . . . well, they're obviously her ideas you're disagreeing with, but you don't bother to rigorously back up your own arguments. And you've definitely mugged poor, defenceless Joyce and dragged him in bleeding to show how tough you are, he's not relevant to your argument at all. I'd bet you had the *Wake* beside you as you were writing this and decided to dip in for a quote just to impress her with your fabulous range.'

This was so horribly accurate that I nearly stuttered again. 'But . . .' I got the quizzical eyebrow. 'But she's so . . . so . . .' I got both eyebrows. 'She has the soul of a *mechanic*!' I wailed. 'She gets *Finnegans Wake* wrong and she gave me a C and you're on *her* side!'

He put his elbows on his desk, cupped his chin in his hands and grinned at me. 'Don't be silly. I'd bet real cash money you haven't read more than twenty pages of the *Wake*' more like five 'so it's a bit naughty demanding her head over an apostrophe. And was it not delightfully human of her to err? Anyway, this essay *is* a C essay, I've changed my mind. You knew exactly who you were writing for and you didn't even begin to try to persuade her. They're A ideas, but you have to bring your audience with you. C, I'm afraid. And I *am* on your side, you schmoo, but that doesn't mean I have to nod wisely and agree with everything you say. Friends frequently don't.'

'Don't want you to be my friend' I sulked. 'What's a schmoo?'

'No idea. I read it in a book. Come on, I'll buy you a cup of muck in the old cantina.'

David mocked me to the lift till my mood suddenly flipped and I did a mad thing. I kissed him, very quickly, on the cheek, as the lift doors closed on us.

'Didn't mean it' I said, horrified, jumping back. 'Just a kiss. Accident. Don't be angry, I really didn't mean it.'

David touched his cheek thoughtfully, as though he'd been slapped. 'Jesus, Juliet, write out the word "mercurial" one hundred times.'

'I mean, I meant it, but I didn't mean to do it, I know you don't want . . . anything . . .'

'I'm just a boy who can't say yes' he sang sadly, pressing the button to start the descent and then, as the old lift lurched down and the floor stuttered briefly from under us, bringing his hand back up to his cheek again.

Oh God, say something. I opened my mouth. 'It was just a because-I-like-you kiss, it wasn't a please-kiss-me-back kiss . . . how's your father?'

David coughed and hid his mouth with his hand. 'Er, yes, he's fine. Still alive and dying' which he said as if it were a quote from somewhere. 'Perhaps a little weaker than when you saw him. It isn't affecting him all that much, physically, yet. When it does of course he'll go down rather dramatically and there'll be a couple of, well, ah, desperately unpleasant weeks.' We gained weight for a long instant, or a short second, and the doors opened. 'Which I'm not looking forward to.' He waved me out first, mock-gallantly? No, absent-mindedly. The way he was brought up.

'I don't even know what your father . . . has' I said. 'I mean, you don't have to tell me.'

'Oh, boring old leukaemia. I thought you knew. Sorry. He had it before, took the chemo, fought hard, came through.'

I was very aware of him as he walked beside me. I could sense the bulk of him, close, shoulder and hip. The left side of my body tingled a bit. 'Maybe he'll come through again.'

'No. He's refused treatment this time. He doesn't want to do it all again. I think, you see, he sort of came to terms with dying and all that the last time, settled his spiritual accounts. And then he got an extra couple of years, which he considered a bit of a gift from God. I think he feels it would be cheating to duck a second time. Besides which he has always missed our mother, you know, and his faith is quite strong although unorthodox. The Far East affected him a lot, you know, going there after our mother died. I'm talking too much.'

'No, you're not, I like him, I really want to know.'

We entered the canteen through the stiff doors, David holding them open for me, and walked towards the smell of coffee. I resisted an urge to put a protective arm around him, and another, more peculiar urge to childishly knock him over and wrestle with him, as Juno and I had done with tall Paul, when we were small.

'Shall we go mad and split a Kit Kat?' he said, examining the austere selection of luxury goods beside the coffee machine. 'My treat.'

'Oh yer honour I couldn't possibly' I said in a thick Tipperary accent, 'In dit to a gintlemin. Compromised in th'eyes of the parish.'

He laughed at me. 'A mere Kat, madam, still less a Kit, hath surely no power to sully so great a Virtue as you possess. Milk?'

'Yes please.'

'Grand . . . So why don't you speak with an honest Tipp brogue all the time?'

'Because I don't want to sound like a pig talking German with his mouth full' I said succinctly.

David coughed hard up his sleeve. 'Sorry . . . Do your parents speak like that, then?'

'Not really. They're more Tipp than me though.'

'More . . . ? Oh, more Tipp, yes.' He was paying for the coffees, a Kit Kat and a Snack Bar, the wafery type in the pink packet. The woman at the till smiled at him, put his change on the tray. Looked past me. 'No, it's a nice accent.'

I snorted.

'. . . but it's odd to hear you speak in it. Me, I sound Irish to the English and English to the Irish. And both to the Welsh . . . you're a harsh judge of your hometown.'

'Yes' I said.

'Nothing for you there?'

'No. Really, I'm sort of glad there's nothing for me at home, or I might be tempted to stay, and that'd be . . . awful.'

'What were you going to say, there?'

I giggled. 'Shite. Or maybe "fuckin' shite",' full-on accent.

'Isn't there *anything* for you in Tipperary? Surely you could build some sort of life there, if you wanted to. I mean, I'm not saying you should, but you could surely.'

I snorted again. 'Yeah, I'm throwing away a corner table for life in Connollys, and a firm offer of a job in Accounts in the abattoir. I'll have to learn to live without the chance to see amateur productions of *I Do Not Like Thee, Doctor Fell* in the town hall, for three quid, with one character missing because some County Council clerk has fallen off the wagon again. I'll have to say good-bye forever to a librarian who sucks in air through her teeth every time I take out a book she disapproves of.' I looked him in the eye. 'Fucking heartbreaking' I said.

'Mmm. Point taken. Points.'

We sat and sipped our coffees in easy silence. I stole half his Kit Kat and dunked it. He did a silent movie scowl of fury and shook his free fist like the mustachioed villain in a Chaplin short. I looked coquettish, batted my eyelids and pretended to blush, then stole the other half.

After the dinner, and the beach, and my rejection, I'd assumed everything would be ruined between us, or at least damaged and strained. But, even from the start of the first tutorial of the new semester, we had talked and argued quite exactly as before; when we'd met occasionally on the concourse we had stopped and chatted briefly, quite exactly as before; and now we were having coffee together and nothing had changed, it was precisely as before. We were getting on wonderfully. Everything was great.

It was infuriating. I hated it. How dare something so important and painful have changed things so little.

'God, this coffee is shite' I said.

That was the nicest thing about him callously rejecting me, breaking my young heart, etc. I could snort and swear all I wanted now and it didn't matter a damn. Didn't matter a shite. Didn't matter a fuck. Didn't matter a shite-ing, fucking damn.

61

Two days later, rain, rain, rain. Blissful, wasteful, useful rain. I walked along the paths and up the ramp and around the library, on the outside, in the dumb, beautiful rain.

I didn't bother entering the university by the doors of the library foyer, as I hadn't bothered entering by the entrance I'd already passed, the one to the tunnel that ran under the library. They used to call me Tinker Taylor when I was in infants, I suddenly remembered, because I wouldn't wear a dress and I stamped in the puddles and the mud like the boys when it rained. The boys called me Tinker Taylor too.

When did they stop? I couldn't remember.

When we got pretty. I couldn't remember, but I knew it had to be then because that was when everything changed.

Raindrops smashed like quiet glass on the smooth, wet concrete as I walked towards the doors of the concourse. The hiss of the rain was really a symphony on one madly repeated very quiet note, tremendously staccato. Hisssssssissssssiss. Pretty lousy symphony. All energy and no talent.

I walked through the doorway into David.

'Hi' I said and pushed past him.

He stopped me and spun me around to face him, somehow. Long arms. Magnets. I don't know.

'You're crying' he said.

'It's raining' I said.

'Bullshit' he said, and brushed the rain from my cheeks with the curve of his fingers. It was so nothing to do with sex you wouldn't believe it. Even if I hadn't already been crying all the way in to college I would have started at that warm stroke along each cheekbone, along the sides of my jaw, stopping short of my ears, gone. Like my mother when I'm sick.

'You said bullshit' I said, and I could feel a tear fall down each cheek at the same speed.

'Why are you crying?'

'Because it's raining.'

'Why are you crying, Juliet?'

'People are looking.'

'Fuck them. Why are you crying?'

'You said . . .'

I began to sob. He took my arm. He walked me around the porters' desk where two porters, still sorting the morning mail, didn't even look up.

The corridor behind it, at the Tower 2 lift. Pressed the button. The door opened immediately. 'I think I was looking for you' I sobbed. 'I didn't think I was, but I was, wasn't I? I thought I was just walking in the rain, but I wasn't, was I?'

When we got to his office he sat me down in his chair, behind his desk. He shoved some books off one corner of the desk and sat. 'Tell me.'

I closed my eyes. 'My sister got a letter' I said, very clearly.

'Juno' he said.

'Yes.'

'You live with her. Your twin.'

'Yes.'

'Go on.'

I opened my eyes and looked at all the lovely books. The different coloured spines. Like a rainbow, I thought. Hundreds of bands of colour. Thousands. Like a rainbow for complicated light.

'Your father could have a bone marrow transplant' I said. 'Not chemotherapy. Not just. He might live.'

'Please, Juliet . . .'

'He might *live*' I said.

'He had one, Juliet, last time. It was my marrow. He won't do it again because he wants to die, he doesn't mind and nor should you. It's not a tragedy, it's not like a child dying, it's a *decision*. You and I, we have no right . . . Please Juliet, the letter.'

I closed my eyes again. 'It was very horrible.' My detached, precise voice. I admired it for a bit. David said nothing. 'I wish he was dead. He made her cry.' David said nothing. 'You don't know how nice she is, David, you don't know. How dare he. How dare he.' Not as precise. Crying again.

'Who wrote the letter, Juliet?'

'Juno's pervert' I sobbed. 'The *bastard* who writes to her. The *bastard*. We thought it was *nice* the first one was *nice*. We thought, I thought he *liked* her. He's a *bastard*. He's a *cunt*ing, *fuck*ing . . .' Not precise at all.

'Anonymous letters?'

Nod.

'How many? When?'

'Third. This is the third.'

'When did they start?'

'September . . . when we came . . . we . . . it was, the first one was nice. He knows where we *live*.'

'Written or typed?'

'Typed?'

'Printed.'

'. . . Printed.'

'Can I see them?'

'What?'

'Can I see the letters?'

'Juno burnt one, the second one. The first one is in Tipperary. She didn't want it in the house after the second one, but she didn't want to destroy it, in case . . . there was another one . . . and she . . .' Sobbing, and so on.

'Have you gone to the police?'

'No.'

'You should go to the police. You should show them the letters.'

'No!'

'Why not? They're nothing to do with you, Juliet, they're nothing to do with Juno. They reflect only on the writer. The guilt is the writer's. They're evidence. They're evidence of pathology. That's all. Please don't cry. Please don't cry.'

He held my hand.

'He made her cry, oh David he made her cry . . .' I was talking over him, we said 'cry' at the same time, the pitches high and low together, like music, mine a harmony to his, or his to mine.

'She . . .' but the words I have can't carry what I feel, so I reach for more, and the crush of words jam in my mouth. Jams. Ten things. Too much. A crush.

She's good,

How could anyone,

Why,
Oh David,
Is it like this?
The *bastard*,
I'm scared,
Please, please, please,
If the world is,
Christ. Christ. Jesus.
'Oh Jesus. Oh David.'

I am holding his hand. He is holding my hand. I feel sick. His hand in my hand in his hand in my hand. I feel dizzy and sick.

'Where is Juno now?'

'We . . . no. God. She's at home, she's fine. She's got friends looking after her. I went to get Michael, she wanted to see Michael, he's, he was, is, her fr . . . boyfriend. Friend. Sorry, sorry, sorry, I'm not doing this very well. She wanted to see Michael, she went out with him, until, recently. They . . . I went to get Michael, he wasn't in so I left him a message. And then I kept walking, I . . . went for a walk, I walked here. I felt OK on the walk, sorry I made a scene, I'm fine. It's just, you understand, it's hard, when I can't help her. You understand.'

'I understand.'

'No, I . . . no. I'm fine now. Oh Jesus, you were going to a lecture.'

'No, it's fine.'

'Oh Jesus, David, I'm sorry.'

'No, no, no. *No.* I'm glad you came to me. I . . . wish I could be of more use. Perhaps, I hope I can be.'

I saw with detached surprise the wet line down his cheek. I touched it with a fingertip. He let go my other hand and brushed his cheek with the back of his right hand.

'You're late for your lecture.'

'It doesn't matter.'

'Go to your lecture.'

'It doesn't matter. This is important. This has to be . . . stopped. This cannot be allowed to go on, because it will go on . . .'

'Go to your lecture. You can solve the mystery after the lecture. We can stop it next week. It's only words. I shouldn't have gotten upset. God, I'm more upset than Juno was. It's only words. You're right.'

'Are you sure your sister, Juno, that she's alright?'

'She's fine, she's with Connie and Dominic. Honestly David, there's nothing you can do. Go to your lecture.'

'But you're still upset.'

'I'm not, I'm not, I was, I got upset talking about it there, but I'm grand now really David, go to your lecture. It's only words. There was no harm done. I'm fine. I'm grand. Really.' I nearly had to push him out the door in front of me.

'You can stay here, if you like. There's a kettle behind all the . . .' helpless gesture back at the mesas and plateaux of printed paper 'and coffee and mugs in the drawer of the desk . . .'

'No, I'll be grand, thanks though. I have an essay to do, there's a book on Aristotle the library's holding for me, I have to pick that up . . . thanks, all the same.'

With the closing of the office door behind us we found ourselves, awkward, too suddenly, in the corridor and the public world. A rush of air. A pressure drop, or rise. From intimate to formal. Rooms should have airlocks, for us to adjust our emotions before we re-enter the world.

'I'll leave it open, if you need to . . . I'm finished at three today, if you need to talk, I don't have a lunchtime because I'm meeting Professor O'Neill about the expansion of the department . . . but, if you want to, to talk. To someone.'

I'd never seen him struggle so hard with the language. His hands were bunched in fists by his sides. He looked like a boxer giving a speech. I laughed. 'You look like you want to hit me.'

A small smile. 'Not you.'

I walked him to the lift. He walked me to the lift. Whichever. We hardly talked during the brief descent, but that was sort of nice. When it stopped at the concourse we got out and smiled with awkwardness and turned in our different directions. I looked back, to see him look back over his shoulder at me. He gave me a salute, I waved a hurry-on at him and he smiled, turned away and began running down the wide expanse of the concourse, really sprinting, dodging the people coming against him, overtaking a nun, Flannery Ryan, a pack of engineers . . . gone.

I turned away. Went to the library. Locked myself in the toilets on the Arts floor to have a good cry. Couldn't. Realised I felt extraordinarily happy. On the way out I wrote 'DH is Fab' and 'JT Roolz' in the steam on the mirror, with my forefinger, and then a couple of badly drawn hearts, with one side bigger than the other, like real hearts. Expressing and mocking my joy with the same gesture, in the modern ironic fashion.

Left the library without remembering to get out the book I'd asked them to keep for me.

Everything would be alright. Juno would be fine. I would be fine. I could feel it. Gut instinct. Just as half an hour earlier I could feel that nothing would ever be right again.

My emotional compass was spinning like a roulette wheel, and my heart felt like the little silver ball.

On impulse, I turned into the Quad as I was passing, hesitated, headed right, toward the college bar. At the doorway of the college bar I hesitated again, and on another impulse turned, walked away from the bar and started down the narrow, dark stairs to UCG Art Gallery.

62

I recognised the paintings. This was very peculiar. I wouldn't recognise the paintings if you walked me into the Irish National Gallery, banged my nose off Leech's *Goose Girl*, and wiped away my subsequent tears with Caravaggio's *The Taking Of Christ*.

These paintings, though, I knew. Hot, bright, hallucinatory. But, like seeing a familiar face in the wrong place, a taxi driver on the beach, without their context I was stymied. Spotlit, high on white partitions, just themselves. How did I know them?

Then an oldish man appeared from behind one of the partitions, conversing with another man. Weatherbeaten, in comfortable old tweed suits, leaning on stout sticks, the two of them together looked like a bit of Connemara hillside talking to itself, and I remembered.

'Mr Hennessey!' I said.

'Well if it isn't the bauld Juliet Taylor! D'ye know Jim here, of course you don't, Dr James Griffin of Spiddal and Paris, a pal of my cradle days and my doctor now at the other end of things, Juliet Taylor, a great friend of my son's . . .' Hallos, pleased-to-meet-yous, and the shaking of hands.

'So these are yours then?' I said. 'I admired them in your house.'

'Ah, I've painted a bit for the past few years. You have to pass the days. 'Twas David made me stick a few of them in the exhibition here. He brought a couple in without tellen me. I said to him one morning last week, where the feck are me paintings on the landing gone and he says he's put them in for an exhibition of young Galway artists. Hah! Sure you've been an artist no time, he says. You qualify, no bother. But them two you fecked are shite, begging your pardon, said I like an eejit. So by trickery he had me picking six for this thing.'

'This one's lovely' I said, which was half true. No, true but insufficient. It was lovely and disturbing. Great angled planes of yellow and blue crumpled suddenly at the heart of the canvas, ruptured and torn. I felt I could put my hand in among the painted shards and pull out . . . something.

'Ah, it's only an auld painting.'

'No, it means something, it must. It's not of something, but it has to mean something, to you.'

'Well it is "of" something, in a manner of speaking. It's a painting of a stress fracture in a load-bearing steel support. Not, now, as the eye would see it, mind, but on a crystalline level. It looks a fair bit like that. That's one of the first ones I did.'

'It's beautiful.' Dr Griffin had wandered off to where some paintings leaned against a bare wall. The girl who'd been crouched by them, screwing cuphooks into the frames, stood up and turned to talk to him. It was Gemma Mannion. Of course, she painted. A boy with a ponytail, the sides of his head shaved, was standing on a chair at the far end of the gallery, adjusting spotlights. 'Am I in the way here?' I asked David's father. 'Your friend, Dr Griffin . . .'

'Oh God no, child. I only had Jim here to help me with the hanging, and mine're hung. We were only having a look at the other lads' paintings and boring each other with our Theories of Art.'

'Bore me with your theory' I said.

'Ah no, you'll suffer enough in this life without that.'

I wandered up to my favourite of his. Broad, thick strokes. Flat, abrupt ledges of oil or acrylic, I couldn't tell. Acrylic, I guessed. Vivid, unmixed. Painted with a knife. Painted with a big emotion, though only God knew what. God and Gerry Hennessey and whoever he'd told.

'But this must mean something' I said. 'It's not just a picture of, whatever it was, steel crystals. A fracture. The way you painted it, and what you chose to paint . . . it must mean something to you.'

'Arra whisht, you sound like David.' He leaned on his stick and squinted with gloomy suspicion at the picture, like a farmer pondering a cow with a cough. 'He's always going on about them and calling them pictorial metaphors for my emotional condition, when he isn't trying to make me get an agent or comparing me to fellahs I never heard of. They're only shagging paintings.'

I laughed. A vivid image of David in the kitchen, embarrassing his father with praise. 'How much are they?'

'Oh, ask my agent, how much are they . . . sure who'd buy them?'

'I would, if I had the money. I'd buy this one.'

'Get away, you'll have me blushing.'

'No, honest to God I would. I noticed it as soon as I walked into your house, it was in the hall wasn't it? The . . . colours. It's . . . I won't embarrass you. But it's good, honestly. Ah no, I will embarrass you, it's brilliant, I love looking at it, I don't know why but I do. It makes me feel . . .'

'Jesus, you're mortifying me Juliet, will you stop. Have it, have it, only stop.'

'What do . . .' I got a couple of words together, but I couldn't make a decent sentence out of them.

'It's yours, take it away when the exhibition's over.'

'But, I can't, I mean, what about David'

'What about him, they're my paintings aren't they, he'll have enough of them soon enough. If you like it you can have it, I'd be delighted and honoured.'

'Oh Mr Hennessey, I couldn't, it's worth money, it's too much'

'And what in God's name would I be doing with money, haven't I money coming out of me arse, would you ever just take it and shush. I'll put it in the book here, sold to Juliet Taylor. I've sold one Jim!' this last shouted across the gallery.

'Oh this world is full of fools' said Dr Griffin, coming over with Gemma to inspect my acquisition. David's dad made to introduce us, 'Gemma Mannion . . .'

'Ah, we know each other well' said Gemma.

'But of course' he said, 'all ye young people know each other in Galway, it's like a club.'

Dr Griffin cast a critical eye over the canvas. 'Oh, one of your finest Gerry, undoubtedly. The modernity of it is only frightening. Sure if it was any more modern it wouldn't be dry yet. I hope you're making the poor girl pay in cash, and upfront.'

'I am of course.'

'Good, good. And you'll have it finished, won't you, by the time she returns with her suitcase of Swiss francs?'

'I will. A good big fishing boat in the middle of it so she'll know which way up to hang it.'

'As long as it's weatherproof. You can't beat the Dulux Gloss.'

'Oh you could hang this one outside in the garden Jim. She'll never rust.'

It was odd hearing men who looked so dignified, so mature, talking easy nonsense for their own amusement. Gemma grinned at me.

A sudden sweet and sour shock, that they'd been young too, once, and that we would grow old and that we wouldn't really feel we'd changed at all.

We stand, very still, on the stage, and the sets change and change, they blur and we are in another play, being treated as a different character, but knowing we're the same.

The true self has no age, or has age the way it has hair colour.

Ah, the old make us philosophical. No wonder we avoid them.

I helped David's father and Dr Griffin to help Gemma hang her paintings, dark sketchy oils of gloomy-looking couples that made me worry about her social life. Both men flirted decorously with us in the relaxed and pleasant fashion traditional to the older, much-travelled Irishman. They flirted with a kind of sophisticated innocence that was much nicer than sophistication on its own, and much easier to accept than the raw innocent regard with which I occasionally caught the ponytailed boy looking at me from the far end of the gallery. The older men weighted their flirtation better. You didn't feel you had to respond to it or fight it, or worry about its implications, or their feelings, or your virtue. They meant it, but they didn't want anything in return. Their compliments were not a speculative investment.

Civilised, dignified men. I liked that brief time very much.

When we'd all finished hanging Gemma's paintings the two men courteously said their goodbyes. 'You must come for dinner again' said David's father to me. 'And you, Gemma, too. Give me enough notice and I'll prepare a proper student dinner for you, baked beans on toast perhaps, and maybe a can of Ambrosia creamed rice for dessert, *Deo volente*.'

We expressed our delight, all shook hands, and the two men departed. Their laughter and conversation echoed down the stairwell behind them as they ascended, sounding like two cheerful boys on the mitch from school. The fire door hissed shut and with a thunk from the hydraulic cylinder the sound of the old young men was cut off.

Gemma stood back and admired her last painting to be hung, a pool of illuminated gloom high on the white wall. 'It's shite' she said. 'But it's accurate. He was a miserable bastard, and his chin really was that long. D'you like the way the two of us look as though we're dying of boredom? He was mortally offended.'

'Who is he?' I said. He looked half-familiar.

'An ex. You wouldn't know him. He's from Ballina, I broke it off with him Christmas before last, after I went looking for a present for him and I couldn't find anything I wanted to give him. I was tired and annoyed with myself so I went for a coffee and a fag in Java's and I realised as I was sitting there that I'd liked the *presents* I'd seen, it was just him I didn't like. So I broke it off and saved myself a tenner.'

'How do people ever stay together?' I said.

'They hardly ever do' said Gemma.

She borrowed the chair from the ponytailed boy and we made final adjustments to the lighting of her paintings.

When the last of the spotlights had been aligned I returned the chair to the ponytailed boy who, as I said thank you, blinked shyly at me, then blushingly looked at my tits.

'Come on' said Gemma to me. 'We're done. Bye Dan.'

The boy said goodbye. So he has the mysterious power of speech I thought to myself. Good man, Dan. God be praised.

Thunk. We ascended the complicated stairs. 'You're a dote for helping' said Gemma.

'Don't be silly' I said, 'I did nothing.'

'No, it was great' said Gemma. We were at the first landing. She stopped, so I stopped. She moved to face me. 'Juliet.'

'Yes?' There wasn't a lot of light on the landing, with its single small window high in the thick stone wall. I wasn't quite sure what her face was trying to say. A second of silence as we studied each other's faces in the bad light. A murmur from the College Bar far above.

'Hang on' said Gemma, and reached out to touch the side of my head briefly. 'Bit of string in your hair, there.' She flicked it free of her fingertip and laughed. 'I forget what I was going to say. That distracted me. Something to do with art, the way the light had you then. Reminded me of something. It'll come back to me.' She turned and we continued on our way.

63

Back home, I walked into a modern Irish drama. Juno was violently making tea in the kitchen, while Michael stood scowling with his back to her.

'Hi guys' I said. Juno slammed the kettle up into the pouring tap. Michael's forehead twitched.

'You OK Juno? Everything OK?'

'Yes.' When she flicked the switch of the electric kettle, it brought to mind a Texas Republican fundamentalist personally executing the murderer of her children. I was surprised a spark didn't leap across the room and fry Michael where he stood. The tension was making the fillings in my teeth vibrate.

'Did you get my message at your place? Michael?' No. 'Let me guess' I said. '*The Playboy of the Western World*?' They seemed disinclined to cooperate with the joke. I couldn't work it out, so I piled in head-on. 'Then did Juno tell you?'

Michael gave a nod as minimal as the flicker back and forth between frames in a video freezeframe. 'Mmm.'

'About the letter?'

'Mmm.' He turned and walked into Juno's room.

'Anything, uh, wrong?' I asked Juno, or the air.

'Apart from Michael being a prick? No' said Juno, un-*sotto* of *voce*.

Michael re-emerged with his jacket on and his black bag swinging from his shoulder. 'Got to go, I'm late.' He went, with a slamming of innumerable doors. The echoes died. The air stilled.

'Fucking hell, Juno.'

Juno tinkered with mugs and teabags and didn't look at me.

'What's up with Mr Sympathy?'

'I kissed Conrad' said Juno.

'Oh' I said.

'It was just to thank him, for being nice to me. For looking

211

after me. The letter had me, had me really shook. Dominic had to go, so Conrad made me hot whiskies and we talked, and he was, you know, *there*, which Michael wasn't, I couldn't reach Michael, we'd tried Druid, they didn't know ... and Conrad looked after me, so I kissed him, a little kiss.'

'Did he kiss you back?' I said.

'Jesus, no. He was a bit shocked I think. I sort of hit his lips by mistake, he was turning his head away. I think he thought I ...' she trailed off.

'Wanted to, like, do it, like' I suggested helpfully. 'Doggy style.'

'Juliet!'

'Wheelbarrow style' I amended.

'What's that?' said Juliet.

'Don't know' I said. 'Like a wheelbarrow race? But with him inside you. And not running.'

'Who stands?'

'I don't know! I only heard it in the college bar. And you're trying to change the subject ... He'd have to.'

She thought. 'Yeah. And you'd be face down. On your hands. Cool.'

'Or you could lie on the bed ... Juno, for fuck's sake. Did Michael catch ye?'

'No, Jesus, there was nothing to catch, seriously. It was just a platonic kiss. But Michael came in a minute after, and Conrad was acting so awkward, Michael said something half-joking about catching us at it, and Conrad like a big innocent gom tried to explain, which made it much, much worse ...'

'Shite.'

'Yeah, so Michael's convinced I fancy Conrad.'

'But you do a bit, you've told me.'

Behind her head, steam began to drift out of the kettle. 'Yeah, but not to do anything! I didn't do anything! And Michael's acting like I fucked him or something and it's all his fucking ego, his fucking hurt feelings, and I was bloody upset and he's done nothing but sulk.' The kettle blasted steam halfway across the kitchen. I adjusted my eyeline so it appeared to be jetting out of Juno's right ear. 'I mean I get a letter where some psycho's threatening to rape me and Michael's *upset* because I *kissed* someone on the *cheek*. He can piss off.'

'He does love you' I said, standing up and heading for the kettle. Thermostat stuck.

'Well if that's love he can shove it up his arse' said Juno.

'How many hot whiskies did you have?' I said, curiously eyeing the half-bottle of Jameson on the table as I passed.

'None! Nearly none. Two.'

I knocked off the kettle. 'Let's have another' I said, digging out two glasses from the washing up, 'Tea is for guuurls.'

'Wish I had fucked Conrad' said Juno.

'You should drink more often' I said.

64

The next day I went with Juno to the Guards.

We walked into a small foyer and looked about us. Four plastic chairs bolted up against the right-hand wall. The chairs faced, across the foyer, a wire reinforced glass window, with a standard doorbell button mounted on the wall beside it. A stout traveller woman stood in front of the window, resting her thumb on the button. Occasionally she would pump the button with her thumb. Behind the glass, uniformed guards could be seen, working at paper-piled desks, or walking about a large room. Now and again a guard would look over at the window.

We sat on the middle two plastic chairs, and waited. The sound of phones and voices leaked through the three-inch gap between the bottom of the reinforced glass and the counter. The drill of the bell. Bursts of laughter. The drill of the bell.

The woman slammed her free palm against the glass. 'Bastards!' Slam. 'What about my son ye bastards.' Slam. 'Are ye men at all ye bastards?' Slam.

It went on.

Eventually a guard came to the window. 'Go away or we'll have to remove you from the premises.'

'I know my rights.'

'You've no right to make a nuisance of yourself in a Garda station. Go away and calm down. We've done all we can. We can do no more.'

She slapped the glass in front of his face and spat at it. He didn't flinch. A younger guard emerged through the security doors and spoke to her with a gentle urgency. She brushed his hand away as he tried to touch her arm reassuringly.

'There's no justice for us, there's no justice for us' she muttered as he escorted her outside. The spit, high in the centre of the window where the older guard's forehead had been, crawled slowly down the window, a bulk of bubbles leaving a shining trail.

I found I had been holding trembling hands with Juno. 'I can't do this' Juno said to me, as we were left alone. The guard at the hatch had gone. The window was empty.

We stood, to go or to approach the window, no way of knowing. The older guard now entered the foyer through the security door, with a big blue sponge bursting out of one huge hand and a tiny yellow plastic squeezy bottle almost hidden in the other. He looked from Juno to me and back, and turned. With a casual swing of his right hand he squirted a line of thick yellow liquid diagonally down the window, from top left to bottom right, slicing across the vertical axis of the dribbled spit. 'Yeah?' he said, his back to us.

Juno tried to speak, couldn't, moved forward so as to see his face, be seen. He wiped the glass carefully with the blue sponge, folded it over like a sandwich, wiped again, both times down along the diagonal of the yellow fluid, then down the vertical of the spit. I could smell the industrial lemon smell of cleaning products. It's nothing like lemon, I thought suddenly.

'Yeah?' he said impatiently, turning to look at Juno.

'I wanted to report something' she said.

'Fire away' he said, folding the sponge over again, into a tight little pad, running it back and forth across the window.

'Someone's been sending me letters.'

The guard turned and threw the sponge past Juno at a tin wastebin in the far corner. The sponge unfolded and expanded as it left his hand, losing all its momentum as it turned from a dense projectile into a handful of air. It landed softly halfway between him and the bin. He ignored it. 'Students, are you?' he said.

'Yes' said Juno puzzled 'in UCG.'

'Anonymous letters is it?'

'Yes'

'Some fella that fancies you?'

'It's, they, the letters are, they're sexual . . .'

'Do you know who it is, or has anyone followed you or threatened you?'

'No, well, he may, he must have followed me, or seen me, he knows what I wear . . .'

'But you've never been threatened, or attacked, or followed at night or anything?'

'Not, well, the letters are very . . .'

'It's just letters, though?'

'Yes' she'd given up.

'There's always a bit of this goes on with the students. I suppose they think it's funny.'

'You don't know it's a student, you haven't seen . . . it could be anyone.'

He ignored her. 'You can report it if you want and we'll put it on file but I should warn you we have higher priorities. There's murders and drugs and rapes and assaults out there, they burnt out three cars in Rahoon last night, and we don't have the resources to chase students with dirty minds. They keep telling us this is the fastest growing city in Europe, but we have less guards than we had two years ago.'

Juno just wanted to get away.

'So you won't take this down?' I said, boiling.

He turned to me. 'I didn't say that. I'll take a statement. I'll take copies of any letters, I'll place it all on the record, but I'm trying to be straight with you here, a lot of people get letters. There's a lot of crazy people out there. There's religious lunatics and queers and lonely auld fellas and mad women and they bother other people and they get notions in their heads and they phone some poor fecker at all hours and they write them and they follow them around. But if that's it, then there's feck all we can do. We can talk to them, but if you don't even know who it is, what can we do? Stake out your house? Have you handwriting, is it . . .'

'No' said Juno. 'Come on, let's go.'

The big guard shrugged. 'Off the record, the best thing you could do is find out yourself who's sending you these Valentines if they're distressing you and get some friends of yours to go round and sort him out.'

Juno nodded. 'Let's go' she said again, tugging my arm. I was staring at him in amazement.

'Are you . . .' I started.

'Come on' Juno jerked me out the door into the drizzle.

At the gate to the garda station car park I tried to turn back.

'I should have spat on his window, I should have spat on his fucking window . . .'

The young guard was standing on the pavement talking to the traveller woman. 'They're bastards' she said to me over his shoulder.

'They are' I replied.

65

I started the next day in college by skipping my morning lectures to chase notes for the lectures I'd missed the previous day. By lunchtime I'd tracked down and photocopied everything, so I celebrated by skipping my two o'clock history lecture. An in-depth look at the Irish Famine, it wasn't my favourite hour of the week.

I figured I'd loop through town and check out Timmy O'Dea's Bookshop for a PG Wodehouse.

On my way across the Salmon Weir Bridge I considered whether or not I should ask for a weekend job in Timmy's, or maybe in Boo's across the road. The money would help. A lot. And I'd far rather a bookshop than waitressing for three quid an hour. I'd tried that in Tipp and only lasted six quid. Had my arse felt or my breasts brushed up against every fifty pence. Dropped two black coffees into the lap of the twelfth feeler, ran home and locked myself in my room, and cried for a pound fifty. As, no doubt, did he.

Boo's first. Boo's stood stiffly in Middle Street on the side that didn't get the sun. I arrived and stood outside it for a moment. I composed myself, gathered my breath. And crossed the road.

I went into Timmy O'Dea's and asked them for a job, and they didn't have one.

So I crossed the road again and went into A Boo shop Of One's Own and walked up to the counter and the two women behind the counter stopped talking and saw it was me and one of them said 'Yes?' and I said 'I was just . . . ah, yes' and I picked up a flyer from the counter advertising a poetry reading in the Atlanta Hotel by somebody I'd never heard of and studied it intently till they returned to their conversation.

I waited another minute to be sure they'd forgotten me before I tiptoed away into the gloom of the sexual politics section.

Bloody bloody bloody bloody bloody bloody bloody fool,

Juliet. Why on earth had I done that? All I was asking for was a job. At worst all they could do was say no, and possibly make me sign a petition about Bosnia. How on earth could I ask them now? Oh Juliet, you must. But I can't. You must. I can't. Must. Can't. Must. Can't. Mustcan't, mustcan't mustcan'tmustcan't . . . My internal debate wasn't very complex. Reason and instinct just ended up making faces at each other. By a gigantic effort of will I managed to lurch a couple of feet closer to the counter, into the alphabetical fag-end of the modern fiction section. Both women looked over at me. Panicking, I picked up a book as camouflage and smiled at them inanely with an oh-that's-where-it-was smile. They looked down at the book. They glared at me. Does your treachery know no bounds, their eyes seemed to say. I looked at what I was holding. Omigod, the new John Updike. *In Urbane Praise Of The Killing Of Women* or whatever it was called. It fell from my suddenly nerveless hands. I scrambled to pick it up. The dust jacket fell off.

I am in hell, I thought calmly. The conversation behind the counter had by now stopped so thoroughly that it was probably going to take intensive post-traumatic stress counselling of both parties to restart it.

I had almost got the dust jacket back on, with fingers that felt like they were wearing rubber gloves, when it tore. Not much. An inch or so, along the fold between backflap and back cover. Loud, though, the tearing noise. I didn't think paper could make such a loud noise, just tearing like that. Gosh, it was loud. In the quiet shop.

I decided I wouldn't ask for that job after all.

One of them opened her mouth, perhaps in preparation for speech. Or possibly in search of oxygen. I took a step backwards, into the children's section. She froze. I froze. Her colleague began to open her mouth, I took two steps backwards and stepped on a child.

'For fuck's sake' came a familiar voice.

I turned around, looked down and with enormous relief and pleasure said 'Juh! J . . .'

'Jimmy' said Jimmy Gleeson. 'Jesus, Juliet, you look like a million fucking ECUs in that yoke.' This of course is back before ECUs became Euros, and euros became real. Both Gleeson twins

were passionate, instinctive Europeans, big, big fans of a single currency and an end to internal border controls. They would quiz
myself and Juno on arcane points of European trade law as though
we were experts, because we read the *Irish Times* every day in transition year. Jimmy had once even shoplifted a copy of *The Economist*
from Healy's for its cover story on European customs union so I
could read it for him and explain the implications, back when they
were starting to distribute smuggled rolling tobacco, cartons of
Marlboro, and lighters. They supported European Union the same
way they supported Liverpool Football Club and Metallica. Their
Europeanism had become another of our private jokes.

That's a ridiculous amount of explanation for the presence of
one word, not even a word, an acronym. European Currency Unit.
One tiny unit of currency in our peculiar love. A shell on that
small beach. I did half-think of changing it to 'a million fucking
dollars' and saving myself the explanation, but once you start that
you're lost. And they're lost. Everything takes an easier shape, but
it's the wrong shape.

Also, digressing like this gets me out of describing what happened next.

I suppose I should just grit my teeth and go for it.

On with the story.

The women behind the counter had closed their mouths, the
better to purse their lips.

'Oh Jimmy, it's great to see you' I said. Jimmy looked pleased
but embarrassed and tried nonchalantly to slide a *Famous Five*
back into the *Secret Seven* section, spine inward. I pretended I'd
seen nothing. 'So what are you doing here?' I said, meaning
Galway.

'Looking for a book' he said, choosing to interpret the question
more narrowly.

'Anything in particular?' I said, resisting an urge to rub his suede
head with gratitude.

His genie-like ability to pop up when I was in trouble had
seldom been so appreciated by me. From scrabbling on the
ground, reassembling an ideologically unsound hardback under
the baleful glare of the guardians of ideology, to having a civilised
conversation about books with an old friend . . . It was a reversal
of fortune worthy of a Shakespearean happy ending. The two

behind the counter were thinking of unpursing their lips. They turned to each other. They seemed to be on the very brink of restarting their conversation. Of forgetting about me. I was going to survive.

'Frogspawn' said Jimmy.

'Pardon?' I said.

'Frogspawn.'

'You're looking for a book on *frogspawn?*'

'Fuck no' laughed Jimmy heartily. 'Tadpoles 'n' shit? No. <u>Frog</u>' he said loudly and carefully '<u>Porn</u>.'

This regained the attention of our tiny audience. I didn't particularly need to check to see if they'd suddenly glanced our way. It was like being hit in the back of the neck by military lasers.

'Porn by Frogs' Jimmy explained loudly and carefully. 'I read some shit by this French cunt last time I was in the 'Dam, classy stuff, none of your *Asian Babes Readers' Wives Juggs* bollocks, a proper book, now, no pictures.' He blushed with pride. 'And it was fucking good, I got to the end and everything.' The clarity of Jimmy's diction was startling. Perhaps he was making an extra effort after the frogporn misunderstanding. And had he been taking voice projection lessons lately? My, the shop was quiet today. I'd seldom heard it so quiet. Not a kook from the women behind the counter, the two or three other customers, the leading minor local poet who stood now frozen in the doorway, unsure if he was interrupting a theatrical event of some kind as everybody stared at Jimmy. And me.

Entirely oblivious, Jimmy continued his book report. 'Brilliant, it was. So I asked Karl, my mate, you've never met him, does a bit of import-export, if he'd any more. And he said I should get this other book by some tart, sorry, but I can't fucking pronounce it, named after a perfume. He wrote it down. French, wrote books.' He looked at me appealingly. 'And I can't fucking find it.'

'The book, or the piece of paper with the name?'

'Neither' he said gloomily. 'I went into Eason's and they said they didn't think they had it. I think they thought I was thick because I didn't know the name. I asked for the manager. Bloke was all right for a Man U fan. Said I should come here, they'd all that kinky Frog shit. But I can't find it.'

'I think you're in the wrong section' I said.

'Oh, yeah.' Jimmy blushed again. 'I got bored. Saw, you know. Paddington and stuff. Going to get something for the kid' his little brother Anthony. 'He reads. You know. This shit.'

I nodded. We shared a smile. Books with pictures. Kids' books. Huh.

'So this book you want's named after a perfume' I said.

'No, *she*'s named after it. Your one who wrote it. Begins with an "A".'

A, A, A . . . 'Anaïs Anaïs!' I said. 'Anaïs Nin!'

His worried little face opened out like a sunflower with delight. 'You're a fucking genius' he said. 'The very one. Annay Annay Nin.'

I felt so pleased with myself I nearly bowed to our little audience.

More used to the layout of bookshops than Jimmy, I led him to the kinky Frog shit section, and we found *Little Birds*. He flipped it open, slowly read half a page, and pronounced himself satisfied. 'Class' he said. 'The Frogs for the porn.' He tucked it under one tiny arm and reached up with the other to take the Updike, the existence of which I had entirely forgotten, from my hands. 'And what are you having yourself?' he said, turning it to see the front. 'Tits on that' he said admiringly. Completely disregarding my feeble protests and explanations, he marched straight to the counter with both of them.

He reached up and, on tippy-toe, slid them onto the counter top. The guardians of ideology leaned over the counter to look down at him. 'How're ya' said Jimmy. He took a roll of notes out of his back pocket, removed the elastic band from around them, ruffled their edges to loosen the tight cylinder of paper, and peeled off a couple. 'Oh, and a *Famous Five*. I'll pick one up on me way out. You don't do Coke, no? The drink? Pity. Or fags? Ah well. It's funny the way bookshops only ever sell books, and newspaper shops sell everything, isn't it. Funny that. Ye should sell fags, every fucker smokes when they read, it's nearly a law of nature. I'd say you'd shift a packet of fags for every book. More. And yer porn's in the wrong place, I nearly didn't find it. You'd sell a lot more if people could find it y'know, because it's bloody hard to get in Ireland. Ah, that's grand, keep the small stuff.' He waved away his non-paper change, hauled the recycled paper

carrier bag containing his purchases off the counter and I practically pushed him out the door, knocking aside a paralysed poet
in my haste. Outside at last. The pure, clean air of freedom.

'Hey, the kid's *Famous Five*, Juliet, for fuck's sake. Hold this'
said Jimmy, breaking free of my grip and dashing back into the
bowels of the shop, leaving me with the carrier bag and my
thoughts.

I mentally surveyed the wreckage Jimmy had made of my prom-
ising career in bookselling, undecided as to whether to laugh or
cry.

'What the fuck are you laughing at?' enquired Jimmy, genuinely
interested, when he emerged a minute later clutching *Five Go To
Billycock Hill* in a tiny hand.

66

'So what are you really doing in Galway' I said. We were walking down Quay Street towards the Spanish Arch where Jimmy had left his bike.

'Ah, expanding the business. You know yourself. You can't stand in the one place.'

'And which business is this now Jimmy?'

'Ah, you know. The E, like. And the auld acid. Bit of hash. But it's the E really, with all the clubs. Galway's crying out for it. Salthill's worse. The distribution in the West is a shambles' he said disapprovingly. 'A fucking joke, it is. Bloody students and amateurs. My fellas had to do something, or the Dublin lads would be in, and we couldn't have that. Dub scuts doing the business this side of the country.' He looked at me for confirmation that this would indeed be a thing that we couldn't have. 'D'ya see what I'm saying?' I did. 'I'm up and down since the New Year, sorting the West. Galway, Ballinasloe. Sligo. Tuam's already sorted. But Galway's the big one, with the students and the clubs. I was testing the water myself out Salthill New Year's Eve, Jesus Christ. I'll tell you the story, you'll laugh. Drugs Squad caught me going into the Castle, three fuckin' plainers, looked more like they were training for the priesthood than raving, real Templemore bogmen on their first day out. Caught me fucking bang on, though, I'd fucking no chance, with fifty fucking E in me jocks. I'd brought a good stash of new stuff from Edinburgh, supposed to be well clean, a harmless cut, none of your poxy speed in there for the flash, or your strick. I thought I'd see how they'd shift in Galway, test the water for the expansion. I don't like flogging a new line too close to home in any case, so it was the two birds, you know? So I'd fifty of the fuckers in a wee bottle tucked in me kecks when suddenly I'm up against the wall, slam. Nearly broke me fucking bottle.' He chuckled nostalgically. 'They were into my pants like Christian Brothers. Found the bottle. Well now I'm fucked, I thought, 'cause I was on bail already. They knew me name. Down to the station. Grand. Charged, no bail, I'm fucked. And here's the laugh. They rushed it away to forensics for analysis, and they analyse it, fifty fucking tablets, and get this: no strick, no speed, no brickdust alright . . . and no fucking E. The cunts in Edinburgh did me. Chalk, aspirin and vanilla fucking essence. Isn't that a gas one? So I walked. Even my solicitor thought that was a good one. I told them they could keep the tablets in case they got a bad head on them some morning.' He shook his own little head. 'Gas.'

We got as far as the Spanish Arch and walked under it in companionable silence. His bike was just the other side of it, the familiar old one with the incredibly low-slung seat designed to push the normal rider's knees up past his ears, but on which Jimmy could ride as straight and erect in the saddle as Arch Duke Franz Ferdinand leading a parade on horseback. 'Oh you still have her' I said, pleased.

'*Jesus*. Look what some of your Galway gurriers just fucking did to my bike' said Jimmy, pointing at the painting on the fuel tank.

'Oh Jimmy.' I laughed, and put a hand over my mouth. Someone had crudely Tipp-Ex'd a bra and panties onto his beloved naked lady.

'Dirty little fuckers' said Jimmy, disgusted. 'I'll have to get some of the kid's Tipp-Ex thinners to get that off.' He scratched at the disfiguring knickers with a thumbnail. 'Little bastards shouldn't be let near Tipp-Ex. Or the toxic markers. They make a right fuck of everything.' He continued to scratch the tank with his thumbnail. 'They had Juno's name up in the phonebox in the square. The square back home now, not the one here.'

'I know' I said.

'I got rid of it' he said. 'Went over it with a marker and a lighter.'

'Thanks' I said.

He looked up and smiled his worried smile at me. 'Made shit of the plastic' he said. 'But you can't read it any more.'

'You were always very good to us' I said. I could feel something was wrong. I'd felt it under all his talk. 'How's Johnny?' I said. He went back to his scratching. Some of the white panties had flaked off to reveal the dark, airbrushed hair.

'He's in the 'Joy' said Jimmy, and looked up at me again, not smiling. 'He's doing my time. I couldn't go in. The thing I was on bail for. He said he'd done it. I didn't want to be inside when, you know. Ah you don't know. I never told you. Nuala Driscoll, I've been seeing her a while, and she's going to have a baby in July.'

I didn't know what to say. He'd admitted it like an infidelity, which was ridiculous. We'd never even kissed.

What was more ridiculous still was that I felt an almost over-whelming desire to pound him with the useless fists that he and Johnny had always gently mocked because I always had my thumb in the wrong place, inside or outside the fist, I could never remember which was wrong.

How could you, how could you, how could you, when you were always meant to be there to protect me?

'That's great' I said. 'That's great. Congratulations.'

He shrugged it off. 'Nothing to fucking congratulate, it was an accident.' We looked at each other and I could find nothing in me to say. Jimmy shrugged again and began to undo the lock that attached his bike to his helmet. 'How's Juno?' he said.

'She's great' I said. 'She's in a play, acting.'

Jimmy slid the helmet down over his face and flipped the visor up. He smiled out at me, a kind of relieved smile, because he'd told me and I hadn't made a scene. 'There's no harm in a little play-acting' he said, and smiled even more in pleasure at his word play, his joke. I couldn't stop myself smiling back, I didn't want to stop myself.

'She'll be giving them some of your trips' I said. 'They're having a party when the play ends, an all-nighter. A trip party.'

'Oh. They were meant for ye' said Jimmy, a little hurt, and I bit my tongue.

'They're friends of ours Jimmy, nice people, honestly. And we never . . . we'd never get through all that acid on our own. It was very good of you.'

Jimmy nodded. 'We wanted to get ye books, but we didn't know what ye'd like. At least I could get you the one you wanted today.' He dug the Updike out of the carrier bag and gave it to me.

'Oh thank you Jimmy. You know you shouldn't have.'

He shrugged and smiled. 'Sure it's nothing. A *mere bagatelle*.'
He said it like it was in French. I'd taught them that. A mere
bagatelle. And, 'Come, we sit too long on trifles'. My favourite
line of Shakespeare. I'd taught them that. My eyes filled with tears
as he tucked the carrier bag under the elastic straps on the pillion
and swung himself onto the bike. 'Tell her I said hello' he said,
rocking his machine back down off the stand.

I nodded. 'Tell Johnny . . .' I said, and faded out. 'Tell him
thanks. For the Christmas present. We didn't get a proper chance
to say thanks.'

Jimmy nodded and started the engine. 'Do you want a lift
anywhere?' he said.

I couldn't hold this together much longer. 'No' I said. 'I'm
grand here. Thanks.' Jimmy gunned the engine, opened his
mouth, closed it. 'Come, we sit too long on trifles' I said, and
closed the smoky visor on his subdued face.

He revved her up and was gone in a smooth surge out through
the Spanish Arch. I walked under the arch and watched as he
mounted the pavement, crossed into the traffic and vanished over
Wolfe Tone Bridge toward Salthill.

I stood under the arch for a while before I went home.

67

I descended rapidly from the stairhead of the flat, swinging my sturdy Timmy O'Dea's carrier bag, its clean lines distorted into a polythene polygon by the trapped corners of the books, notebooks and pens I'd hurled into it at random in transit on my sprint from the bedroom.

'That's *cheating*' wailed Juno behind me, 'I wasn't *ready*.'

'Save it for the Second Coming' I shouted up 'And it'll be no excuse then, either.'

While I waited for her, I had a half-hearted rummage through the slurry of junkmail slopping over the edges of the hall table. I noticed it just as Juno was slamming the door on the top landing. It was impossible to tell how long it had been there. I felt sick.

Oh no, I thought. That's not fair. It's her first night tomorrow night.

I grabbed the familiar envelope in the dark hall and slid it into my carrier bag as Juno clattered down the last few stairs.

'What?' she said.

'Fairy Liquid vouchers' I said. 'Might use them.'

'Miracle the mouse-people didn't grab them' said Juno as we stepped out of the gloom of the hall into the gloom of the day.

We were both quiet on the walk into college. She was trying out line-readings under her breath, I was sick wondering what to do. I couldn't show it to her, not today, it would wreck her head. But she'd want to know, needed to know. And when I did tell her, I'd have to tell her I hadn't told her. Beside me, Juno mumbled the word hopeless with different intonations. Hopeless. Hopeless . . . Hopeless? Hopeless!

Fucking great help you are, I thought.

Juno actually took notes during the lecture. Unbelievable. What in God's name was she doing at a lecture the day before a first night anyway? Jesus Christ. An actress at a lecture. It was unnatural. I knew non-speaking extras in lunchtime pantomime who'd repeated the year on the back of it. I invested the fifty minutes in circular argument with myself. As we left the lecture hall, I didn't even know what subject it had been in. Our fellow scholars dispersed in a cloud of complaint. I caught the word 'potato'. Ah, History, I thought to myself.

'I'd better go to rehearsal' said Juno.

'Grand' I said. 'Good luck.'

'See you back at the flat' she said.

She walked away, looking so heartbreakingly vulnerable and delicate and innocent I felt fear rise again like sick in my throat. I went straight round the back of the porters' desk to the lift and up to the second floor.

In the English Department toilet I sat on the closed lid. I rested my forehead against the cubicle door till the tide of nausea went out. Then I rooted in my bag for the envelope, found it between the pages of *Catch-22*, and took it out to look at properly. Same small, white, nondescript envelope as before. Typed, same as before. No stamp this time, to let you know he'd physically been at your door. It was odd how I knew without even opening it. It was odd how we could tell so much from so little. From absences.

Then I read the front of the envelope again. No. No I didn't know.

Juliet Taylor, it said in neat type.

14 McDonagh Quay,

Galway.

68

It said everything you would expect. About me, about what he wanted to do to me. About what he would do to me.

He described clothes I had worn, things I'd done, to let me know how close he'd been. It was very clever. I would have preferred the ravings of a madman. He described only my actions in crowded places, things I'd done often where anyone could have seen me, where hundreds were, that narrowed down nothing. A walk on the prom. Shop Street, watching buskers. And the language was deliberately flattened, dead. No adjectives. No floweriness. No style. Cold descriptions of actions. What he could have done to me. What he had done to others. What he would do to me.

What he was going to do to me.

69

By the time I got to David's office I could hardly see.

The door was unlocked, I pushed through and inside. The opening door smacked into a small heap of paperbacks, they tilted and slid, pushing the door back, half closing it, half blocking it.

The room was dark. The blinds were drawn against the heavy overcast. Some sort of underfloor heating had come on automatically and the air was stifling. There were no controls visible to turn it off. David's chair seemed empty in the gloom.

I closed the door behind me and started to pick up the paperbacks and stack them, all the same cover, familiar. *Heart of Darkness.*

Heart of Darkness.
Heart of Darkness.
Heart of Darkness.

When I'd finished I sat on the grey nylon carpet-tiles in the grey half-light. Then I lay down, bunching my fists under my cheek to keep my face away from the dead, dusty smell of the floor. With the dead air rising forever from the warm floor past my knuckles and my face, I waited for him.

When I woke up my jaw was stiff and my mouth was half-open, harsh and dry. I lifted myself out of a dream like a swimmer out of a river, and forgot the dream at once, a place, a face, and gone. My fingers tingled as the blood returned, my knees cracked as I stood. I walked to his chair and sat down in it. I swivelled it till my right knee hit something under the desk, then I swivelled back till my left knee hit something. The action of the chair was totally smooth, no squeak. I reached out and picked up a plain blue mug, brought it to my nose. Coffee. Cold. I touched the lip of the mug to the hollow under my nose, brought it down to my lips. Cold. I tilted it and sipped some of his cold black coffee. My dry mouth moistened. I held the mug to my lips, rolled it slightly against my teeth in a cold kiss.

I wrote him a note, and left.

70

The first night was very well attended, by Dramsoc's appalling standards. More than forty people were milling around the draughty shed of the IMI by the time I arrived. With the crowds Dramsoc traditionally got, milling wasn't an available option. It was not unknown for Dramsoc productions to pull in audiences insufficient in number not merely for milling, but for the playing of a decent game of snap, or, by premature close of run, solitaire.

This crowd milled, though. I brushed the rain out of my hair, thought of fixing it up a bit, didn't bother. I hadn't seen Juno all day, as the entire cast and crew had been busy making nine or ten hours' worth of last minute changes. I stood in the doorway and looked around.

The IMI was a disastrously bad theatrical space, smack bang in the grand old tradition of bizarre and inappropriate Galway venues. They've ruined Galway now of course with their modern theatrical spaces, but in my day it was all sheds, pubs and garages, oh beautiful it was.

Strictly speaking, the IMI wasn't a shed, it was three sheds, all enormously long, enormously high, enormously narrow, and parallel. Ideal for, say, the mass production of railway trains complete with carriages, it made for a tricky theatre. Only used for drama when the Aula was unavailable, and entirely empty but for pigeons the rest of the time, it was, as one might say, a Challenging Space. Juno had told me of the problems the venue posed, and I could see what she meant. The speed of sound being as slow as it was, you couldn't really use the full length of the place. By the time a line of dialogue had made its lonely way from the front of the shed to the back there was always the danger that the language would have evolved and the audience's descendants wouldn't understand it. Of course you could always bunch everybody up one end, with the audience huddled round the footlights for warmth, but the enormous ache of space behind them made them nervous. It was like watching a play with your back to the steppes of Central Asia. People kept looking around into the darkness to their rear, thinking they'd heard a wolf.

So a smaller space had been compromised into being, with a flimsy partition closing off the far end of the first shed, with behind it even flimsier, jerry-built raked seating that left splinters in you, and a small stage. A cosy space. Apart from the odd pigeon flying over the partition and into the lights, it seemed to work.

As I stood in the IMI doorway then, what I looked into was a kind of giant, fluorescent-lit reception area, with the actual 'theatre' down the far end behind its partition. Along the left wall were scattered, at large intervals, huge closed doors behind which lay the next enormous shed, behind which again lay the third of these absurd empty cathedrals dedicated to some industrial God in which the People had long ceased to believe. I felt somewhat dizzy on the brink of even this one vast room and was glad the doors weren't open into the others.

Forty people, no matter how hard they milled, weren't going to fill all this space, so they'd sensibly decided to concentrate on the area just inside the door. Gemma was helping out by selling coffees. I greeted her with relief.

'Hiya Gemma, is Juno around?'

'Juliet, how're you, she's not. It's nearly starting, I'd say they'd be backstage, pissing themselves. Do you want a coffee, for nothing?'

I took it. The thin plastic beaker was impossible to hold without burning your hand. I quickly put it back down on the black formica tabletop, without spilling much. 'Thanks' I said. 'Good crowd.'

'All the blaggards who dropped out of *Cavalcade*' said Gemma. 'Coming to bury it, but they'll stay to praise. I've seen the dress rehearsal. It works. They know their lines. Even the long ones. All the way to the end. You wouldn't believe how fucking rare that is, they all smoke too much dope in Dramsoc to be memorising anything.'

A woman by the left wall cleared her throat in that I've-an-announcement way. We all looked over. 'The play is about to begin, so if you'll take your seats . . .' People began moving obediently toward the partition at the far end. 'Ah, excuse me, sorry.

Tonight's performance is taking place in the *middle* unit, not, ah, in this unit as is usually the case. Just use this door here, and you may sit where you like. You may move the chairs if you wish, and of course there's no smoking anywhere in the building, is there Joe?'

She looked over at the UCG security man standing by the front door. Several people laughed and he cheerfully put his hands up, palms out. 'Nothing to do with me' he called back, and people laughed again.

The big door was swung open from the inside by two people, one of whom I recognised as the play's lighting technician, from Juno's pointing him out to me the week before. The two scurried back into the dark, to their positions I supposed. I felt a little tingle of excitement. And then I felt a hand on my shoulder, heard a pleased voice. 'Juliet!'

I turned. 'Michael! I was wondering if you'd come.'

'Ah, had to see her first night, fuck Druid.'

'She'll be delighted' I said.

'Coffee, Michael?' said Gemma.

'Bless your bones, Gemma, no. I've had a gallon of it today.'

A familiar figure passed behind Michael, heading for the queue. Shite. Dominic. I'd been dodging the Tampon Kid for weeks. I was suddenly mortified by memories.

Michael was saying goodbye to Gemma. We began to drift towards the doorway. In the queue ahead of us Dominic could be seen glad-handing the faithful and soaking up the good lucks and best wishes. The last back slapped, he turned and began walking towards us. I grabbed Michael's hand and as Michael gave me a startled look I whispered 'So tell me all about Arsenal' and stared adoringly into his eyes.

'What the fuck are you on about, woman' said Michael, baffled, as Dominic tried to catch my eye, failed, and turned back. I kept up the adoring gaze a moment longer just in case.

'Oh, nothing' I said, dropping Michael's hand. 'Got a sudden craving to learn about football. It's gone now.'

Dominic disappeared through the dark portal. Horrified at my cowardice, I felt terrible, but not half as terrible as I would have felt trying to hold a conversation with Dominic.

As we handed our tickets to the woman who'd made the

announcement I remembered I'd left my coffee on the formica table. Oh well. It'd probably be cool enough to pick up by the time the play was over.

We walked through the doorway. A dim light came from our right, away down the far end, where I could just about make out traces of a human settlement. We walked towards the light.

As we approached it we came across the occasional chair, then couples of chairs and finally clumps of chairs clustered close to what had to be the playing area because it was up against the back wall. We picked seats and sat next to each other. The rest of the audience lay shipwrecked all about us, sat scattered among groves of black plastic chairs that rose from a Ukraine of concrete floor. Dominic had obviously decided to go for the steppes of Central Asia option.

I looked nervously into the darkness behind me for wolves.

71

It worked. The great void at our backs had pushed us up timidly into the tiny and only oasis of light and what went on in that light over the next hour worked very well indeed.

Dominic had casually turned the play on its head, and with Juno as Clov and himself as Hamm he had made the play a giddy hybrid, both cold and warm, desolate and erotic. I had read Juno's copy in an hour the day before, and thought it harsh and sad, the humour funny but freezing. It was without hope, without sex, without love. It was a wry essay on aloneness and death.

Changing Clov from male to female gave a bizarre, sexy sitcom spin to the play, lines were played for a warmth that simply wasn't there. It was very unsettling. A ghost of sensuality simply shook the play apart. They were talking about death and acting about life. I couldn't tell if Dominic was a directorial genius or simply didn't understand the play.

Juno made my heart hurt. I had no idea if what she was doing was acting, or if she was any good. I just watched her with helpless, hopeless love. She seemed to me to be simply herself, but somehow, under the lights, speaking those words that weren't hers, she hurt my heart. I became so painfully aware that she wasn't me that I almost rose from my seat in a panic the first time she left the stage, for fear she would never reappear, because she had become completely unpredictable to me under those lights. So utterly herself, so utterly alien. If you don't understand, that's alright, I hardly understood.

Dominic was very, very good.

What the bare words were saying and what the actors were saying without the words were totally different things, and yet it held somehow together, and that could be put down to Dominic. He was simply a tremendous actor. The actors playing Nell and Nagg were weak, but it didn't matter. They were irrelevant. Dominic and Juno burned.

It wasn't perfect, it wasn't a revolution in theatre, I've probably enthused too much and I've skipped over the flaws. But it was so much better than I think anyone in the audience had really expected and it really had something good at the heart of it so that when it was over we rose without thinking to our feet and applauded until several pigeons, awoken and distressed by the noise echoing and re-echoing through the sombre shed, flew the length of it and passed low over our heads with a whoop of wings into the lights of the stage, which lit them serene for an instant before they flurried and panicked their way back into the darkness of the girders overhead. Their sudden appearance out of the light made the actors duck in the middle of their third curtain call so that they and the audience laughed and the tension and the applause and the crowd slowly dispersed, everyone talking excitedly like they'd just come out of an adrenaline-pumping action movie, not a Beckett play. Or were all his plays always like this? My God, was it the play? Who'd hidden this from me?

Michael went to congratulate Juno, but I was too moved and confused. I walked out into the reception area, where Gemma was packing away the coffee machine. 'Isn't it great?' she said when she saw me.

'Oh yes' I said. 'I'm all . . . I don't know how I feel.'

'It's doing two things at once, isn't it?' Gemma said. 'They don't let you settle. I loved it, I snuck in down the back. Better than the dress rehearsal, the crowd makes it.'

'It wasn't at all what I expected' I said. 'It was . . . oh, it was lovely. Michael's gone to tell Juno she was great.'

Nonsense phrases were going through my head, She isn't me, I'm all alone; I felt exhilarated and sick. Little groups and couples stood about talking.

'Have you seen David?' I said.

'David who?'

'Hennessey.'

'No. Why?'

'Nothing. I just thought he might be here.' I looked around. 'Did Conrad not come?'

'Back on the bottle.'

'Oh no.'

'It's not unusual.'

'Juno likes him.'

'I know, it's her has him back on the booze. Upset he made a mess of things between her and Michael.'

'Oh, that's terrible, it wasn't his fault.'

'Ah, nothing's ever anybody's fault. Don't we all mean well?'

I didn't know what to say. The play had unsettled me, my mind was all over the place.

'I think your coffee's cool enough' said Gemma.

A shockwave of nervous energy arrived, immediately followed by Dominic.

'Did you like it, did you like it?' one each for Gemma and me. Juno and Michael washed up in his slipstream as we assured him we did. They looked good together but they didn't look right. It wasn't fixed. The trust thing. 'Wasn't it great? Wasn't it great?' he cackled, the stereo effect still on. 'I want to marry Juno, I'll have my bed extended.' His glee erased my unease. We'd forgiven each other without talking about it. If he was over it, so was I. A sigh of rich relief.

'What . . . did you *do* to it?' I asked, and he understood immediately.

'We betrayed the text' he said, hopping with glee. 'We did the dirty on Beckett. We flooded the whole fucking play with affection and love. Oh, he'll be rotating like a chicken on a spit tonight. We didn't change a bitter word of it, but did you see, did you get it, didn't we fill it with life, fill it with love? Because he was wrong, he was wrong, he was wrong about *the whole thing*. I love him, a genius, but wrong. Life is wonderful, he was talking beautifully out of his terse, eloquent arse. Come on, College Bar for a pint, fuck the Students' Union coffee machine Gemma, leave it, they're just being pricks wanting it back every night, fuck 'em, Jesus, forty-six paying fucking customers, it's the *Batman* of Dramsoc openings, it's *Gone With the* fucking *Wind*, to the Batmobile, come on, before they stop serving, come *on*.'

72

I was standing outside his office when he arrived after his last lecture of the day. 'You didn't come to the opening night . . .' I said as he said 'Juliet, I only just got your note . . .'

We stopped. 'Go on' I said.

'I wasn't in my office till this afternoon, Dad had a bad night, he's fine, but I took yesterday off . . . you said you wanted to talk, was it urgent?'

I felt a peculiar reluctance to speak. I didn't have the energy to start this conversation. If I didn't mention the letter to anyone, then it wasn't yet real. It had no consequences. The pain didn't have to start. Please God put this off a little longer. 'No' I said. 'No.' And suddenly, 'Do you want to buy me a coffee?'

'God yes, love to, but I can't' said David. 'I'm a man on a mission, I'm just collecting some discs and I'm gone.'

My face fell. Well, OK, I could have hidden my disappointment if I'd wanted to, so strictly speaking it didn't fall, it was pushed. Even David, noted insensitive oaf, callous swine and casual breaker of my young heart, noticed. I'd pushed it pretty hard. 'That was the wrong answer, wasn't it?' he said.

I nodded glumly.

'Give me another go' he said.

'Want to buy me dinner somewhere expensive?' I said vindictively. He laughed. I stuck my tongue out at him. Flannery Ryan came round the corner and walked past, pretending not to see us. I left my tongue out and rolled my eyes. David snorted with amusement and turned to stand beside me, sticking his tongue out at Flannery Ryan's retreating back till Ryan disappeared round the next bend.

We turned back to each other, still sticking our tongues out. I crossed and uncrossed my eyes at him in a fashion meant to be comic. The English Department secretary came round the bend around which Flannery Ryan had just disappeared, and gave us a very startled look. David, to his eternal credit, continued to hold the pose. 'Weh dust stigging ow tongues oud ad ead udda,' he explained in a casual aside as she passed.

'H'llu' I said politely.

'Good work, keep it up' she said, and continued on and around the corner.

We went back to normal. 'No time for coffee or an expensive dinner right now' he said, 'but you're an idle student with nothing to do for the next hour or two aren't you?'

I looked at my watch, checked the position of the sun, and consulted my folder of notes. 'Yes' I said. 'Why?'

'You can join me on my mission if you like, it's a boring one.'

'Gee, thanks.'

'Well it won't be as boring if you come along. I can drop you back in town in an hour or so.'

'Fine. What's the mission?'

'A friend of mine's gone to a wedding in Sligo, and I have to feed his fish.'

'You turned down coffee with *me* to feed somebody's *fish*?'

He grinned. I didn't. Gah!

'If I don't feed his fish before five o'clock he might lose his job. Come on, got to run.'

He grabbed his discs out of the office and we ran.

73

The bay was like glass as I lay on my back in the moving boat and in the chill blue sky white flecks of gulls circled high.

'*How* many fish?' I said again.

From the wheel David looked back at me. He groaned. 'Between twenty-five and thirty thousand. *Must* you do that?'

'I want to get a tan' I said.

'We are, you realise, some few months away from summer.'

'I don't mind. The sun's out. I'm hardy.'

'Indeed.'

In fact it was quite cold, but the warm glow of pleasure from winding up David more than compensated for that.

'Are *you* hardy, David?' I said in my best Lauren Bacall. The back of his neck slowly went red.

'Almost at the cages' he said after a while. I sat up on the bags of pellets I'd been lying on and looked. It was very unspectacular; a large, dull, floating, metal walkway with a safety rail, forming a big rectangle, maybe thirty yards by twenty. Black and orange plastic floats seemed to be keeping it all just above the water and there was an impression of bulk beneath it, of suspended structures. The entire thing rose no more than three feet above the calm surface of the bay.

'They call this a farm?' I said, disappointed. I think I'd expected acres and acres of . . . something. Fences, sticking out above the water. Floating barns of indeterminate purpose. A windmill on a raft to power . . . whatever. Electric fences for electric eels.

'Fish farms are as dull as it gets' said David apologetically. 'Some metal cages and a couple of anchor lines. I told you it was a boring mission.'

'Who's getting married?' I asked.

'Hey? Oh. An old girlfriend of Eamonn's. They're good friends. This is one of his more reasonable excuses for skiving off.

Sometimes I get a phonecall from Donegal at four in the morning and it's Eamonn saying, Can you feed the fish before ten a.m.? I'm stuck in the middle of a poker session.'

'And you do it?' I said.

A shrug. 'He's a friend. His boss is a very decent man, an old friend of my father's actually, but he's very intense, very uptight.'

'So unlike you' I interjected.

'Ouch . . . he expects Eamonn to do everything by the book, but Eamonn . . . is not a big fan of the books.'

'So he's your bit of rough' I said helpfully. 'A horny-handed son of the sea-soil. An honest working man. The two of you have a couple of jars and talk about greyhounds and hurling, and none of your booktalk.' I felt skittish, my mood was light but fragile.

'Mmm' said David as he concentrated on bringing the boat in to the floating walkway. He looked lovely in the watercolour light of a sunny spring afternoon, silver ripples of light racing across his face and neck, under his chin, from the sun on the rippled water. I wanted to kiss him and I wanted to kick him overboard. His idiotic scruples and his dumb idea that he was somehow protecting me, and protecting himself. From *what* for God's sake? Nobody move, nobody get hurt.

The boat touched the metal frame, softly, and the whole structure rang deep like a low bell. The water shivered inside the frame.

David tied the boat loosely to the handrail, nose and stern. 'Shift, you' he said, not looking at me, and began to heft the big bags of fish-food pellets over the gunwale and the handrail and onto the walkway's metal mesh floor.

I stood behind him, doing up my buttons. When I'd done up the last one I swung back my right foot till the sole touched the side of the boat. I thought for a second. Looked at him, heaving another bag over the gunwale. The gold of the sun in his hair. The tight curve of the sober black jeans over his almost perfect behind as he bent to lift the last sack of food. Better than almost perfect. Perfect.

I kicked him as hard as I could.

He gave a little dance of wordless pain, which lasted for some while.

'*What* the . . . *giddy* . . . *blazing* . . . *hell* was that about?' he came up with eventually, leaving the realm of wordless pain rather slowly, a painful word at a time.

243

'It's all right' I said consolingly. 'I feel much better now.'

'*Jesus.*'

'Your face has gone very red' I said, interested. I looked closer. 'Oh, wow!' I said, excited, 'Tears of pain! I thought that was just a book thing.'

'That' he said and breathed deeply for a moment, then another moment, '*hurt.*'

'Well it was either that or kiss you' I said. 'And I knew you didn't want me to kiss you. So I *had* to do it. For your sake. Don't worry, I've got it out of my system now.'

'Good . . . to hear.'

'Actually, I didn't think it was going to be quite that dramatic.'

'You got me . . . right on the tail-bone . . .'

'*Cool*, it felt like I'd hit something solid alright. Hey, if you break your coccyx, can you end up with a paralysed, you know, arse? I mean, medically, could you walk around and everything but not feel anything in your bottom ever again?'

'Interesting . . . question, Dr Taylor . . . I'll get back to you . . . on that one.'

I skipped nimbly over the gunwale and rail, and onto the walkway beside the pile of sacks. Their weight tilted the structure almost imperceptibly in the water.

'What's keeping you, come on, I wanna feed the *fish*.' I did a childish impatience dance.

David wincingly joined me. I was glad he wasn't mad at me. I'd have been furious. 'Glad you're not mad' I said.

He waved a pained, dismissive hand. 'Useful research' he said. 'For my thing on pain in fiction.' His breathing was almost back to normal now, and a healthy paleness was returning to his cheeks.

'How's that going?' I said. 'I loved the bit you showed me.'

He began lifting a sack, winced. 'It's going quite well.' He turned and very, very gingerly sat on the sacks, then lay back across them, shielding his eyes from the sun. 'Excuse me a moment, I think I'll rest for a minute or two before I try that again.'

I leaned on the handrail and looked out across the vast sea at the vast sky. I covered one eye with my hand until my perspective went and the sky looked like a distant cliff of infinite height rising straight up from the flat ocean.

'Tell me more about pain' I said.

'Pain in fiction?'

'Whatever. You're the expert.'

'The surprising thing' he said in a dreamy voice from behind me 'about pain in fiction . . . is that there is so little of it. Physical pain hardly exists. Writers are by and large only interested in psychological pain, distress and trauma. Physical damage and the feeling of it, the sensation of actual pain . . . is seldom described, analysed or discussed. Psychological pain is described, analysed and discussed exhaustively, across the entire range of literature, across almost all genre boundaries. Psychological pain is at the heart of the novel, physical pain is absent.'

I noiselessly lowered myself to the metal mesh and lay along the walkway full length, my head on my arms. The motion of the platform seemed exaggerated by my closeness to the surface of the sea. The great blue desert of bitter salt water tipped and tilted gently around me. The suck and plash of the water beneath me was intimate, very close and quiet. Lazy. Overheard, not heard. Behind and above me, David sounded like he was talking to himself now as he lay on his back, facing the sky, arms across his eyes. He had adopted a pompous, self-mocking tone as though he were reading aloud something he didn't wish to be associated with. 'Is it that writers, then, have no interest in physical pain, or is it that they know nothing of it, or nothing special of it, and everything of psychological pain? Writers are not, by and large, of the warrior class.'

The sun flashed on something, and again, very bright. I squinted. A Coke can high in the water, not far away, rising and falling with us in the middle of the bay. It swung lazily around as a light breeze, gliding across the smooth rolling plain of the sea, caught on its aerodynamic snag. The bottom of the can swung to catch the sun in its silver dish, a silent bang of light out on the ocean. Dazzled me. The high-floating can and the sea and the light were effortlessly, elegantly beautiful. A sculpture by God. Just a little something he dashed off, blush-blush.

And a thought spoke quietly from under that thought, there is no God. God is a pattern we impose on the chaos. Just like beauty. Saying, there, look at that, there he is, in this moment. No, not that one. Don't look at that one. God's not there. Nor beauty. He's over here, look. The red can cupping the silver coin of light.

God's beauty. In the desert of salt that we can't see at all, that surrounds us.

'If writers knew pain, physical suffering . . . would they give it more weight, pay it more attention? It seems so. Dennis Potter, with his skin in foul revolt against him, Dick Francis with his shattered and mended and re-broken bones, they write of worlds where disfigurement is not simply a symbol and pain not just a metaphor, but also things in themselves, very real, very hard to bear. When they write of skin and bone, we worry about, we care about the skin and the bone, not just the soul within. Because the soul is also in the skin, not merely under it. And the soul is not merely supported on a crutch of bone, the soul is also in the bone . . .'

'Why are you writing a book about pain?' I said, out to sea.

No answer from the sea. No answer from behind me. I held my breath. Released it. 'Does your father . . .'

'Nothing to do with it. My father has absolutely nothing to do with it.' I heard him sit up. I didn't look around. 'If you think I'm writing this because my father is dying, or because he was saved once and now won't save himself, you're quite wrong. It's not a . . . displacement activity. My father has had a long, extraordinarily happy remission period and he has been hardly affected by the return of the cancer. He is certainly not in pain. When the collapse of his white cell count goes far enough he will . . . it will all be relatively quick, a week or two, and there's morphine and so on. He should have died months ago, who knows, perhaps, it's quite possible, he won't die at all. Of leukaemia. The body is a mystery, the cancer may have stopped, gone, come to terms with the body. He won't let us test him any more. We don't know what's going on in there. Perhaps nothing. Perhaps miracles.'

I turned to face him. 'The soul is in the bone' I said.

He smiled. 'Maybe it's on my mind a little as I write. But it's not . . . the reason.'

We looked at each other. I don't know why I felt the right to ask this, but I did. I don't know why I wanted to push him so hard, but I did. I knew it was a question that he didn't want to hear. I knew he'd forgive me. The question, anything.

'What happened to your mother?' I asked.

He said nothing. I looked away after a while. The Coke can had drifted further away. Beyond it, above it, out in the mouth

of the bay, the hard smudge of a cargo ship was still smaller than
the can to me. I waited till the can flashed again. Waited.

I sat up, crossed my legs under me. 'Sorry' I said.

'No' he said. 'No need.'

There was another silence. Suck, plash. A gull's high skree.

He started slowly. 'We aren't explained, you know, by a bad
thing. Something terrible, when we're young, it can change us,
of course it can, change the whole shape of our life, but it's still
our life. Under our control. The bad thing that happened, it
doesn't explain us. You know what I mean, don't you?' Yes, I
knew. 'And that bad thing, it is not an excuse for our life being
all wrong, we can't just say, well of course I'm unhappy, a terrible
thing happened long ago. We have a duty, to ourselves and those
around us, to deal with it and move on. Both are important. We
have to deal with it and we have to move on. If it is difficult, and
if it takes time, well what else is a life for?'

'That's very lonely' I said.

He shrugged. Shook his head. 'No. But to make room for the
other things in life, that task, perhaps in itself a lonely one, has to
be performed. Do you understand me?'

I nodded. I understood him.

'So if I say that I don't want to talk about something, that
doesn't mean it's not important, but it doesn't mean it's the secret
key to my life either. It just really might be that I don't want to
talk about it. That it's bad, but it's not that bad. Not that I'm
afraid to tell you, or unable to tell you . . . but that I'd just prefer
not to. That it's just something I'd rather . . . you know.'

I nodded. He looked at me for a moment. He half-smiled. I
half-smiled. 'Yes, I'm sure you do' he said. 'I'm sorry for preaching
again.'

'Didn't mean . . .' I trailed off.

'No, thanks for . . . let's change the subject before we both die
of embarrassment.'

'Let's feed the fish before they all die of hunger.'

'Oh my God, the bloody fish.' He stood up.

'How's your rump, Yugoslavia?' I said. A topical joke, from the
headline in that morning's *Irish Times*.

'A peaceful settlement is hoped for shortly' he said. 'There's a
knife in the toolbox in the boat, will you get it?'

I got it.

He hefted a sack and cut a corner off it with the knife. He began tipping the musty brown pellets over the inside edge of the walkway, through the unobtrusive wire tops of the cages. He swung the bag gently and the stream of food arced from side to side.

The water frothed and stormed with instant life, a thousand mouths and bodies battling to get to the surface and the food first, whipping the water to foam in seconds, and as David began to move along the walkway, pouring great swathes of food across the wire tops of the cages, the frenzy spread and followed him, cage by cage, the flat yards of water churned and bulged. By the time he reached the near corner of the walkway the sack was empty and all the sea between us spat and danced with life as the salmon broke the surface of the sea to feed, their bodies thick and supple with life.

74

I got to pour the second bag, and the fourth. They were heavy, and it was satisfying and right the way they lightened as you walked from cage to cage till their weight had disappeared.

When we had poured the last of the pellets into the hungry sea, we stood for a minute by the boat, unwilling to leave immediately. The surface of the sea grew calm under us as the last of the food sank, was eaten, vanished, and the salmon calmed and allowed themselves to drift lower in their cages until all that was left of them for us was that sense of bulk and suspended mass beneath us.

'Beautiful' said David. I nodded.

We faced the mouth of the bay. Nothing between us and America. To our left the water, to our right and behind us the low coast of Galway.

The cargo ship was closer now and beginning to swing about to make its approach to Galway harbour. We watched it, didn't bother talking. It was nice.

I got into the boat first, put the knife back in the toolbox. David started the engine, cast off. It was a quiet journey.

When we were almost halfway home 'Look' I pointed, 'A seal.'

David throttled back the engine. The seal rose and fell with the roll of the ocean as she looked at us, sixty or seventy yards away. David cut the engine completely and we drifted closer in silence.

The seal gave a hoarse bark and disappeared, to reappear ten yards away, the slick head and big eyes slipping up out of the water without the water seeming to notice. Not a ripple.

'Ah, too much beauty' said David. 'It hurts.'

I looked at the seal and she looked at me. To be so easy in the world that there was no barrier for you between the elements of air and water. To glide through life. For a stupid second I envied her. 'She has Juno's eyelashes' I said facetiously.

'What a coincidence' said David, 'so have you' and I was startled to realise that I'd actually forgotten that. I'd managed somehow to see the resemblance and make the remark without remembering that I too was inextricably involved in the equation.

The seal looked from me to David and back, barked again, and dived. When it reappeared briefly it was a hundred yards away and it didn't look back at us before vanishing again.

David restarted the engine. He offered me the wheel with a nod of his head. I took it and steered for the harbour.

We crossed the exhausted wake of the cargo ship close to the open harbour gates and entered the harbour as the ship was still tying up at the far side of the docks.

I gave David the wheel and he brought us in to the stone steps close to Juno's and my building. He held on to a rusted chain that looped along the stone face of the quay as I clambered out onto the steps.

'Do you want to come to see Juno's play tomorrow night?' I said. 'It's the last night, there's a party afterwards if you want . . . I mean, you don't have to go to the party . . . or . . .' I could see it in his face, in his shoulders. 'Oh David.'

'I'd love to. But I just can't.'

'Why, what are you doing.'

He couldn't even lie. 'I just can't.'

'Nobody move, nobody get hurt' I said. He breathed out but he didn't say anything. 'Go home' I said eventually and turned and started walking up the steps. When I looked back down he hadn't moved. He swallowed and his mouth moved. I was afraid. I didn't want to hear almost anything he was likely to say.

'. . . Thanks for thinking of me' he said.

I do little else, I nearly said, but was afraid he wouldn't take it as a joke. I turned back and kept going.

When I reached the top step I turned and gave a dramatic, *Gone With The Wind*, Cinemascope wave. He pushed the boat off, engine idling, and waved back. I could see the line of orange rust across his palm from where he'd held the chain.

'Safe home, Ulysses' I shouted down as he let the throttle out.

'We'll always have Paris' he shouted back sadly, and turned the boat towards the gates and open water.

We don't even have Galway, I mumbled to myself as I turned and walked towards my front door.

75

As Juno got ready to leave the flat for the IMI and the preparations for her final performance, I felt like our mum.

'Have you got everything? Are you sure now? Have you the acid somewhere safe? And the tapes for the party?'

Well, maybe not exactly like our mum.

'Juliet, stop worrying. Everything's grand. I'll see you after the play. If you decide to head in early, give us a shout, we're only running through the lighting cues with Eddie's replacement.'

'OK, I might. Good luck.' I gave her an awkward kiss. I was aware that there were other types of kiss on the market, which were supposed to be just as good or, theoretically, even better, but I didn't hold with them, not even with Juno.

The bell rang. 'That'll be Conrad' said Juno.

'Conrad?'

'He's only walking me there, we're going over some lines on the way in. He offered to help me. That's all.'

'I didn't say anything.'

'Yes you did.'

'God bless your hearing.'

She went.

I flicked on the radio, flicked it off again before I'd even recognised the song, a '*Da–*' of voice and drums immediately cut off by the little 'whump' noise the machine made when you turned it off.

I picked up one of Juno's books from the table, looked at the back of it blankly, might as well be in another, oh, it was in French, that explained it. I put it down.

Small pile of dusty tapes beside it, obviously not Michael's or there wouldn't be dust on them. *Hounds Of Love*! That's mine. Can't believe I haven't played it in so long.

I put on Kate Bush very loud, thought about my brother, thought about how big the world was, thought about nothing, danced around the room.

76

Was that the doorbell?

I banged the machine's stop button with my petite fist in the way that always made Michael cover his eyes with horror. The room was suddenly silent. It was like a huge pressure drop. I imagined I could feel my eardrums bend suddenly out like tiny sheets of rubber. A tiny avalanche in the stove. A click, a creak of the building settling.

The doorbell rang, loud as gunfire. I opened our door and ran downstairs, opened the front door.

'David'

'Juliet.' He produced something from behind his back. A rose.

'It's white' I said, disappointed.

He rolled his eyes in probably only half-feigned despair. 'What's wrong with white?' he said.

'You can't lecture me for ten million years on the importance of symbols' I said 'and then expect me to faint with delight over a white rose.'

'But, God damn it, it's a symbol of . . . *friendship, affection.*'

'It's a symbol of *grannies* and *nuns*' I said. 'It's about as sexy as . . . as . . .' I couldn't think of anything. 'You might as well have given me a bunch of lilies for my lonely grave, because I'm obviously beyond *passion* and *sex* and being remotely *attractive.*'

'Er, I wouldn't go quite that far' said David, blushing infuriatingly attractively. 'I mean, you're a red rose sort of girl', he bowed at me and I bowed back to acknowledge his concession of this important point. 'But if I'd given you a red rose, well, you might have interpreted it, ah, as . . .'

'Yup' I said, nodding vigorously.

'Hmm' he said. 'Yes. Well I would . . . if it's not too late . . . I would like to accept your invitation to the play. After all. If you haven't . . .'

'Come in, I'll cancel the gigolo.'

'Will you get a refund?'

'Oh I get freebies, I'm special. Come in, come in, it's freezing, I'll dress.'

He stood awkwardly by the stove the whole time I was dressing. I left my door open a crack as I dressed, but didn't hear any of the giveaway floorboards creak. When I came out he was exactly where I'd left him, he hadn't moved to sneak a peek. What did I have to do? At least he swallowed hard when he saw me.

'You like?'

'I like. Well, come on, granny, or we'll be late.'

Our conversation on the walk to the IMI was, disappointingly, as relaxed, enjoyable and friendly as it had ever been. It was agony. The backs of our hands brushed against each other once, as we turned into the college grounds, and we both jerked our hands away as though from a glowing hotplate, apologising profusely.

I made one last attempt. 'David . . .'

'I want to be friends' he said immediately, cutting me off. 'It has to be possible.'

'Some friendships shouldn't be, can't be, platonic' I said. 'It's in the fucking stars David, look up.'

He looked up. I looked up. The clouds looked like they started ten feet above our heads and kept going till they ran out of atmosphere. I nearly laughed. Nearly.

There was an extraordinary turnout, by Dramsoc standards. 'We're packing them in tonight!' gloated Dominic, buzzing past us as we queued to get in. 'We're within fifteen of the fire regulations!'

'Packing them in' was a relative term in the context of the IMI. Well, no, it was a lie. Or metaphor. We got good seats up near the front, as did everybody else.

The play was wonderful. Dominic was wonderful. Juno was wonderful. The new lighting man only missed his cues twice and I wouldn't even have noticed that if I hadn't seen the play already. The two in the bins had improved alarmingly.

I cried at the end, but then again, when don't I.

I went up afterwards with David to congratulate the cast. They were completely hyper. Dominic shook my hand for about a minute and said 'Jesus Juliet I'm fucking tripping already and I haven't touched a tab I've an ounce of Moroccan are you on for the party' in one explosive unpunctuated breath, and did not stay for an answer. We couldn't even get to Juno, who was buried in blushing admirers.

Dominic now wandered back from out of the darkness with a large dustbin over his head and most of his body while the thin, habitually unhappy boy who'd done the costumes followed him, grinning like a maniac and loudly slapping the dustbin with a very baggy old hurling or football sock in the county Galway colours of maroon and white, which lent it the look of a senior ecclesiastic's surgical stocking. Occasionally the words 'I'm a fucking genius!' boomed from beneath the dustbin. The stand-in lighting boy was hanging upside down by his knees from the lighting rig, kissing the tiny girl who'd played Nell, who was standing on her upturned dustbin to reach him. To my innocent eyes it already resembled a drug-debauched party, and the audience hadn't even finished leaving the theatre. Dear God, what would the introduction of actual drugs and the commencement of the actual party entail?

Juno finally broke free, came over, hugged me. David stood respectfully back as some serious sisterly bonding went on. I cried in her ear, told her how impressed I was. God, I nearly gave her another awkward kiss. Emotions, yuck.

'How's the Big Date?' whispered Juno giddily, nodding at David, when we'd both run out of ways of saying how much we liked each other without actually *saying* it.

'Oh shush' I whispered, squirming.

She squeezed me. 'No, really.'

'Terrible' I said, 'I took him to this play about dustbins . . .' She pinched me. 'Fine' I said, 'We're still . . . the best of friends.' Perhaps it came out a smidgen bitter.

'Oh Juju, you probably . . .'

'I don't want any words of wisdom or consolation' I interrupted, 'I'm fine, it's fine, it's wonderful, it's perfect, I don't even have to worry about getting pregnant. Mum would be delighted with me.'

Juno squeezed again. 'Well you're doing better than me, none of my harem have turned up.' A handsome, gangly boy, no doubt a friend of one of the company just arriving for the party, gave us a curious stare as he passed. Hugging each other and whispering, heads together, shielded by Juno's long hair, we must have seemed to present a curiously narcissistic, Sapphic spectacle, impossible to see as innocent in the context of the increasing debauchery all about us. I kissed Juno's ear and he looked hurriedly away.

'I'd say you could assemble a new harem in no time tonight' I said. Beyond Juno's shoulder, David seemed to be talking to Dominic about Beckett. Dominic was still wearing his dustbin, which made conversation more difficult, but he had also just walked into a pillar and fallen over, which made conversation easier. David had merely to bend and talk into the open mouth of the dustbin, from which Dominic's voice and feet emerged. For Dominic, the party had definitely begun.

'I don't want a new harem' said Juno. 'The harem I've got's difficult enough. I've got to go now and find Connie and drag him back to the party. He wouldn't sit through the play because of some stupid row with Dominic. He's probably sulking in his office, thinking the world doesn't love him. Unless he's sulking in the College Bar thinking the world doesn't love him.'

I thought about Conrad and his air of being stranded in a time he was afraid of and didn't understand. 'I don't think the world does love him' I said.

'True enough' said Juno sadly.

'Are you kissing him?' I said.

'No . . . it's not really like that' said Juno. 'It sounds silly . . . he's desperately sad, and I want to . . . save him, or something.'

'I know exactly the feeling' I said drily, looking at David leaning over, happily discussing Beckett with a drunken, talking dustbin.

Juno gave me a last kiss and swirled away in a cloud of happy blondness. Twins my eye. I lugged my raincloud over to David. Maybe I should dye my hair black.

'Juliet's legs, by all that's holy' boomed Dominic from his cave. 'Did you bring Juliet with you by any chance?'

I kicked his ankle. 'No' I said, 'She's at home practising dress-making and subservience.'

'Ouch. Good to hear. She'll make some happy man very lucky. If you see her tits, give them my warmest regards.'

I sighed and walked round to the bottom end of the bin. Kicked it a few times and came back.

David applauded ironically. 'Well put.'

'I thought it rather witty myself' I said modestly, in a refined accent not native to my tongue.

Dominic wriggled out of the bin clutching his head. 'You are a bounder and a cad, Flashman' he said, 'And there is no place for you in this school.'

The general theatrical air was having its usual effect on all our human voices. Irony, accents and references. I felt a mild welling of panic but fought it down. We do not have to be ourselves all the time, I reminded myself. It's not like I enjoy being me lately. And I remembered the letter, tang of sick suddenly in my throat. Nothing is real. I shook my head to shake the memory. Crushed it back into the attic. Forget it. Forgot it. Nothing is real until I say so. Nobody can impose their reality on me. Enjoy the party.

77

I enjoyed the party very much. The crowd swelled. Alcohol and those small foodstuffs unique to parties appeared in great profusion. 'Eat the profits!' cried Dominic, standing now on Nell's dustbin, Little Nell having left it for a Better Place. 'Drink the surplus! They'll only spend it on Brecht! For God's sake eat up!'

Everyone (bar the Dramsoc treasurer, a couple of the more responsible committee members and the unfortunate youth who'd directed the previous year's Brecht disaster) cheered. Trestle tables were improvised from chairs and the flats of the set. Somebody made a raid on Dramsoc's props, stored in the third unit, and these began to flavour the party. Nagg mounted an old black bicycle and cycled away from the party into the dark of the epic shed, ringing his bell.

The hugeness of the space began to be used, life spread out from the light of the stage and the twilight immediately around it and the party colonised the darkness. High above us, the ramshackle lighting box, strapped to the girders with a web of nylon ropes, had pulled up its ropeladder. It swayed in its cat's cradle (and elsewhere a spotlight above the stage blinked on and off in mysterious rhythmic sympathy) as the stand-in lighting boy and Little Nell got to know each other better.

'Is it a full moon or what?' I said in bemusement to David.

'Thank God' he said. 'I thought you were taking all this in your stride.'

We walked further into the dark to avoid standing under the shuddering lighting box. A distant tinkling sound grew louder and Nagg sailed back past us out of the darkness on his bicycle, ringing his bell. Swerving to avoid a group of revellers, he ran straight into a clump of chairs and lay among the ruins, still ringing his bell in the wreckage, till the revellers pulled him out, lifted him onto their shoulders and ran roaring toward the stage. Nobody they passed paid them a blind bit of attention.

Dominic wandered up wearing a Minotaur's head. 'Where's that sister of yours?' he said, offering us plastic cups of punch to supplement the plastic cups of punch we already had. We declined the offer gracefully.

'She's gone to collect a friend from the College Bar' I said, naming no names. I strongly suspected David wouldn't approve.

Dominic nodded the great bull mask and poured punch from his cups into our cups till our cups overflowed.

'What play do you plan to do next?' asked David, 'I'll definitely go to it.'

'Fillum' said the Minotaur. 'Fillum's the business. I want to make a filllllum.' He swayed and nodded. 'Or maybe an advert' he said. The party roared behind him. Someone had done something funny. The Minotaur with Dominic's body continued to nod. 'That's where Orson Welles went wrong' he said, nodding. 'He should have *started* with the sherry ads and *finished* with *Citizen Kane*. Then you'd have none of this poor Orson what a wasted talent bollocks. Poor eejit did it the wrong way round, that's all. You should save your triumph for the end. Only an eejit starts with it.' He abruptly stopped nodding. 'I'm drunk' he said. 'And I've a bull's head on me.' He dropped the empty cups he held, and carefully pulled the head off. He handed it over to me and stood rubbing his ears. 'That's a secret now, mind' he said. 'You won't tell?' We said we would not. He nodded again, pleased. 'I want to live Orson Welles' life' he roared into the darkness 'Backwards!' Then he looked at us, frowned, grabbed us both and pushed us together. 'That's better' he mumbled and, putting a finger to his lips, looked from one of us to the other. 'Shush now. Secret' he said, and turned and walked back into the crowd and the light.

I snuggled closer to David before he could pull away, and he said 'Christ' and dropped his cup.

I gave up.

78

I've probably talked enough about the party, haven't I? I should just take another deep breath and plough on.

We socialised, we mingled, we talked to other people, we talked to each other. We kept ending up on the edge of the party. When we'd washed up in the darkness at the edge of things for the third or fourth time, I said 'We're just not party people, are we?'

David had somehow acquired two tennis racquets and a ball. 'Tennis?' he said.

We walked further into the dark away from the noise, past couples writhing in the gloom, a drunken smiling boy trying to catch pigeons with a ladder and a butterfly net, and (I swear to God) a fire-eater, till we were in a limbo barely illuminated by the distant stage lights, and the occasional gout of blazing petroleum. The money Dominic had paid Security to patrol elsewhere had been wisely spent. Already not a fire regulation remained unbroken, there was serious talk of toasting marshmallows on a bonfire on the concrete floor, and the night was yet young.

'Something's up' said David. 'Something's up and it's not just me. That note, where you wanted to talk. It was something important, wasn't it? It wasn't just us.'

I was silent. David served. The ghostly ball floated gently down, bounced startlingly close. I lobbed it back. The pock . . . pock of our shots was very soothing against the ambient noise of the far-off party. I didn't want to answer.

I didn't want to make it real. Nothing is real until I say so. But that's not true.

Pock . . . pock. Zen tennis, with no scoring system and no attempt to beat each other, because if we lost track of the ball we'd never find it again.

OK, deep breath. Gemma appeared out of the gloom. 'Where's

Juno?' she said. I lowered my racquet, and the returning ball bounced past me and away into the dark.

'She's not back yet?' I said. I'd assumed she was around and I'd missed her in the crowd.

'Well I've not seen her and I've been looking' said Gemma. 'Some people were thinking of maybe taking it now so if you see her give me a shout, I'm over at the punch table.'

'Righto' I said. Gemma winked and left.

'David' I said, 'I might have a look for Juno in the College Bar, she's probably stayed on for a pint. She has some stuff Gemma needs.'

'Want a handsome gigolo escort?' said David, striking a pose with his racquet.

'No, you'll do' I said. We got our coats.

We found the door from unit two into unit one.

We found the door from unit one into the world outside.

It was raining. We found Juno.

79

Deep breath.

'Juno' I said.

'Oh Juliet' she said and collapsed into my arms. I held her weight as she cried. Her hair was soaking and it stuck to my face. My arms felt numb around her. My body felt numb. Everything felt numb except my face. I leaned back against the concrete wall of the IMI, holding up her dead weight as the rain patted the tarmac. David stood, pale eyes widening and then he blurred on me and I couldn't read his expression at all. My eyes were very hot, hot strokes on my cheeks from abrupt tears, and the cold, wet weight of her hair.

'Oh Juno, oh please, oh Juno'

'He wrote the letters, oh Juliet, he wrote them all, he wrote the *letters* and I told him, I'd told him, and he, and he never said'

'Who wrote the letters? Who wrote them, Juno?' David's voice didn't sound right, the words jerked out through a tight throat.

'Conrad Hayes, Conrad Hayes' her sobbing was shaking my body.

'Oh, sweet Jesus' said David and took a stride away from us.

'David don't *leave* me' I sobbed.

He froze, stuttered forward, came back to me. Us. His face was clenching and unclenching like a fist, his jaw and his mouth and his forehead.

'Oh Juliet' said Juno, sobbed Juno, oh God 'It felt all wrong, I knew, I knew it was all wrong, I should have known, it wasn't *nice* Juju it wasn't *nice* and when he'd finished it was all wrong he was drunk but that wasn't it that wasn't it at all, it was, I could tell, there was something wrong, oh God he wrote the *letters* how could he do that Juju?'

I couldn't say anything. I felt like I'd been in a carcrash and airbags had bloomed in an instant inside me as well as around me and now I was all protected and empty as the crash continued all about me.

80

David talked to her as I held her in my useless arms and my shoulder blades ground through my thin wool coat against the concrete wall behind me.

She talked into my shoulder to David and she calmed against me, growing lighter in my arms as the words came out of her and she could take back the weight of herself from me.

As David coaxed the words from Juno he placed a hand on my hands where they joined on Juno's back and my mouth opened in an O sucking in little shudders of breath, o, o, o, o, o.

When her tears were fully words again David grew silent but his hand on my hands meant I didn't have to open my eyes. I didn't want to open my eyes.

'We hadn't even really kissed, I never thought that was what he, we talked about plays, his play, the other times, but he was drunk and he wouldn't talk, he wanted, I said, well he wouldn't stop and I knew it was safe I said yes, so it wasn't . . . I could have said no, I'm sure I could've, and he wouldn't have, would he? But it felt all wrong, because it, he wasn't, I didn't like it but it was too late to say no, I thought it was in my head, I was imagining, I don't know, but the way he, and he didn't speak to me, I felt like I was someone else, and when it hurt he didn't, he didn't, oh Juju it wasn't like'

I couldn't bear it and my mind filled with visions to distract itself, to stop any more of this coming into me. I felt the ache of my shoulder blades against the concrete wall and my mind in one sharp moment transformed them into the stumps of severed wings, so that all the muscles of my back bunched and tensed at the vivid illusion.

David's hand clenched around both mine.

'. . . and when he'd finished, it was the place he sleeps in there, it's a terrible kip Juju' she laughed, which hurt me worse of course because it was her laugh in the middle of this, which made it real and I didn't want it to be real 'there's no bathroom even, he just walked out, he left me there and the smell of the pillows oh God I got up and I was, I don't know, I was restless or maybe, I don't know what you'd call it but I felt awful, it had all been wrong Juju, I mean he hadn't asked, you know, checked, it was like he didn't like me or that he didn't care and we'd been talking about, about the *weather* and *books* and everything yesterday and it was *grand* then, I couldn't think if I'd said anything wrong or what so I was, I wasn't happy and I sat in his chair at his desk and I rooted around in all the papers there, I'd never do that Juliet would I you know that but I felt all wrong and I wanted to know, I knew, I think I knew already does that make any sense to you' and I nodded yes and held her, so strange for me to be holding her, it wasn't meant to be like this, who would hold me up now if I took the full weight of her sorrow and what if I fell under it I'm so lonely can't bear this oh Juno 'Oh Juliet at the back it was all big envelopes with names and my name was on the top one and I pulled out these pages and the top one was the first note to me, with all these changes, the changes were the note I got, he'd written me a letter and taken out the long words and made it like the others and I thought, maybe it's only the first note, he just wrote the nice one it's a coincidence, the others, he couldn't, because I *knew* him for the last one how could anyone . . .' Oh Juno, how could anyone and all the muscles of my back tried to lift me free of it with my sister in my arms and her breath on my cheek was like the wind going past I had to open my eyes to check.

'And I read the other pages and he'd written all of them.'

She lifted her head beside mine so that she must have been looking at the concrete wall in front of her, or at nothing at all, or maybe she hadn't opened her eyes, I didn't want to turn my head to see. David was looking at me and his face was almost calm and I was glad because I'd been afraid when he'd begun to move away that he might do something terrible. Juno was calmer now. Everything would be fine.

'He had copies of the other letters he'd sent me and he'd copies of forms I'd filled in to sit exams and copies of exam rosters and some of my essays, things in different subjects, like a file on me.

And more stuff like in the letters, for himself. There were other envelopes like that, for other girls. And . . . oh Juju, he's started an envelope for you.'

'Oh, dear God' said David and took his hand from mine.

81

Juno laughed, an oddly little-girl laugh, as though she had been naughty and knew she shouldn't be laughing but couldn't help it. 'Shall I tell you what I did then?' she said. 'Oh, maybe, no I shouldn't have done this . . . I took his bottle of Jameson from the desk and I took all the acid tabs I had for the party and I put them in the bottle and shook it. And I crushed the little microdots with a biro and I put them all in too, folded a piece of paper and poured them in. Was I terrible? I wanted to hurt him or, I don't know. Was I wrong? It seemed . . . I got all the bits of paper out with the biro they were floating on top. And I left . . . I left the envelope with all the things about me, I left it on his desk, so he would know, I wanted him to know . . . It won't hurt him though will it? The acid I mean, all the acid in the whiskey I mean you can't overdose so, I mean . . . but,' she said with sudden anxiety 'It just seemed, I thought, I wanted to get him back, it was stupid wasn't it, I shouldn't have done that' she was upsetting herself oh don't, please don't 'But I'd said yes and I wouldn't have if I'd known so it was like, it was like he'd' oh don't Juno don't 'and if only he'd liked me, why did he have to do that when I liked him anyway there was no need to do that'

'I could have stopped him' said David calmly oh Jesus Christ, don't be part of this I love you 'This is all my fault. When Juliet told me you'd gotten these letters I thought it might be Conrad, because of things I'd heard about his time in Austin, rumours I'd heard here. But I didn't want to damn a man on hearsay, I talked to him, he swore on his honour, he was upset, I believed him. I had to apologise. I had to apologise. Oh, Jesus Christ. I could have stopped this. I could have warned you. I could have done more. I could have checked, told the guards. This is all my fault.'

'Oh, David . . .'

'How could you know? It's not . . .'

But he turned and walked away from us and as I followed he began to run.

82

Juno came and took my hand and I looked in panic from her to where David had gone, and back to her. 'He'll do something stupid' I said, but I couldn't leave her.

'Come on' said Juno and pushed her wet hair back off her face and together we ran, her hand in my hand, my hand in her hand.

83

It wasn't far from the IMI to the Quad.

We came through the Quad gate close behind David. He'd stopped running, we hadn't. The rain faded out as we ran, the fickle weather of Galway. The few people we'd passed had paid no more attention than usual to two girls running, hand in hand. As they'd paid no attention to Juno as she'd stood outside the IMI in the rain, afraid to go in, afraid to start crying, waiting for me to come looking and find her. The things she'd said, do you think I've told you everything? I had a sick, exultant sense of just how dark the world would be if we could see into the lives of all the strangers passing by us.

We caught up with him by the door at the foot of the tower, in the corner of the Quad. Light came from Conrad Hayes' window high above, as it almost always did. From the College Bar behind us came the muffled chorus of a Pogues song was it, yes, 'The Sickbed of Cuchulain'. I remembered the foggy morning I first heard Conrad Hayes, singing unseen from a window high above. And if that fog had lifted and he'd seen me then, would I have found myself befriended, would he have supervised my fraught exams, a pleasant and a helpful man?

'David' I said 'Don't'

'I have to talk to him.'

The door wasn't even closed, after Juno's flight. He pushed it wide. A dark space, dim stairwell rising.

'Please David, leave it, we'll call the guards, tell the department, they'll deal with it . . .' But we could see it in each other's eyes. He touched the tip of my nose sadly with a fingertip. Juno said nothing.

What charge, when it became a kind of rape only in retrospect? How subtle a law is required, for a violation where only the evil-doer knows at the time the truth and the depth of the evil? Letters, bad sex. Nothing.

I held Juno's hand and made no move to stop him as he walked through into the hall.

He took the stairs two at a time. I felt a tremble in my hand and couldn't tell if my hand was shaking in hers or hers in mine. I looked at Juno and brushed her hair back off her face again with my free hand. We followed David up the stairs into the dark. Through my head like an irritating jingle ran the title of a Browning poem I hadn't even read though I'd always meant to because I'd liked the title, *Childe Roland to the Dark Tower Came, Childe Roland to the Dark Tower Came, Childe Roland to . . .*

We followed David up the stairs into the dark.

How rich and dark the world would be if we could see into the lives of all the wives and daughters we call strangers passing by us.

84

A sense that we were now in a realm of sorrow and darkness shook me somewhat as we approached the final landing. My mind was, I think, a little loose in its moorings by now. Tears and adrenaline and high emotion had lifted me to an unstable peak from which the world seemed transformed. I think some sort of gap had opened up between all of us and the ground of the ordinary world.

But Conrad's actions had transformed the ordinary world, we couldn't fight him on the old ground, he didn't truly live there. Up here in the sorrow and the dark, we were perhaps right to allow the transformation of ourselves into these unstable things that came running up the winding stairs, somehow laughing. At what? God knows. God knew. I kissed Juno and she me.

A crashing sound as we came up the last steps to the final landing. It was only David's knuckles on a wooden office door. We ran up behind him, snorting back our laughter because it was too loud on the tight landing with its thick, still air.

No answer. Another clatter of knocks, incredibly loud on the landing. No answer.

David turned the handle and the door swung open, a thin crack of grey fluorescent light widened and a wave of light gushed over us, flooding the small landing, pouring down the stairwell into the dark. I watched David's eyes narrow and blink, before he took a step into the room. We followed.

85

Conrad Hayes sat in a leather armchair behind his desk. He faced us, with the window behind him framing chair and man against the black of the night sky. He clutched the arms of his chair with hands which were longfingered and strangely beautiful. His head was thrown a little back, the neck supported by the back of the chair. The resemblance to one of Francis Bacon's paintings of a screaming pope was at once hilarious and frightening.

His stare was so fixed that I thought he was dead until Juno moved uncomfortably beside me and his eyes followed her. Neither David nor I seemed to exist for him at all. His throat convulsed and we waited for him to speak.

'What have you done to me?'

A stale smell rose from the crumpled sheets of the camp bed along the right hand wall and my mind mixed it up with the terror in his voice, so that I thought for an eerie second that I could smell his terror. Juno couldn't look at him, buried her face in the hollow of my neck and shoulder.

'What have you done to me?' and now he was looking into my eyes and I knew with absolute certainty that in his mind he was seeing Juno as he looked on my face.

'What have you done to her?' said David quietly and Conrad's head jerked so abruptly round that a droplet of spittle at his mouth corner was left to drag across his cheek by the movement.

David had walked around the desk to stand by Conrad. The two now looked into each other's eyes along a line of sight as taut with tension as a yard of bridge suspension cable. Juno turned her face from my shoulder at David's question and looked at the tableau. Her hand tightened. Her hand in my hand. My hand in her hand. I was suddenly embarrassed, as though somebody would see us, frightened, holding hands at eighteen, and mock us. But David was looking into Conrad's eyes and Conrad was looking into the abyss. And I had a moment of, what would you call it? Secular clarity. An agnostic vision. I saw not the light, nor the opposite of the light, but . . . the back of the light, the light going elsewhere. I saw in this room, very clear, not the face of God but the enormous and distant back of His head. God was altogether elsewhere, vast, supervising the suffering in Africa and Asia, suffering the children to come unto Him. Working industrial miracles of suffering. Upping production. Making His quota. We, here, in this room, were too smallscale for the personal supervision of God. And, also, overqualified. We were grown-up, educated, European. We knew all about suffering, theory and practice. We'd read books on it. We could suffer without benefit of plague or hunger. We could suffer while wealthy and healthy. We had a genius for suffering. God trusted us to get on with it. He knew we'd see it through.

David sat on the corner of the crowded, messy desk and leaned down a little to bring his eyes level with Conrad's. Conrad looked back and from his acid-drenched and melting, drowning world whimpered 'Who are you?'

And David said in a calm and even voice with no trace of the bunched fury that had shuddered through him outside the IMI, 'Your conscience. A mirror. Nothing.'

And Conrad whimpered in genuine and frightening horror.

I couldn't look. My eyes dropped from his face, and my gaze snagged in passing on a word on a page upon his desk, in the centre of the mess. The loose page was the top page of a small stack, on an envelope. I reached my hand out cautiously into the electric field that overspilled the space between the two men, and picked up the top few pages. Behind me Juno started to speak, stopped. Handwritten. The ink was black and the writing very even, a good strong hand, well-formed letters, almost copperplate. I turned it round, and reread the first line, that had caught my eye.

My dear Juno.

'My' was crossed out, replaced with another 'dear'.

I know that you don't know me, and I make no claim to know you.

He had replaced the 'don't' with 'do not', simplified the 'make no claim to' as 'do not'. I read the original, in his beautiful old-fashioned handwriting, beneath the bleached and dead replacement words.

My dear Juno, I know that you don't know me, and I make no claim to know you. You will think this letter foolish, perhaps. So be it. All I wish to say is that on a recent day when my life had darkened to the point where I was contemplating quitting it, I saw you pass, you shone: I followed you. I know it is inexcusable, and had courage been equal to desire I would have thanked you then, but please accept even these coward's thanks. In contemplating you, I cured myself somehow. Your beauty pulled me through. That's all. And I thank you.

A love letter. Oh this will end in tears Conrad. I read the next sheet, the second letter, in the original, so beautiful, darkening, vicious, black with blood and hate. '. . . *I will have you like a whore. You will whimper on all fours . . .*' This will end in tears.

I looked at Conrad, my eyes dry. He had ceased whimpering, and was silent. He was listening now. David was speaking.

'I'm not here to punish you' said David soothingly. 'I'm not here to hurt you. I'm just here to show you exactly what you've done. To explain it to you so you understand. Because you've done a very terrible thing, Conrad. You've hurt a girl very terribly, you've made her afraid and you've made her cry, Conrad, you've made her cry. You've treated her as though she wasn't real, as though the hurt you caused her wasn't important, hardly mattered, didn't really exist.' Conrad's head jerked round like a damaged toy to stare blankly at Juno, at me, his eyes flicking, helplessly, and Juno couldn't bear to look at him and turned to me again, buried her face again in my shoulder, so that now Conrad looked straight at me with my short hair and my sister's face. He saw Juno in me and I felt curiously relaxed, as though that were entirely correct under the circumstances. As Conrad looked on me and saw Juno, David spoke of Juno and I knew (I could see it, as clear as a photograph) that the picture in his mind was of me.

'This girl is real' said David. 'The hurt you have caused her *exists*, just as much as this book exists.' He picked up and slammed down the *Concise Oxford English Dictionary* on Conrad Hayes' desk so that the empty Jameson bottle shivered on a swaying stack of paperbacks and Conrad's frightened eyes snapped free of mine to lock back into David's steady gaze. 'The hurt you have caused her stains this universe in which we all must live. You have caused real damage in the real world, Conrad. A damage you would never dream of doing to yourself. How could you conceivably have had any right to damage her, Conrad?'

'I'm sorry I'm sorry I'm sorry' said Conrad Hayes.

'Put that in writing, Conrad.'

Conrad groped for a pen on the crowded table without taking his eyes from David's eyes. The pile of books and the bottle fell to the carpet. A mug fell, and papers in a long, fanning slide that took them yards across the carpet. When he found a pen in the wreckage he brought it up to his face, into line with their eyes.

David nodded. 'Write a letter to all of them, Conrad. To Juno. To Juliet. A letter to all the girls. One you can sign your name to. Are you sorry you hurt them?' Conrad nodded and whimpered like a beaten dog. 'It's a terrible thing, isn't it, to deliberately add to the hurt in the world.'

Conrad nodded, 'I'm sorry I'm sorry'

'Write it down. Tell them you're sorry.'

'I'm sorry I'm sorry . . .'

Juno let go my hand and turned and walked to the desk. My heart slapped into my ribs but I didn't try to stop her. I felt like a ghost, invisible. Conrad turned from David to face her. Only the desk between them now. His face rippled with fear, a thing I had never seen, the muscles in spasm from his neck and the jaw under the trim beard to his forehead and temples. It was as though a stone had been thrown into his liquid flesh. The spasms passed, to leave a tiny muscle twitching under his right eye and another on his right temple.

I drifted closer, like a ghost. I leaned on Juno's shoulder, looking over, like a ghost in a waxwork museum, among the exhibits. Juno looked at Conrad and I couldn't tell what was in her mind. Conrad looked at Juno, and I didn't want to know.

The tableau unfroze. Conrad pawed a page from a pile of pages. It had a few lines of print on it, upside down to him, but he treated it as though it were blank. In a drugshattered hand, a debased, collapsing form of the perfect calligraphy of the original of his first and charming note, he convulsively wrote 'I'm sorry I'm sorry I'm sorry I'm sorry' until the words ran out onto the desk and he lurched his hand back for another line 'I'm sorry I'm sorry I'm sorry'

'You shouldn't have hurt them, Conrad' said David sadly, almost to himself.

'I'm sorry I hurt you I'm sorry I hurt you I'm sorry I hurt you' wrote Conrad, line after line, until the writing reached the typed lines and ran over them. They were the last lines of a poem I half-knew, by Yeats. Juno reached behind her to find my hand as Conrad wrote 'I'm sorry I hurt you' again and again in a broken hand across the scrap of Yeats turned upside-down to him,

> 'Transparent like the wind
> I think that I may find
> A faithful love, a faithful love.'

It was perhaps the most savage thing I had ever seen, but I could not make myself intervene, to stop it. Because I did not want to stop it. Because I believed it was just.

86

'Now sign it' said David. Conrad's hand fluttered over the packed page before finding a space where two scribbled lines of his apology had diverged to form a long blank island of white. He wrote his name on the island. David picked up the sheet and looked at it. He nodded. 'Very good, Conrad. Now give me the envelopes, and we can leave you in peace.' Conrad looked up at David and his mouth moved. David leaned down again to his level. 'Yes, Conrad?'

And Conrad said quietly, in a child's voice, 'Am I in hell?'

David shrugged sadly. For the first time tears appeared in Conrad's eyes, welling on the lower lids and spilling down his cheeks into his beard. David stood up, holding the apology, and walked around the desk to us.

'Here you are' he said to Juno and handed her the page. She let go my hand to take it from him in both her hands. 'Thank you' she said.

'Am I being judged?' said Conrad from the far side of the desk. His voice had grown even smaller. He was collapsing into himself like a dying star, the words were barely able to escape him now.

We looked at him. I felt something like pity, or compassion, at the last. Very late. I am not as kind as I would like to be.

'Is this judgement?' he asked again.

'No' said David. 'We have no right to judge you. Only you can judge yourself.'

Conrad closed his eyes. He nodded, and tears fell to the cluttered desk. Opening his eyes again, he pulled out the top drawer almost all the way, pulled out the envelopes and piled them on his desk. He looked up at Juno. At me. At Juno. 'I'm sorry I hurt you' he said. 'I'm sorry I'm sorry I'm sorry'

David gathered Juno's pages, I gave him those I held. David reached for the pile of envelopes and Conrad shrank back in his

chair, so small a man now, so broken. David picked up the envelopes, turned to go, saw the name on the top envelope now. My
name. He hesitated, looked from it to me. 'And you've received
a letter haven't you?'

'. . . Yes.'

'That was what you wished to tell me, why you wished to meet
me'

'. . . Yes.' His face asked me a question. I didn't know the
answer. 'I was afraid . . . ? Of . . . what you would do.'

He nodded and slipped the slim single page out of the envelope,
still looking at me.

'Childe Roland to the dark tower came' I thought, in lieu of
thinking.

David read the letter.

'You two go on, I shall join you' he said when he had finished,
and handed me the letter, the letters, the full envelopes. There
was something so certain in his voice that we did, without thinking.
Juno held my arm as we walked out the door, leaving it open
behind us to spill light down the stairwell as we walked down the
shadowed stairs. Behind us we heard the murmur of a voice.
David's voice, conversational. A moment of silence. A murmur of
reply.

And then his voice was like a thundercrack, an avenging angel's
roar, a weapon of execution. We were afraid and we ran, pursued
by the crash and echo of our footfalls through all the long spiral
down.

Outside in the rain we held each other. Then David came quietly
out through the great doorway and put his arms around us like a
brother or a father. 'It will be alright' he said and we walked
towards the Archway in the rain.

At the Archway I stopped. We stopped. 'What did you do to
him?' I said.

Drunks passed us going to and from the College Bar. 'Babe
alert!' shouted one. 'Babe alert!'

'I helped him come to his judgement' said David.

I looked up at the high window of the dark tower, to see Conrad
in silhouette against the light. Where first I heard him sing. Conrad
seemed to be staring up at . . . I looked up. Nothing. The bellies
of clouds. Darkness. David, looking too where Conrad looked,

spoke. Not his own words, a quote, his voice heavy, saturated with sorrow. '"Two things fill the mind with ever new and increasing admiration and awe, the oftener and more steadily we reflect on them: the starry heavens above and the moral law within."'

The featureless night poured past us. The mercury vapour lights that illuminated the Quad denied us the sky. I didn't mind. My neck stiff, I moved my head a little, to look again at Conrad, framed in the window.

I wanted to leave but couldn't, the night was unfinished.

'What is he doing?' asked Juno.

'Coming to judgement' said David. 'It's probably best if we leave.' But we didn't leave. Another drunken boy wolf-whistled as he passed us.

A girl and two boys entered the Quad behind us, swaying, joined us, looked up.

High above, Conrad, swaying, dark against the light, hands raised, looking up into the night.

'Too late' said David sadly, beside me.

As Conrad swayed behind the glass, he looked like someone underwater, in a flooded room, a drowning man.

'I'm so sorry' I said suddenly. To whom? I still don't know.

Conrad came towards us, then, and the window turned white and vanished and he was through it now and falling and all the shards and fragments of the shattered glass about him spun in the harsh light in a gush of diamonds.

His dark bulk with arms outstretched outpaced the glass and light and even as he fell I thought quite calmly, oh that is the air slowing down the smaller bits of glass, as the wheat is sorted from the chaff.

His dark arms outstretched he began to turn slowly in the air and then with the most astonishing shock for I had forgotten the inevitability of this he ran out of air and the sound as he hit the ground was strangely wet and muffled with drier sounds inside it, breaking sounds like plastic forks snapping in the canteen. He lay there, astonishing, and then the glass began to fall on him like diamond snow.

In the silence that followed the last of the glass the sky broke and it began to rain.

87

David rang the police from the porter's office inside the Archway of the Quad. He re-emerged to find us standing in the bright electric light of the Archway, out of the rain. In the Quad, under the rain and the mercury vapour light of the high lamps, people moved in ones and twos toward the body and away. Others drifted out of the College Bar to see. Joe from Security, who should have been at the IMI, quietly kept them back from the body with words I couldn't hear from here.

We stood there in the Archway, silent. Thinking, I suppose. No, not thinking. Adjusting. A lot to adjust to.

'I'm glad' I said. Juno leaned on me, nodded. I brushed her hair back from her face again and smiled at her. She closed her eyes and rested her head on my shoulder again.

David glanced over at the body in the rain. 'They're coming. Five minutes.' He looked exhausted and depressed. 'I failed at everything' he said, 'I couldn't save you, I couldn't save Conrad . . . I've misjudged and I've messed up everything, God . . .'

'No you didn't' said Juno.

'David, you haven't' I said. His hands were fists. We put our hands on his hands. 'How could you have known?' I said. 'What more could you have done?'

'I've practically killed a man.' His fist jumped in my hands.

'*No.* Don't be stupid. Shut up' I said, furious. '*He* did it. *He* lied and he deceived and he hurt Juno and now he's done this awful thing to *himself.* He did it. Not you.'

'He was obviously out of his mind with guilt and fear and I goaded him, I pushed him . . .'

'If he felt guilt it was because he was guilty, and he felt fear because he was right to be afraid. Don't be so *stupid* David. Everyone can't be a victim. He was a *bad* man, David. So you told him to judge himself. Well, he judged himself. And I'm *glad.*'

David shrugged and rubbed a hand over his face. 'When the police come' he said to Juno 'don't tell them you put the acid in his whiskey. It's a class "A" drug and the coroner is likely to judge it contributed to his death. You can't be associated with it. If he took it himself it's straightforward guilt-induced suicide by a depressed man about to lose his reputation, made all the more likely to do something foolish by drink and drugs. There's no need for you to mention the acid.' Juno nodded. 'Everything else, if they ask, we tell the truth.' We nodded. 'We came to confront him, took the envelopes, left, and he killed himself. We've what's practically a drunken suicide note, a thick file full of reasons, and a Quad full of witnesses. I can't see them investigating this too thoroughly. But if you've any more acid I would strongly advise you to get rid of it.'

'No, I've none. I used it all.'

'What did you do with the paper tabs once you'd fished them out?'

'I wrapped them in a tissue in my purse.'

'Jesus. Well, flush them down the toilet or something when you get home. And don't blow your nose while the police are questioning you.'

88

In the event the police were a huge disappointment. Two of them eventually arrived, on foot. One was the young guard I had seen at the station, who had been talking to the traveller woman. He didn't recognise me and I said nothing. They seemed bored and depressed by the body and the circumstances, and hardly asked us any questions at all. The note and the envelopes and our story seemed to explain everything to their satisfaction. The position of the body met with their bored, sad approval. The several drunken witnesses, now much sobered, who had also seen the fall told their confirming stories. The guards didn't even bother to separate us all, to get our stories independently. I was astonished to realise, very, very late, that this wasn't a murder investigation. Despite all my words of reassurance to David I quite firmly believed he had essentially killed Conrad Hayes, that he had quite deliberately magnified and reflected Conrad's fear and hatred back against Conrad's disintegrating self. David knew he had carried out an execution. He had acted as a mirror, and a conscience. As he had promised.

But as the two guards put away their notebooks and an ambulance arrived quietly, with no sirens, I realised that even if the police had been in the room and witnessed everything, they would have seen only a suicide.

I walked out of the arch toward the body on the slick black tarmac, just short of the soft blue grass. Past the solemn couples, to the broken man.

His head looked half sunk into the ground, his skull and cheekbone shattered inside the skin. Diamonds flecked his clothes, his face. The blood pooled in his open mouth, a trickle ran from the corner. Something shifted inside him and a trickle of blood ran from the nostrils. Blood welled and filled his ear, flooded its curves, filled its pool to the rim and ran, and was slowly thinned from his face by the rain. I knelt. His face lay in a pool of blood and water. I looked into the dark pool. I studied Juno's face, my face, in the black mirror of his blood under the mercury vapour light. I could smell iron and urine.

'Ah, Miss' said the older of the two gardat from behind me. 'Miss'

I could hear the clink as the closed half of the big gate swung open in the Archway. Joe, letting the ambulance in. I stood and turned. Its blue lights pulsed out through the Archway ahead of its coming.

'Miss, if you could just move back a little' said the older officer in a kindly tone. Escorted by the two guards, I walked back and joined Juno and David. We moved aside as the pulsing ambulance passed us almost silently. It stopped by the body. Its blue light flashed around slowly, casting a tint all along the high walls of the Quad.

As I stood beside Juno she gave a mischievous little sneeze. I giggled and David glared at us which made me giggle more. The younger officer looked at me sympathetically. Obviously delayed shock. 'Are you alright love?' he said, trying to sound reassuringly world-weary and experienced but his voice went squeaky for no reason at the end. I saw the older guard give an amused glance across and I clenched my jaws shut to stop myself laughing. I gave a serious nod, bowed my head. I was alright, love.

89

The three of us walked out through the Archway. I was almost shocked, no, I *was* shocked at how normal the world felt. How unchanged.

'So back to the party then' I said. Juno and David looked at me. 'Joke' I mumbled.

'I should talk to Michael' said Juno, and then to me 'Will you walk me there?'

'Of course' I said. 'Oh God. Conrad split you up deliberately'

'I've judged Michael too harshly' said Juno, and I winced.

'Am I in the way?' said David awkwardly. 'If you want to talk or'

'God David, I'm going to hit you if you don't shut up apologising and being all soggy' I said, not as harshly as it sounds. I hope. 'You've just slain the Dark Knight in his tower for God's sake, don't be so modern and angsty about it.' I grabbed him by the hand as we walked so the three of us were linked, Juno, me, him. 'You were brilliant, he deserved it, you did no wrong. Shush. Help me walk Juno to Druid. There might be dragons.'

'Dragons are extra' he said, smiling. *Childe Roland to the Dark Tower Came*, I sang to myself, *Childe Roland to the Dark Tower Came*, everything's going to be alright. Anything can happen now. Everything can change.

90

When we got to Druid, Juno took both David's hands, and kissed his cheek in the warm foyer. 'Thank you for everything, for what you did' she said as he blushed. 'You were kind and brave for me, and anything bad that happened wasn't your fault. Juliet's right.'

'Nothing bad happened' I piped up. 'I'm glad the *bastard* is dead', which wasn't very Christian of me but had the slender virtue of truth. A woman in paint-spattered overalls, emerging from the box-office just in time to hear me, gave me a strange look and I gave her a strange look back. She smiled and put up her hands in a 'sorry!' gesture as she left the building. I'd probably super-charged my look a little. Everything I did now felt a little super-charged. David let go Juno's hands.

'I'm terribly sorry about the whole mess' he began.

'*David*' I said threateningly, and he smiled.

'Good luck' he said. Juno kissed his cheek, kissed me.

'We'll wait' I said. I pulled a couple of chairs together and we sat down as she bounded up the three steps and through the soundproofed door into the theatre. When the door had swung shut I said 'You did it for me.'

He shrugged. 'What do you mean?'

'You did it because it could have been me.'

'Did what?'

I frowned at him, and he sighed and rubbed his jaw and cheek. 'Perhaps. Look, you can't expect me to feel good about this. I set out to destroy a man and I probably did. Christ, what right had I? How can I be happy discovering that's in me?'

It sounded fine to me. I tried to hide my surge of primitive pleasure, and didn't quite succeed.

'You bloodthirsty creature' he smiled.

'You think too much' I said. 'You worry too much. We're only responsible for our own lives, really, in the end. His life and his death were his own decisions. Can we shut up about him now?'

'Absolutely.'

So we talked about ordinary things, and I told him about the Gleeson twins, just stories, not what they'd meant to me, and made him laugh. And he told me about his childhood friends and their tiny crimes, funny stories, charming, far more innocent than the amusing thefts and the comedy beatings I'd regaled him with. And I realised how innocent he was, compared to me. He thought the world was honourable and decent in a way that I only fantasised it was to cheer myself up. In his innocence, he had destroyed Conrad Hayes. A less innocent man couldn't have done it. Not like that. So pure and cold.

When Juno came back out to rejoin us we were chattering away like children, and he sat up straight, guilty at his happiness, as she came down the three steps. I sighed. Lot of work to be done. Ah no, he was lovely the way he was. Madly annoying, but lovely.

'I'm staying with Michael' said Juno. She looked radiant. 'His sorrow and remorse are only brilliant. Will you be alright?'

'God yes' I said. Ouch. A little pang that she hadn't chosen me as her harbour in time of trouble. A little relief that she hadn't. I made a pretty turbulent harbour. And I was glad, I think (I hope) unselfishly, that she had someone who liked her or loved her so much for herself. Bleuch, I'm making myself sick. But you know what I mean. The feelings he had were actually for her, as she was. They meant something.

'I won't be back home tonight' said Juno. 'Is that OK?' She was acting like I was the one who needed tender concern and delicate handling after the traumas of the day. I felt a fizz of unsisterly, well no, incredibly sisterly irritation.

'Of course it is, nitwit. You'll be alright?'

She nodded. Smiled. More than one great weight seemed to have been lifted from her. She was luminous with happiness, and I'd been so scared she'd fall to pieces. What the *fuck* had Michael said to her? Or done.

Whatever. All couples are mysteries. 'Walk me home?' I said to David.

'Honoured.'

We goodbyed Juno and set off on the brief journey to the

harbour. As we walked away from the theatre down Druid Lane I said 'David, who was Childe Roland?'

'Childe Roland who came to the Dark Tower? Browning invented him. He dreamt the story of the poem, it's all made up. It's just a dream, I'm afraid.'

'Hmm. How old was Childe Roland?'

'No age, he didn't exist . . .' David saw how dangerous this style of answering was, and switched off the teasing before I started to cry. 'Well he wasn't actually a child. He was a Childe, with an "E". It was a sort of rank in medieval society. A young man who could still become a knight.'

'Hah!'

'Pardon?'

'Nothing.'

I felt great. I felt like air after a thunderstorm. I absolutely knew that Juno would be fine. I knew it like I knew my name, I felt it like I felt happy, it was just a fact that was true that I knew. You can choose not to be a victim. No, we were never victims. If you let them fuck your life up, they've won. And I knew that Michael would be good for her, and she wouldn't do him any harm either, and they'd work it out, for at least a while, and that I hadn't wrecked it, that the dumb thing that I'd done with Michael didn't matter. And Jimmy Gleeson's having a baby, I thought. Jesus, poor Nuala. Childe Gleeson to the Dark Town Comes. Slouching towards Tipperary to be born, with a fag in his mouth and fifty E down his Pampers. Childe Gleeson with an E. Goodbye Jimmy. Goodbye Johnny. Good luck, Jimmy Jr. I'll visit.

I'd always felt I was the wrong shape for the town I was born into, scuffing my cramped and awkward way through childhood, catching myself on the snags of the town as I tried desperately to grow up without damaging myself too badly, choking on claustro-phobia and ducking low expectations in a town with a tripwire for a horizon. As I walked and talked with David, as we rounded the corner onto the docks and walked to the quaysteps in front of my house with his boat at the bottom of the steps, my life at last felt big enough to stand up and move around in. Stretch out. Swing my arms. My life would never fit back into Tipperary now, and that was fine.

We stood at the top of the steps. In the cheap sepia of the

quayside's sodium light he looked monochrome, tired, Bogart-beautiful. Very lovely. Very lonely. I almost reached out to touch him, didn't. He stirred, as if to, I don't know, say something, do something. I made a wish in my head. Say something. Do something.

We stood there, in the sodium light. A great roar from Brennan's Bar, further down the docks. The slap of the water against the quayside wall. Nothing. A gull wheeling into the light and then gone and very far off another gull's cry. A heart-piercing sound. Harsh and high. A sound made to carry far, across wide ocean water. A cold scream of loneliness without a trace of self-pity or any pity. A sound that reminds you that birds are reptiles that took to the sky. Maybe the least intimate sound in the world. Nonsense words. Why do you fly? The better to be alone, my dear, the better to be alone. I trembled.

'I'd better get back' David said abruptly. 'You'll be OK?' pointing across, without looking, toward the building.

I nodded, my happiness cooling and freezing in the chill of another gull's scream, miles away, distant, high. Could he feel that?

He nodded as though in answer, but he turned, and walked down the steps, away from me. Oh Jesus. Into that dark night. No. Over that cold deep water, alone. Leaving me here on the cold stone steps, under the frozen single frequency of this monochrome light, alone, why for Christ's sake? I ran down the steps, slipped, grabbed onto his jacket and he turned, held me up, startled.

Deep breath, turned off my mind, opened my mouth.

'You said you didn't want to get involved with me, that one of us would get hurt and how you couldn't bear that. Well that just isn't good enough. Look what happened to Juno, and she didn't want to get hurt. Look what happens to people just living their lives. They get *hurt*, it's not *fair* they get hurt but they *do*, all the *time*, no matter how careful they are. Somebody can just come along and hurt them, for a stupid reason or no reason, and I *like* you David, I *like* you an awful lot, way more than you imagine, and if you still like me as much as you said you did when we went shopping and you invited me to dinner, and if all that's stopping you from . . . from *getting involved*, is that you just don't want anybody to get *hurt*, then . . . I don't *care* if I get hurt, and you shouldn't care either, because we like each other', I was crying now 'and we're going to get hurt anyway, so what.' I felt utterly miserable. I didn't think I'd said it right at all. I looked up and blinked the tears clear. 'Do I sound like an American?' I said, and he laughed and put his arm around me and as his face moved towards mine I saw just before I closed my eyes that a tear had squeezed awkwardly out of his right eye and hung from an eyelash, heavy and clear. Our lips touched and I felt his tear fall on my cheek. He must have closed his eyes. I opened mine as he opened his. So close. We closed our eyes again. Love, I thought to myself abstractedly. Not 'This is love' or 'Is this love?' Not a sentence, not a certainty, not a thought with moving parts or direction. Just love, all of it, as it is. Whether it's enough or not. Whether it's real or we're making it up. However shoddy it gets, or bent out of shape. It's still extraordinary. However foolish, however vain. However badly it ends. Love.

We kissed, and I contemplated, static, accidentally transcendent, love.

Time passed. The world turned beneath us. Later, it spun.

Eventually the kiss ended. I was warmer than the sun. David held me while we practised breathing, got the hang of it again. I took it as a sign of God's special favour that we'd managed not to fall off the steps into the harbour. We kissed again. We were getting very good at it. Practice makes perfect. Like anything, you have to put in the hours.

Time passed pleasantly.

'You've convinced me' said David. 'I was completely wrong. Get in the boat.'

91

I set out to tell you Juno's story, Juno's and Michael's, and Conrad's. Looking back, I seem to have ended up telling you mine, and David's. Perhaps that was the story I wanted to tell all along, and I had to trick myself into telling it. Who knows. I've given up thinking I'll ever understand myself, or anybody else. It's a great relief.

Certainly we're too complex to judge ourselves. Conrad Hayes was almost certainly far too harsh in his judgement of his poor, whimpering self. But then again

> 'Seldom went such grotesqueness with such woe;
> I never saw a brute I hated so;
> He must be wicked to deserve such pain.'

I've read *Childe Roland to the Dark Tower Came* since, as you can see. It's very silly, but it ends well.

I've read a lot since, done a lot. Where a story ends is a choice you have to make when you're telling the story. Choosing to end it here makes it a happy ending, almost a Shakespearean comic ending, with happy couples all over the shop, Juno & Michael, David & me. Almost a Hollywood ending. The starcrossed lovers kiss under the, well OK it's not moonlight but it's close, they've made it through somehow, audience dabs eyes and files out happy. Happy ending.

And some people are suspicious of that, because lives *don't* stop with a kiss and stay happy forever. They think, and I appreciate their point, that a happy ending is cheating, because if I'd chosen to end it a day earlier it would be an ambiguous ending, an hour earlier and it would be a sad ending.

So I think it's only fair to say that I really have thought about this, and both the story I've tried to tell and the story I've ended up telling really do have happy endings. I'm not saying we all lived happily ever after. Christ, not only would that be ridiculous but it wouldn't even be half as much *fun* as the more complicated truth. I'm not even saying that Juno and Michael stayed together and prospered, or that David and I did likewise. That's not the point. That would just be me, now, putting another arbitrary end on the story. I mean, ultimately we all *die*, all stories end in death and all endings short of that are a bit dodgy, they all rock a bit in the wind. So if you're very, very uptight about happy endings and a stickler for not being manipulated, well there's an honest answer for you, we're all going to end up dead.

But it's truthful to give this story a happy ending. Because we were all happier afterwards than we were before. And if all that extra happiness eventually led to a little extra hurt because we'd all more to lose, well so what. Hurt is part of life. To be honest, I think hurt is part of happiness, that our definition of happiness has gotten very narrow lately, very nervous, a little afraid of the brawling, fabulous, unpredictable world.

But what harm. If we won't come to life, well, life will come to us. You can't avoid it.

So I'll end the story now. No. Not on the dock. I think I'll end it the next day, and you can take these kisses as shorthand for a million kisses.

The next day, in David's father's house, well not exactly *in*, I was standing on the roof of the tower, leaning my hips against the low stone wall and feeling like God had polished and serviced me. The sun on Galway Bay, not up long. Mist burning off Connemara behind me. The pale blue empty sky above. Love, love, love. A gull swooped in front of me, a few hundred yards away, level with the tower. I stuck my tongue out at it, pressed my hips against the wall and shivered with a kind of happiness I'd never known before.

Up the stairs behind me came footsteps. 'Breakfast' said David, his head appearing through the trap. 'Another of Dad's bloody dinosaurs, with fried eggs, fried tomatoes, fried mushrooms and coffee. Or would madam like to see one of the specialist menus?'

'Look' I said.

He came all the way up, stood beside me. Looked. 'It's going to be a lovely day' he said. 'Yes' I said. I turned, and kissed him, a little kiss, a lovely kiss.

We stood on the tower, in the sun. Breakfast noises came from the kitchen far below. A clatter of cutlery. Pan on the stove. Kiss, break. Kiss, break.

David's father's voice, faint, from down in the heart of the house. 'Breakfast, Juliet! Breakfast, Romeo, you big eejit!'

We managed to squeeze in a last quick kiss before breakfast.

No, I was wrong earlier, I gave in to the modern fear of the happy ending. The devil take our fashion for irony, misery and ambiguity.

Here's what really happened.

We all

lived

happily

ever

after.

THE END.